THUG GIRL

Butterflies With Concrete Wings Still Fly

O Lorr William
A NOVEL
Part I

Thug Girl
Butterflies With Concrete Wings Still Fly
All Rights Reserved.
Copyright © 2019 O Lorr William
v6.0

UNCOMMON LIT PUBLISHING COMPANY

ISBN: 978-0-578-22220-2

PRINTED IN THE UNITED STATES OF AMERICA

Our hearts belong to time.

TABLE OF CONTENTS

Part I

OPTIONS

Chapter 1

TWO OF THEM BECAME THREE

For years, California soil had run dry.

The dark storm clouds that loomed above the howling winds and blanketed the chilly streets were long overdue.

On almost each of the twenty-three days that October rain had fallen on San Fran.

Flash floods and car accidents were a daily topic on local news but everything was business as usual.

Public Buses still drove the puddled streets and highways. Cable Cars still operated along the slippery train tracks. Ferryboats still sailed the choppy whitecaps of the bay and the word from the reporter on the weather channel was drought season might have finally come to an end.

Lillian Auroya Webster changed the television from the weather channel to catch the mid-morning traffic report on a different news station. She was supposed to be on bedrest and had only three weeks to go until she was due to deliver her baby but she was about to drive herself to an appointment.

Her plan was to return home from her appointment and spend the remainder of her three weeks in the house but that did not end up happening.

Instead of her leaving to drive herself to where she was going she had to be rushed to the hospital.

Her baby had decided on an early arrival and what otherwise would have been a quiet Friday for the hospital labor and delivery unit became lit when it filled with Lillian's family and friends.

I

Lillian's appointment was with a longtime client that only did his business with her.

Her client's drive was more than two-hours from Lake County to San Fran and her client told her that he would be in town after the morning's busy commute. The television said traffic was clear enough for Lillian to go meet him and she acquired her boyfriend's car keys to be on her way.

Lillian took two steps out her boyfriend's front door but her water broke no further than his doormat.

Dion Jacob Hayes was seated on his living room futon.

His thumb and index finger from both hands were fanatically entering fighting combos on round two of a game of Mortal and he heard Lillian yell. He paused the game in time to hear her say their baby was coming and he dropped the videogame controller. He yelled back to Lillian he knew what to do and as she got into the car he grabbed an umbrella, her favorite blanket and her pre-packed designer baby bag.

Within the minutes of the water soaking Lillian's maternity jeans Dion was honking his horn and running streetlights to get her to the doctor.

II

Lillian wished she could have asked Dion to go in her place to meet her client.

She trusted he could make the sale but he detested crack and that made him uncomfortable with selling dope.

In Lillian's first trimester Dion lacked any imagination for fatherhood and he did give dope-selling a try.

He let Lillian convince him they should get money together but on day one of him becoming a dope boy morning sickness made it impossible for Lillian to train him. She told Dion that with her in no shape to leave home they would start another day but with him being so adamant about being able to go alone he made Lillian go against her better judgment.

She placed fifty-dollar's worth of plastic wrapped product into the palm of Dion's hand for him to go and sell and as she gave him the small amount of crack a sour smirk imprinted on his face.

His frown wrung Lillian's gut. He made her want to breakdown and confide in him that the streets she grew up on were marked with stories of her mother's crackhead antics and there was no part of selling dope she felt good about. It broke her heart to flip crack but she said nothing to Dion but good luck on the block and she sent him into Death Valley.

Death Valley was a multi-unit multi-block public housing project not too far from the Tenderloin where Lillian grew up.

She warned Dion before he left home there would be many crackheads trolling the grimy pastel pink dwelling to buy crack. She said he would see people he knew and that some fiends he would have had no idea were smoking the glass pipe because they were on the down low.

She told him they would be the main ones to act embarrassed of their addiction but soon as they got what they paid for they would be the main ones to shamelessly beg him for more than they could afford.

Dion headed towards his front door and told Lillian enough with her prep talk. He said it would not be his first time in Death Valley but Lillian followed behind him saying this time would be different. She doubted he was listening to her point out he was not going to shoot the shit with a friend or bang a chick. She said he was going to slang dope and he had better not take pity on them beggars begging but without a word Dion kissed Lillian goodbye and left.

He was gone close to two hours before he returned asking Lillian for a second fifty-shot but he only handed her fifty-dollars.

Lillian accepted his fifty dollars but she thought no way he assumed his first fifty-shot was free. She wanted to know why he was not handing her one hundred dollars to pay for both fifty-shots but she did not speak on what he owed her and she gave him what he asked for.

A couple of more hours later Dion came to Lillian and gave her fifty-dollars to buy a third fifty-shot but she figured she would get her money after all was said and done. His enthusiasm was making an impression and reminding Lillian of her younger self.

She started in the dope game with a fifty-shot same as Dion and if he was anything like her they stood to make guap. Her crack-Connect profited greatly from how hard she hustled and when her crack-Connect retired from being the crack-Connect he taught her to make her own product though he told her it was not enough to know how to move dope.

The words he gave her to abide by was that her longevity would not be earned on a corner or in a trap house. He said for her to really maximize her money it was one thing to control the quality of her product but equally she would need a loyal base of steady clientele who pushed weight for her.

III

The night of Dion's debut as a drug dealer he was out late and Lillian was left restless on his living room futon. She was in and out of sleep writing rhymes in her journal and she turned her thoughts of their earning potential into song lyrics about their bright future ahead dealing dope. The title of her song was Money Made Double and Dion came home to find her fingertips still flooding her journal pages.

Lillian had moved from lying on the futon to sitting in a single seat recliner chair adjacent to the futon and she was waiting up to hear something about Dion's day.

She figured he would have a laughable moment or a dispute to say a word about but like any other night and like they had not taken on a new venture that morning he said nothing.

He came downstairs from his shower and entered the living room.

He was wearing sweats and a t-shirt and carrying his dirty clothes.

He dropped the clothes under the lid of the bamboo hamper next to the futon and he raised the futon to the upright position to have a seat.

Dion turned on the giant wall-mounted living room television and Lillian went to heat him a plate from the dinner that was cooked earlier in the evening.

She served him a glass of water with his meal piping hot from the microwave and he said thank you in between blowing multiple times on his first bite but he said not a thing else.

The household upstairs was sleep and the only sounds in the home came from their television airing a sci-fi rerun.

During a commercial break Lillian got up from her single seat and walked to the corner of the living room. She slid back their privacy curtain to open the last cabinet at the kitchen border and she grabbed a large bottle of vodka with an old fashioned gold-rimmed glass.

She poured Dion a double shot over fresh ice cubes then she mixed his drink with cran-apple and peach juice and she went over to sit next to him.

Dion placed his meal scraps aside and he traded Lillian the vodka for a cigar. He did not have to ask her to slice his cigar open and empty it for him to roll up the weed.

It was usual for them to smoke in silence and have little small talk but Dion was more quiet than usual and their small talk included not a word about one sale.

Lillian initiated some foreplay with the weed smoke. She straddled Dion's lap to give him a charge and they took turns blowing smoke through the blunt into each other's mouth.

Halfway through the blunt they did not get undressed to start having sex but before they finished the futon was in the flat position and they were naked.

Lillian was breathing heavy and could hear Dion also breathing heavy.

His lips were at her ear and she could feel the heat of his breath.

She asked him how much he made off flipping the three fifty-shots but he did not respond.

They were spooning with their drenched bodies connected and Lillian was waiting patiently. She could not see Dion's face because he was pressed to her rear so she sweetly called out baby and he responded yes but not with a response to her question.

Lillian twisted her neck to look over her bare shoulder.

Dion's arm was bent with his head on his forearm and his elbow was pointed at Lillian.

She could see his bare shoulder shrug up then down before he mumbled about not knowing for sure.

Lillian scooted from him a few inches to roll onto her back and her shoulder pressed into the crease of his chest. His elbow almost touched between her temple and forehead and they were eye to eye.

Lillian no longer used a sweet baby tone to ask Dion what exactly did he not know for sure and was he saying he had not counted his money yet and if so, why not.

Dion threw the comforter off exposing his naked body and half of Lillian's and he yanked his legs from their entangled position to stand up.

Lillian pulled the covers up over her body but she did not look away from Dion or his dick. It was thick and hung and it was swinging as he moved to get his jeans out the hamper.

Dion took money from his pants pocket and threw it on the bed saying that was all he had.

Lillian unbent the money and turned each bill the same direction before she counted three tens, four fives, two two-dollar bills and five ones.

She folded fifty dollars and put it to the side and she said that was hers to keep but she left the five dollar bill and four ones on the bed. She told Dion he should have more than nine dollars and she started calling off amounts. She asked was he sure his pockets did not have twenty more dollars, ten more dollars, five more dollars or even one more fucking dollar to round shit off.

Dion raised his voice to reiterate the fifty dollars she had just taken from the bed and the nine dollars she left for him was it.

Lillian lifted up straight from her pillow-propped position with her hands pressed to the mattress. The comforter dropped to her lap exposing her bare cumbersome breasts and she asked Dion was he seriously saying he made no money slanging in crackhead heaven all day.

Dion went to the dresser by the single seat recliner next to the opened living room closet door. He pulled out a drawer for a clean pair of boxer briefs and he put them on. He opened a different drawer for a clean t-shirt and socks and he went inside the closet to get a clean pair of jeans off a clothes hanger.

Lillian was yapping about him being in too much of a hurry to get out there when he should have waited for her but Dion dressed like he was disregarding her blasting him for bringing home less than his product was worth. She said had they gone together they would not have come home with less than one hundred profit. She told Dion she got that he was new to the hustle but she questioned if he thought it was okay to have come up in there with nine dollars as if the other ninety-one dollars required no discussion. Her way of trying to get him to say how his loss happened was by asking did he spend it, did he break off too much and sell it for too little or did he give a little extra a little too many times but that did not work.

Dion sat in the single seat recliner chair and he put on one of his socks and Lillian sighed a deep growl. She told him to stop with the theatrics of trying to put on socks to put on shoes to go nowhere. She said they had all night for him to come clean about how he had fucked up the church's money but Dion refused to explain. He said he felt no need to explain what he did with money he took the penitentiary chances to make and he told Lillian to be satisfied with the bread she made off him.

Lillian told Dion taking a loss of any kind did not satisfy her. She proclaimed that if it were her in crackhead heaven all day she would have the fifty dollars he gave her and the ninety-one more dollars that went with his nine but them talking about dope turned into a mean blowup about more than dope. It became about maybe they were not meant for each other and maybe Lillian should go home but by sunup they brought their anger and aggression down and went to bed after agreeing Dion's training day selling crack was his last.

IV

Dion had money when he met Lillian.

He was a Street Knight for the Unknown Dynasty Family.

Street Knight's were paid on retainer and he received a stipend regularly to perform assignments whenever needed. If he got an assignment he could be gone for days, weeks or months with no guarantee he would return home but Dion expected his life to be short prior to accepting his invitation to join the UDF.

Dion was affiliated with Fillmoe Kings Get Paid by age twelve and FKGP was a respected and feared multigenerational multiracial gang. They organized well-attended sideshows and competitive street fights that people had to pay to see and by age thirteen Dion was making money as one of FKGP's top street fighters.

Anytime Dion was not training for a fight he was enjoying his young fame. The most he did for fun was smoke weed, drink dark liquor and have sex and he had his lion's share of girls and young women. The alcohol he would sip on here and there but he had it around more for the other people. He did not drink too heavy to be sure he could turn down for the tossups that like to try and ease the condom off during sex or for the ones who tried to talk him out of wearing protection.

By the age of fourteen Dion and three others from FKGP had become Street Knight's.

His UDF induction alleviated any doubt his life would be short but he continued to see another day and after three years in the fast life a regular bed-buddy came to him saying she was pregnant and he had a baby on the way.

Dion's UDF affiliation required blood in no matter what but blood out had two exceptions. One exception was getting out to raise a family and UDF accepted Dion's resignation to go and be a father to his child.

V

Dion's money dropped low after his UDF resignation but he did not want Lillian to think he could not support their family.

He told her he had his ways to get money but she told him he was irreplaceable. She begged him to promise not to risk abandoning their son or daughter to chase a check and Lillian said she made enough money for them to live on but Dion was not okay having her take care of him.

He said for her not to worry and he eased her mind by promising to never abandon her with their baby but it was a promise that carried no weight because the only way Dion ever went about getting money was by risking his life to get it.

Lillian and Dion shared sleepless nights on his futon mattress wrestling separately with thoughts and fears of becoming parents.

She manifested her thoughts into verses on the custard-colored pages of her journals and most of what she wrote she kept to herself but some things she reflected on with Dion.

Dion never reflected what was on his mind. Even as Lillian and their baby forever becoming part of his life was happening he could not stop his mind from going blank anytime he thought of the day the *two of them became three.*

Dion did not care to finish high school and if that was cool once he had a kid he did not know and he did not have a job history but did he need one to be a father he did not know.

He did not know what having a family meant but him pillow-talking with Lillian during their sleepless nights helped him to ascertain that he was gaining something valuable to care for.

They both wanted to change their lifestyle and rather than keep spending money on expensive dinners, trips out of town, events, the newest electronic device and designer wear they wanted to save that money for their child but they faced a dilemma.

Turning their pillow-talk into a savings account did not simply occur and a step in a better direction was nowhere to be found.

The risks of death or jail was what was familiar to them being kids who had survived the streets.

The streets called to them from the morning until the night leaving no roadmap for how to leave the streets behind. There was no blueprint for a different life and without a blueprint, Lillian kept up with her crack sales and Dion kept his ear to the ground for a quick money lick.

Chapter 2

A KID IN A CANDY STORE

Lillian learned she was pregnant at age nineteen and during her entire pregnancy she echoed often she did not plan to get pregnant. She was ten days from turning twenty when she delivered her baby and Dion was seven days from turning eighteen. Had their baby come on or after the due date, she could have said she was technically not a teen mom and her baby-daddy would have technically not been a minor.

Lillian and her four best friends were told by their elders not to become teen moms. To become one would be their oneway ticket into the poor house and each of them had experienced poverty in some form or fashion.

Whether from wearing shoes down to the soles talking or pants flooding or patches sewn on clothes to cover holes or whether from waiting in long lines for a government handout or to recycle bottles and cans for cash or whether from having almost everything passed down secondhand.

The thought of putting a kid through any of that made them have no interest in teen-parenting and their summers, weekends and evenings after school were spent hustling for money to do whatever they wanted to do.

I

Dion learning of Lillian's pregnancy caused them to be at odds.

Their beginning was not built on a foundation of commitment and from their initial encounter their affections were a confession and expression of lust.

It all happened haphazardly on a warm spring day when Dion was in the car with Lillian's former crack-Connect. Her former crack-Connect was someone she thought of like a father figure and he had invested in the growing and distributing of marijuana. He had given Lillian an eighth of his hybrid strain of weed to sample and the day she laid eyes on Dion she was meeting her Connect to buy more of his weed.

Lillian's second encounter with Dion was same as the first. She came to buy weed and he was again in the car but this time she nonchalantly asked her Connect about him and he told her Dion was his little brother.

She honestly did not care what their relation was. She just knew if she saw Dion too many more times she would have to pop at him and on their third encounter she almost missed her opportunity.

Lillian had come to meet up with her Connect to buy weed and he mentioned getting gas, cigars and something to drink before taking his little brother home.

The light bulb in Lillian's head went off telling her that her Connect stopping at the gas station would leave Dion in the car alone a few minutes for her to make a move.

Lillian did not let her Connect know she was following

him to the gas station.

She pulled to the gas pump behind him and when he got out his car to walk to the gas station convenience store she got out her car to walk over to his passenger window and tap on the glass.

The slightly cracked window came down and Dion's smooth honey brown skin was shining.

His long black hair was styled like a Mohawk in one braid down the center of his head with his sides tapered nicely and the end of his braid was laid neatly over his front right shoulder.

His shoulders were broad and muscular like he did one hundred pull-ups daily and his full dark brown lips were moist with what Lillian figured was lip balm or petroleum jelly.

Dion did not give Lillian a chance to say hello. She opened her mouth to speak but Dion spoke first and with his smile stretching ear to ear he asked what made her finally decide to say something.

Not many more words were exchanged before Lillian invited Dion to take a ride with her and without hesitation he got out his car.

Lillian's Connect returned to the gas pump. He started the premium gas flowing to his tank but before he got in his car to wait for his tank to fill up he looked over and saw Dion was outside the car. He then gave Dion the peace sign after Dion gave him a head-nod towards Lillian's car and Dion walked to Lillian's passenger side door. He got in as she started her car and they pulled off slowly.

II

Lillian turned onto the highway and signaled to get over one lane but she stayed away from the far left fast lane.

Her car was an old beige-colored four-speed BMW that could use a fair share of bodywork but the car ran good. She just could not go faster than the posted speed limit.

She drove them across the Golden Gate Bridge into Marin County and they chitchatted about favorite foods, places they liked to go and things they liked to do and the talking helped to keep the focus off how slow Lillian was driving.

She was up front with Dion about her being a non-licensed seventeen-year-old but she was livid to learn he was only fifteen.

Her impulse was to flip a bitch and she almost turned her whip around to take the kid back to her Connect but something he said wrangled her in.

Dion admitted to Lillian that seeing him the first, second and third time was not by chance. He said he first saw her from his sister's living room window one night.

Lillian asked Dion where his sister lived and she was amused to remember the night he was talking about was the night her Connect had her to stop by to give her the weed he wanted her to sample.

Lillian asked why Dion had not said anything the first two times. She was curious why she had to make the first move if he was interested enough to ride along three different times to see her and Dion admitted to having never pursued a girl.

Lillian would have initiated a kiss if they were stopped. She wanted to drop her panties for Dion from the moment she saw him but they were not stopped they were driving with the music on the car radio playing low.

They were smoking the weed she bought not tracking the swigs from the pint size cognac bottle he pulled from his back pocket and they were laughing so much they got lost but getting lost was okay with Lillian. She was liking the kid's vibe and the time seemed to be whisking by.

They found themselves near Napa wine country on highway 37 and Lillian turned off highway 37 onto highway 29 to take them towards San Fran through the city of Vallejo.

In Vallejo they pulled into the parking lot for a burger bistro.

Lillian parked furthest from the entrance to be furthest from the streetlights where it was dark and she turned off the ignition. Turning off the car triggered the inside car light and she took a good look at Dion. She had thought of what to do when they finally stopped in those silent seconds before getting out her car but she decided to wait and not do anything right then.

Lillian walked somewhat in the lead through the glass front door of Nation's Burger Bistro and she was speaking low but Dion heard her say he could order what he wanted it was her treat.

The couple in line in front of them took long enough to order giving Dion plenty of time to decide what to get. He kept saying he was not hungry but he could eat and he insisted they share something small but he did not say what they would share until his turn came to order.

He got a bacon cheeseburger with mayo and mustard, ketchup, pickles and no onions, turkey chili-cheese fries with sour cream and chives, a large strawberry banana milkshake and a slice of fresh baked cherry pie.

Lillian had to hand the cashier two twenty-dollar bills for Dion's meal and tax.

The cashier handed Lillian back some change saying the wait time for her order would be ten to fifteen minutes and Lillian thanked the cashier while she counted her change.

Her face expressed she was flabbergasted at the cost but she dropped the coins from her change and two one-dollar bills in the cashier's tip jar and she went to grab a seat in a window booth. She was still looking flabbergasted wondering was it her hearing incorrectly or did the nigga not say he was not hungry.

Dion sat at Lillian's side with his arm over her shoulders and they both faced the empty intersection blinking yellow streetlights in all four directions.

Their food was brought to their table and Lillian pushed away every bite of the burger Dion tried to get her to take. She said it was too messy for her taste but she did share his plastic fork to eat more than half the fries.

She washed the fries down with more than her fair share of the milkshake but with the cherry pie she let him give her the first bite then she said for him to take the rest to the neck.

III

Walking to the car Lillian asked Dion could he drive a stick shift and Dion said yes.

He asked did she need him to drive and she slipped her hand into his hand to give him the car key and she thanked him she could lay down for the thirty-minute ride back to the city.

Dion stuck her car key in the ignition but Lillian said for him to wait and let her see his dick.

Dion laughed and asked Lillian what the fuck was she on and Lillian laughed saying she had to see his dick to determine if she wanted it.

Dion asked was she trying to get down like that right there in the restaurant parking lot and Lillian said yes if he was not too scared to pull it out.

Dion laughed harder and asked if his dick was small would she still want it and Lillian did not say yes or no.

She said for him showing it to her she would give him a kiss and he asked would it be a kiss on his dick and they both laughed.

Dion left on the emergency break but he put a foot on the clutch and a foot on the floor brake to turn the ignition. He pulled the stick shift from first gear to neutral and turned on the defrost pretending to ignore Lillian's dick-peek request.

He looked at her with a smile that made her smile and he kept his eyes on her eyes as he unzipped his pants. He pulled his dick out and Lillian's eyes dropped to his lap then bulged and she reached for his dick like *a kid in a candy store.*

Dion blocked Lillian's reach and asked what she thought she was doing and he said her asking to see was not asking to touch and Lillian asked to please touch.

Dion said not unless she was about to put her mouth on it and he pulled Lillian's hand into his lap.

She started stroking him and she leaned towards him for him to lean towards her and she started sucking his tongue. She licked and sucked his earlobe and his neck and when she had him moaning for more she kissed the tip of his dick making him moan louder and pant in anticipation of her sucking him off but after she gave his dick a kiss with some spit she only jacked him off.

Dion erupted in Lillian's palm and apologized for the gob of cum he left seeping down her hand but she said not to apologize. She used her clean hand to pull a pack of wet wipes from beneath her passenger seat and she sat the pack between them.

Dion pulled out two thick scented moist wipes. He gave them to Lillian then he pulled the next two wipes for himself and in silence he wiped off his dick and she wiped the front and back of her hand.

IV

Over the next year Lillian and Dion's relationship was sex and more sex.

Whenever Lillian wanted Dion she sent him a text message requesting an appointment and Dion would drop what he was doing short of a UDF assignment.

Whenever Dion wanted Lillian she would hold back and say she was busy. She made him wait to purposely drive him crazy then after a while of being unavailable she would pop up at his house.

Dion was not home for every pop up but Lillian knew he loved their cat and mouse game.

When they would finally see each other he acted mad at Lillian but by the end of virtually every visit he made sure to surprise her with a gift she outwardly expressed gratitude for.

She would tell him how perfect of a gift it was but she dared to show it to anyone for fear he may have been siphoning the gifts from his sister's lair.

Lillian and Dion's friendship-with-benefits grew into them being together almost daily and when they got pregnant Dion thought automatically Lillian would get an abortion.

For Lillian abortion was not an option and even Dion becoming violent did not change her mind.

The day she left the hospital confirming what she already knew from a home pregnancy test she went to Dion. He was expecting her to show up at his house and help finish packing his moving boxes but when she gave him the news he did not want her help. He was not happy and after she kept refusing to say anything different than no to an abortion he slapped her face hard enough to make her stumble.

Lillian took a minute to gain her footing then she lunged at Dion and tried to smack him like he had smacked her but she was too slow. He pushed her backwards and she fell over a brown cardboard box.

Dion lifted Lillian from the floor as if her swinging fists and feet were doing nothing and he slammed her against a wall.

He grabbed her by the throat and squeezed both his hands around her neck not to stop the flow of air but hard enough and Lillian clawed at Dion's face, hands and arms until he released her but only to pull his gun from the crease of his back.

Dion put his nine-millimeter handgun to her temple and he said she needed reminding of the fuck type of nigga he was and he pulled the trigger.

Lillian winced with a high-pitched screech until she realized she was still alive and the fear she felt was quickly turned to rage.

She had no reason to think Dion's gun would be empty so she rightly thought a bullet was about to blow off her head but then Dion had the nerve to laugh at her terror and with all her strength and fury from her shorter frame, she slapped his face temporarily crooked. She punched him multiple times, kicked him just as many times and Dion did not block one hit.

He gritted his teeth and he looked steadily at her and was calmly taking his beating like he deserved to be beat until she got tired but Lillian was not getting tired.

Her hits went from openhanded to closed fist and she went back and forth between smacking him and punching him.

Lillian's inner voice was saying fight. Fight his ass. Fight. Kill or be killed. Fuck him up harder. Kick him. Punch him. Look around grab a weapon but Dion grabbed her wrists.

He asked Lillian why she thought she could keep hitting him like that and Lillian yanked away.

She told him he could not be serious about slaps or punches because unless he thought waving his punk ass gun was the thing to do he had seconds ago played her like she was the biggest sucka alive.

Dion sat down on one of the surrounding cardboard boxes and he acknowledged he lost it for a minute. He said he was out of pocket for his reaction to her keeping their baby and he offered Lillian a seat on a box next to him but she said he could go fuck himself for offering her a seat on the very box he knocked her over. She called him and his apology a piece of shit and Dion said over and over he was sorry.

He said he was wrong to put his hands on her and he promised to God to never touch a hair on her head and after so many apologies and promises Lillian forgave him.

V

The day Lillian and Dion fought they were alone in his sister's living room.

Dion's sister shared a son with Lillian's Connect. He had moved her and their son and Dion to an upper echelon neighborhood of San Fran but Dion's sister was relocating them back to her and Dion's side of town.

Dion's sister was called away by her child's school the morning of their move and she had to rely on Dion to supervise the movers with their belongings until she made it back.

Dion and his sister were parting ways from the only home her son had known. From the day she was released with her son from the hospital they had lived for six years in a three unit Victorian building. Their unit was airy because their building was second from the top of a step hill but they lived in the sunny top floor flat with a cityscape view.

Lillian's Connect had easily afforded Dion's sister a luxurious lifestyle in San Fran's Uptown Fillmore District until he violated parole. He went to jail about a month after Dion and Lillian hooked up and Dion's Sister was left paying the rent.

She was good paying the rent when her baby-daddy was supposed to do three-months in county jail but when he picked up a more serious charge while in county, his three months turned into more than three months.

Dion's sister did not want to uproot her son but her baby-daddy had left her with access to a boatload of his money and without upper echelon rent to pay she could stretch that money further.

Dion and his sister still had their two-story two-bedroom place to live in the Double-Rock public housing projects and his sister did not ask anyone's permission to move back.

She scheduled the movers and told Dion to start packing they were moving back to their childhood residence.

Their aunt was the one who had Dion and his sister keep Double-Rock. She said for in case of an emergency they would never be homeless but it was a smaller space and Dion would either have to share his old bedroom with his nephew or share the living room with their aunt.

VI

Emerald Day stepped into Dion and his sister's lives as guardian when their mom died.

She battled with her addictions and she was clean when she accepted custody of her sister's kids but months into parenting she relapsed. She started drinking heavily to hide she was smoking crack-cocaine again and she was popping an opiate for every minor ache and pain.

Aunt Emerald's sobriety was short-lived but she held up a job for over a year to try and be a good example. She had relapsed and was still functioning as an intake worker for a family violence intervention house because of how clients and staff loved her when she showed up but she had to be let go from missing too many shifts.

Aunt Emerald was telling Dion's sister and their social worker she was spending her free time volunteering and finding a new job.

She knew to show up and clean up for welfare appoints to keep the courts from meddling with her family but her days away from home became nights and weeks and months away from home.

Dion had the talk with Lillian about the drastic change in space and scenery but Lillian let Dion know his ghetto could not be worse than hers. She had survived filthy, rodent-infested, dope-centric buildings, businesses and parks as a kid and was more interested in what Dion's bedroom situation would be.

In the top floor Uptown flat Dion dwelled in his sister's living room but the living room had a door with an inside and outside lock on it.

Dion described the Double Rock living room to Lillian as an open space.

It was accessible from the back door and the kitchen but it was downstairs from the two bedrooms and the bathroom.

He said he technically would be sharing the living room with his aunt but she was never home and not because Dion and his sister had any problem with her being there.

Lillian wanted to know was Dion not concerned about discretion and he partially assured her when she came to get fucked there would not be an issue but he told her to make no mistake about one thing. If his aunt were to need somewhere to lay her head she would not be turned away.

He said he owed her that much and more for keeping him and his sister together and out of the San Fran foster care system.

VII

There were still open boxes to fill and seal with tape when Lillian showed up for Dion's move.

She dropped the I-am-pregnant-bomb on him amid lending her two hands to help close and tape boxes and she expected him to at most not be happy but not violent.

Violence had always been a deal breaker.

Any other relationship Lillian would have ended and never looked back but she believed Dion's apology was genuine and she accepted he was young and had a lapse in judgment.

She blamed his youth again for ruining the apology after she took the seat next to him on the cardboard box and he asked her why she was not scared of him.

Lillian had to take a deep breath.

She slid off her box down to the black Persian area rug onto both knees and she crawled to the front of Dion. She wanted to respond to him in his face not talk to the side of his body and she lifted her finger to his chin.

She brought his face to meet her eyes and they aligned with one another and she placed both her palms on his knees. She stared a few uncomfortable seconds into his round dark eyes and said her being scared of him was irrelevant and her feeling fear did not make her weak.

She said she knew he was not in love with her and she could accept they had no deeper connection than sex before knowing of the baby but now that her womb was giving him a legacy to hurt her was to hurt himself.

Dion gripped the base of Lillian's head but she kept talking.

She said if an abortion was what he wanted she would fight him to the death for her baby and he had to press his lips to her lips to stop her mouth from running and their kiss became wet and long.

Their kiss was uninterrupted by Dion helping Lillian out of her panties but there was a quick pause for Lillian to help Dion out of his shirt.

He slid onto his knees and let Lillian unbuckle his belt and when his pants dropped his dick sprang out.

Lillian stopped kissing him to look down at her hand giving his balls a hand massage and she massaged as they kissed some more touching the front of their bodies together.

Lillian then brushed her ass against the tip of Dion's dick as she turned to bend over on all fours.

She used one hand to keep her face from the floor but her other hand she used to spread one ass cheek.

She twisted her head to watch Dion over her shoulder and his eyes were down. He was watching himself go inside her and with every slow stroke he went deeper and deeper widening Lillian's pussy more and more and as she got wetter and wetter she was bucking for Dion to go faster. She was begging for him to do it to her the way he was doing it and when he hit that right stroke she reverberated his name for the length of her orgasm.

Lillian collapsed onto the floor and Dion fell on his back beside her but she barely let their heart rates slow to normal before she got on top of him.

Her knees were at his waist and her legs were along his hips and she moved her lower lips up and down his dick and as they kissed her wetness engulfed his erection for another round.

Lillian got her a second nut but Dion gave her no recovery time.

He rolled over on top of her while still inside her and he started pummeling her pussy to the finish line.

He was chasing his nut at top speed when the moving company laid a long finger on the doorbell and completely distracted Lillian.

She tried to tell Dion they should stop and get the door but his eyes were closed and he was panting he was almost there.

She could see she was not getting him to stop for the movers and the movers would not stop pressing on the doorbell. They rung it another two times before finally Dion shuddered a short low gruff yowl and came to the end of his release.

He lifted himself off Lillian but not to go let the movers in.

Lillian saw her panties and bottoms were next to her and she slid them on to get up to get the door but Dion threw his arm over the top of her chest.

He stopped her to say he did have feelings for her. He said he did not know if what he was feeling was love and he was not saying what she felt for him was love. He was saying he was cool if she wanted to make things more official by taking things to the next level.

As Lillian was about to ask him what the next level meant, Dion kindly asked that she hurry to the door. He wanted her to let the movers in before they bounced.

Chapter 3

MOOLAH

The morning Dion and Lillian's baby decided to come into their lives, he sped his charcoal grey mustang to the Children's Hospital.

At every twist and every turn he was burning the rubber off his spinning sixteen-inch rims.

Dion drove fast but steady with his body on autopilot and for the short time he and Lillian were driving inside Golden Gate Park they passed a pond. It was a pond full of wishes from Dion's childhood and having lunch at that pond was the last memory he had of his family together.

His mother was sober and vibrant and could make up a song about anything.

She led them to a patch of grass she chose for them to sit near the pond and as she carried their lunch basket with both hands she sang of the trees the butterflies the sun the rocks the birds the dirt the sky and about how weighty the over packed basket was in her hands.

Dion's sister was behind their mother trying to keep up

and sing backup but her hands were holding a book with her head down and her eyes were perusing the pages of her novel.

Dion was holding his father's hand as he hopped along his father's side from the car where his father found them a place to park.

His father dragged his feet and complained to Dion about there being dogs off their leash and the fleas and bugs he said were in the grass and the insects he said were trying to bite him but when they caught up to Dion's mom and sister by the pond he wore a quiet smile.

Dion's mom splayed their feast on the blanket their father laid down.

They had homemade tuna sandwiches, buttery cheesy corn on the cob, sliced melon with chocolate covered almonds and strawberry lemonade but Dion and his sister did not get to finish eating their melon or chocolate covered almonds.

Their father asked for some privacy with their mom and they were sent to the water with breadcrumbs to feed the ducks and coins to toss in and make a wish.

—⟫•⟪—

Dion reached the street outside Golden Gate Park and realized his wish upon that last coin he tossed in the pond was the last wish he ever made and he looked over at Lillian.

She had been absolutely quiet on their drive to the hospital and Dion asked was she good and she told him she was gucci but truthfully her mind was heavy.

She had a client in town to spend what she could live on for months and she could not stop thinking of how to somehow meet and make the sale to her client without raising a red flag.

I

Lillian had contemplated the many ways her life would change when the baby was born.

She would be breastfeeding and Dion would be there burping, bouncing and bathing their baby but they needed to be homebound to grow together as parents and the need for money was the only part of motherhood Lillian had focused on.

She kept money stashed in three different locations but she had saved nearly nine thousand dollars and her money put together with Dion's would be enough for her to not have to sell dope her baby's first year if they only bought necessities and kept to a tight budget.

More than half of what Lillian had saved was in a bank safety deposit box no one knew about and she had a little under a thousand dollars in the floor of Grandma Dah's studio apartment. The rest of Lillian's stash was in Dion's living room.

Dion only knew about Lillian having the twenty-nine hundred dollars she kept with his money and combined they had roughly fifty-three hundred tucked in random shoeboxes behind his futon.

The shoeboxes stretched the length of his queen-size futon frame and stacked five boxes high.

They placed a thick rectangular piece of glass atop of the

shoeboxes and covered it with a cloth that stretched to the floor to create a makeshift table.

The table lined the bottom of their gated living room window and with the futon in the flat position it was no obstacle getting to the shoeboxes.

Each shoebox had the face of the box sliced on three sides making a flap that folded up and down for Dion and Lillian to easily take a pair of shoes out but they made it impossible for anyone to find which shoeboxes they put money in.

The money was divided and inserted into the soles of unworn baby shoes and into the soles of his and her shoes both worn and new in different designer brands, styles and colors.

⇒»《◉》«⇐

Kamber Diamond Perry arrived at the hospital after hospital staff admitted Lillian into a private room.

She darkened Lillian's doorway with balloons and flowers and she was the first of Lillian's four best friends to arrive.

Lillian saw Kamber and called her name in a pitch just below a scream but not for the balloons and flowers.

Kamber showing up when she did was perfect timing to escort Lillian to meet her client.

Much as Lillian wanted to ask Kamber about her split lip and the bruised cheekbone beneath her oversized dark shades, she already knew Kamber's boyfriend had probably socked her again.

If she reacted to Kamber's display of a beat down her time would get wasted on Kamber telling the same story about the boyfriend who took such good care of her went crazy vicious on her because he thought she was cheating.

Kamber needed to hear that cheating was no cause for her to take any abuse. She needed to be urged to think more highly of herself and Lillian would have given Kamber the girl power speech but Lillian had a twenty-four hundred dollar sale waiting to be made and she could not be distracted by Kamber's drama.

Her priority was to send a follow up text message to her client giving him a location she could get to while in labor and she provided him the street names intersecting in front of a dog park half of a block from the corner of the hospital.

Kamber saying her hellos to other people in the room gave Lillian time to send her client the message before Kamber reached her bedside to hand her the bouquet of balloons and flowers.

Lillian put her phone down to take the bouquet into her bosom.

She reached her arm out to get a hug from Kamber and Kamber hesitantly leaned into Lillian's hug.

Lillian laid a kiss on Kamber's cheek and Kamber gave Lillian a peculiar look but Lillian held her arm over Kamber's shoulder carrying on her affection like it was normal. She thanked Kamber for always being there for her and she called Kamber her anchor saying Kamber was solid as a rock then she told Kamber to take her for a walk to get fresh air.

Kamber shunted from Lillian's clutch forcing Lillian's

arm from around her neck and she told Lillian she would have walked her waddling ass outside without her getting sappy about it.

Lillian set the flowers and the attached balloons next to her bed and she grabbed her phone and her big purse bag but she handed Kamber the purse.

Kamber pulled the umbrella Lillian had sticking out the top but Lillian told Kamber not to take anything out her purse.

Kamber said she was already carrying an umbrella and she asked did they really need two and Lillian's answer was yes she needed her own.

II

No one in Lillian's hospital room interfered with what was transpiring between Kamber and Lillian.

Lillian expected her grandmother to say something when Kamber began to help her stand up from the hospital bed but nope.

Dahlia Frances Orlenne Mendoza was Lillian's maternal grandmother and she had tunnel vision behind her reading glasses. Her eyes were locked on penciling in letters in a crossword puzzle book almost the size of her small lap and much like Lillian she was always cold. She had her full body nestled in Lillian's hospital room window seat with Lillian's favorite blanket draped over her head and shoulders.

The attending nurse was minding her medical procedures and adjusting equipment near Lillian's bed and Dion was sitting in a chair scrolling his smartphone but he was paying attention. He asked Lillian did she want him to walk with her and Kamber but Lillian did not have to say no thank you because Kamber said she had it handled.

Lillian held her phone in her hand as she got to her feet but nervousness was crawling under her skin waiting on her client to reply to her text messages.
She had sent him an earlier message letting him know she unexpectedly went into labor but was still trying to meet and she got no response.
Her fear was that he might have left to go back home.

Lillian told her nurse Kamber was taking her for a walk. The nurse said for Lillian to wait and consult the doctor but Lillian said it was no need to alert the doctor and she wobbled out of her hospital room door saying she would be gone a few minutes.

Kamber trailed close on Lillian's heels to the elevator but when Lillian got to the elevator she did not push the button to call the elevator to their floor.
She stood at the elevator door and looked at her phone.
She was staring at her phone and Kamber was staring at her but Kamber staring at her did not make Lillian stop staring at her phone.

Kamber pushed the button to call the elevator and she asked Lillian what was it with her staring at her phone on some psycho shit but Lillian ignored her.

The elevator ride was long with medical staff and

other patients getting on and off at different floors but for Kamber's whole ride she watched Lillian stare at her phone. Her looking at Lillian made other people look at Lillian but Lillian would not look up and allow her dingbat bestie to get in the way of her making some serious *moolah.*

Their elevator reached the ground floor and soon as the elevator doors opened Lillian's phone lit up with four text messages from her client.

Her client's first message said he got her text and was on his way to the dog park.

His second message, which had to have been the first message he sent Lillian, said he had arrived.

The next message said he had been waiting nearly twenty minutes.

His fourth message, which was surely the message he sent before saying he was on his way to the dog park, said he was getting on the freeway to go back to Lake County.

III

Lillian and Kamber walked all the way from the elevator to the hospital entrance before Lillian slowed to a pause. Her face looked as if she entered a transient state of paralysis and the onlookers saw it too but they bustled by.

Kamber watched Lillian's scalp begin to produce beads of sweat that raced down her temples and many seconds passed where Kamber believed Lillian possibly did not breathe. She had to tell her to breathe and once Lillian got her breath together she held onto Kamber with one hand.

Lillian held her stomach with her other hand and she

breathed through her first contraction using the breathing technique her and the nurse upstairs went over when she was admitted.

Kamber again questioned why they were not turning around and going back upstairs to labor and delivery but again Lillian ignored Kamber and disregarded every gawk and when her contraction passed she kept Kamber moving forward.

IV

Kamber reached the dog park first.
She stood in front of an empty bench waiting for Lillian to catch up and after Lillian sat down she sat a couple feet away.

In the twenty minutes it took for Lillian's client to arrive Lillian asked Kamber to be the Godmother of her baby but what Lillian thought would be an excited yes became a deeper conversation.

Kamber did not simply accept. She asked Lillian why her and she let go of a couple tears that she wiped so fast Lillian thought the sight of them was unreal.

Lillian answered Kamber's question with a question and asked what type of question was that and Kamber pretended to be joking but she asked why Lillian did not pick paleface bestie.

Eliza Bethany Kerry was the Whitest-shade of Black girl whenever Lillian brought her around. Not just Kamber made it a point to say so but Kamber was by herself calling

Eliza Lillian's trophy piece saying Lillian brought her every-where like a show puppy she found to be her best friend.

Of course Lillian called Kamber ridiculous but Kamber stood by the claim she and Lillian were not as close because Eliza integrated into the clique and changed everything.

Lillian abruptly corrected Kamber to say Eliza was not only her best friend. She pointed her finger from herself to Kamber a few times rapidly to emphasize Eliza was both their best friend and Lillian said she thought Kamber was done faking like she did not know Eliza was also her blood cousin.

Lillian held up her hand to prompt Kamber to swallow whatever stupid shit she was about to say. Being accused of worshipping Eliza made Lillian think she was being called superficial and she pointed to her stomach. She told Kamber in a mild angry way she was pregnant by a man the shade of the darkest chocolate bar and she asked Kamber had she ever ate the darkest chocolate bar.

Kamber admitted yes she had ate the darkest chocolate bar before and Lillian asked was it darker than dark choco-late and Kamber said yes but she told Lillian to make her point. She said she did not need reminding of her baby-dad-dy's jet-black skin and Lillian yelled her point was to ask Kamber who the fuck was she calling superficial.

Lillian stuck her index finger up in front of Kamber's face. It was not close enough to be disrespectful but it was close enough to stop Kamber from talking.

Lillian said the finger she was holding up represented the Spanish and Filipino ancestry of her maternal grandparents and she put up a second finger. She told Kamber her middle finger represented her Irish paternal great-great-grandmother she was named after and who she shared with Eliza.

Lillian put up her ring finger with her pinky finger representing her Black and Native American mixed father and she stretched her four fingers towards Kamber's face. Now she was close enough to be disrespectful and she asked Kamber was she unfamiliar with any race or ethnicity mentioned and Kamber said no.

Lillian asked did anything she was mixed with make her less Black and Kamber said no.

Lillian asked Kamber was her being a mixed Black girl not the same as Eliza but Lillian silenced Kamber again and put her opened hand up to block Kamber's mouth.

Lillian's mild anger turned to full anger as she told Kamber the only reason Eliza came out lighter-skinned was Eliza's maternal grandmother was White. That made Eliza's mother more White than Black but she was still a Black woman and she had Eliza with a mixed race man. That made Eliza mixed with more non-Black than Black but Lillian asked Kamber did that not mean Eliza was still Black.

Lillian shook her head with her shoulders squeezed indicating she had become irritated and she roared about Eliza's grandfather being her grandfather's brother. She said they were both Black men raised by the same Black ass father in the same fucking southern Baptist home so no it did not fucking matter Eliza's skin was fairer than other Black girls but Lillian told Kamber she had defended Eliza's Black card for the last time. She said Eliza's feelings would be hurt to know

Kamber was a backstabber and Lillian asked if Kamber preferred Eliza to be her baby's Godmother but Kamber blurted hell-to-the-no. She told Lillian to stop going evil bitch on her and Lillian coolly said she had no problem asking Eliza to do it but Kamber tried to clean things up saying how she beaucoup loved Eliza.

Kamber put on a performance professing Eliza was her girl for life and she claimed to have not remembered being told by Lillian her and Eliza were cousins. She said she did not know what had come over Lillian to get her so upset but she was sorry Lillian had misunderstood.

Lillian gave Kamber the side eye until Kamber reluctantly affirmed she might have gone a bit far but she said Lillian would be going too far if she gave her future Black-skinned baby a White-skinned Godmomma.

Lillian asked what Kamber really meant with her color bullshit and Kamber told her.
Being of a darker-skinned complexion born into a family of all lighter-skinned men and women was something she may never fathom but whether she had a boy or girl her child would need some Black balance.

Lillian asked Kamber what if the White-skinned Godmomma was Blacker on the inside than say someone like Kamber's bourgeois Black ass was on the outside and Kamber cracked a laughing-smile. She said touché and with glimmers of truth but heaping portions of shade she began highlighting Eliza's Blackness. She checked an imaginary box in the sky and said that box was for the finger licking good fried chicken Eliza knew how to throw down and make the best.

Kamber checked a second box for the watermelon she said was never safe when Eliza was around and she checked a third box for Eliza being the reason they won almost every double-dutch competition. The fourth box Kamber said she was checking for Eliza's ass still being bigger than Lillian's even with Lillian's ass temporarily being the size of a whale's tail and Lillian let go of a fart with a sudden flurry of laughter. She had to brace for a contraction just as her client's car came into view a couple streetlights back but when her contraction came to an end she released her breath slowly and she told Kamber she was about to take that ride around the block.

V

Lillian shared with Kamber on the walk to the dog park why they were out of the hospital and what her ride around the block was about.

Kamber had to help Lillian off the bench and over to the curb where her client's car was stopped in front of them and as Kamber helped Lillian into her client's passenger seat she winced from the pangs of her passing contraction.

Kamber was waiting for Lillian to get situated enough to hand her her purse and close her inside the car but Lillian must have thought Kamber was waiting for instruction and she told Kamber to go back to the hospital and meet her at the entrance with a wheelchair.

Kamber closed Lillian's passenger door but she asked would wheelchairs be waiting in the hospital lobby for anybody to use or was Lillian now confusing her with somebody's fucking orderly.

Lillian barked through the window that she sure was not the fucking orderly and she asked Kamber did she look like the muthafucka to ask about a wheelchair. She told Kamber she should be running to the hospital fast enough to go figure the shit out and get it done before Lillian got to her and Lillian's client started to drive from the curb but he had to stop for Kamber.

She was running but not towards the hospital. She was alongside his passenger door saying labor had scrambled Lillian's brain. If she was asking her for a favor like that telling her to figure some shit out without saying please Kamber said she did not talk that crazy talk.

Lillian tried to then say please with sugar on top but Kamber told her to try again.

For Lillian to get Kamber to budge, she had to say please Queen Almighty Goddess Kamber The Great One.

Chapter 4

DIRTY MEMOIRS

Royal Dior Hayes was born the evening of Friday October 23 at exactly seven twenty.

Lillian pushed her baby into creation and passed out not too long after. She came to consciousness slowly and was fuzzyheaded with no idea how long she had been out.

She could not assemble the strength to open her eyes right away and she idled in her bed quiet with her eyelids shut.

Her head was rested against her pillow as she checked in with her body and listened to the voices in her hospital room.

She remembered being unable to move then feeling Royal's warm body against her chest and now she was freezing with her arms at her side.

She almost fixated on her arms being cold and wanting her favorite blanket but she thought of her daughter. She rotated her neck around searching the room without fully opening her eyes and she found Royal cuddled in the arms of Dion's sister.

Dior Joy Hayes was sitting in the chair next to Lillian's bed. She did not have the chance to notice Lillian watching with how fast Lillian turned her head back to Dion standing at the foot of her hospital bed. He was holding an open blunt of weed in his hand and he was carefully lacing the weed with white powder from a small plastic baggy.

Lillian knew Dion did not mess with anything harder than liquor and weed. On special occasions he might take some mushrooms or he might pop an ecstasy pill with her but he never even took a whole pill.

Dion handed the plastic baggy to the person standing beside him when he needed both his hands to roll the blunt and Lillian's eyes followed the plastic baggy into the person's pocket.

Reddy Lawrence Rich Sr. was Dior's baby-daddy and the one who brought Lillian and Dion together. His street name was Reddy Rich until his firstborn son became his junior and he inherently became Big Red.

Big Red's hands had become unsteady and he did not know why but he refused to see a doctor about it. He settled for relying on Dion or his oldest son or Dior to roll his blunts for him two to three and at times four to five times a day.

I

Dior's world revolved around Big Red and their son but also around Dion.

Eventually little sister privileges included Lillian but they were not automatically tied to her being pregnant.

Following Dion learning of Lillian's pregnancy she stayed a bunch of long weekends with him.

One long weekend turned into her staying every night and she was around Dior to witness her daily preservation of their home.

Dior kept the common areas spotless and the plants watered and she had Big Red bring fresh kitchen flowers weekly. Her bedroom was pristine and her lush seashore by the sea decor and bedding looked like it was never in use. The wall art and home furnishings were perfect all over the place. The smell of great grandmas soul food kitchen was the smell of every breakfast and every dinner and Lillian not once had to lift a finger to keep her fat belly full. She did not have to take her own clothes to the wash and fold or dry cleaners because Dion and Dior would switch off doing the laundry for the household.

Lillian had no reason to bring up to Dion in a tetchy way that her grandmother raised her to cook and keep a clean house but not to the standard of trying to hang a price tag on it.

Dion asked Lillian what was her problem and her problem was anything Dior touched turned to gold and she was not about to try and measure up to his sister who did not like her or want her around.

Dion said his sister was cool with her and whatever she was on was in her mind and Lillian let it go but she knew it was not in her mind.

Dior was always cordial with Lillian around Dion but even after she knew Lillian was having Dion's baby she continued to give Lillian stale energy when they were alone.

She was standoffish for weeks into Lillian's sleepovers until in the final three months of Lillian's pregnancy they had a bonding moment.

During a summer afternoon Dior and Lillian were home alone.

Dior came down the stairs to the kitchen on a call as Lillian walked in the kitchen from the living room where she and Dion slept.

Lillian could hear Dior's side of the contention. She knew she was speaking with Big Red and when Dior hung up the phone she rashly shared with Lillian why the conversation had her tight.

Big Red had called to say he was not coming over at the time he promised.

It was the third time in a week he would not be tucking their son in for bed and Dior asked Lillian could Big Red actually be expecting her to be good with him dismissing her like that.

Lillian knew it was not a question for her to answer and Dior went on. She said her and her son were no longer the top spot on Big Red's priority list and she had been racking her brain but could not pinpoint when things changed or why.

Lillian sat at Dior's tastefully draped kitchen table listening nearly an hour to Dior expose pieces of her life Lillian would have never imagined.

The Dior Lillian knew carried herself crisp like new money and she had manners, spoke polite and did not say too much. She had impeccable posture and moved effortlessly with grace in everything she did and she always held her head high with a smile. She chewed with her mouth closed and refreshed throughout the day with breath mints or gum, lotion, perfume and she had the press powder for when that shine crossed her face.

Dior was completely dissociated from classless behavior, which made Lillian feel real special she was permitted to see Dior that afternoon in rare form trash talking Big Red with bad words. She spoke phrases like no hoe held a candle to her, niggas be testing her character and little did bitches know she was not the muthafucka to be fucking with.

Dior asked Lillian whether to give Big Red an ultimatum and demand that her and their son come before his stupid drugs and dirty money but it was another question for Lillian to nod and not respond.

Lillian was concerned if Dior somehow thought the money Big Red spent on her and their son was not dirty but she squeezed her fingers over her mouth to not tell Dior she was concerned. She looked perturbed to get Dior to ask what was on her mind but Dior was deep in her feelings looking through Lillian and not seeing a thing.

She kept confiding about Big Red paying a high price to be the man she shared her bed with but she was finding his money to have lesser and less value making her feeling like a fool for believing in their relationship. She said there was not any amount of money that could make her not have doubt and Dior let her words stream into silence.

Lillian did not know what to fill the wordless space with and she decided to be patient.

It took Dior a half of a minute to find her words but to Lillian's shock Dior began venting a new narrative that went back to the beginning of her and Big Red's relationship.

She said before she met Big Red she was an emotional loudmouth that had never heard of table manners. She wore cheap antiperspirant and over oiled her unwashed hair and she credited Big Red for helping her say bye-bye to armpit stains and good riddance to ring around the collar.

Lillian commented to Dior she must have been very young first meeting Big Red and Dior said yes they met on the last day of her first semester of high school.

She said she took the bus downtown to Market Street and walked into his popular clothing boutique Four One Five that he co-owned with his wife.

Ivory Rose Rich was the mother of Big Red's oldest son who Lillian heard was married to Big Red but Lillian had never seen Big Red wearing a wedding band and she had never met nor seen his wife.

Dior's casual mention of Ivory by name made Lillian want to interrupt her to ask what she thought her and Big Red's side relationship would ever be. Knowing he was married from gate Lillian could not believe Dior was missing the irony in the cheated with getting cheated on.

Lillian wanted to be messy and say to Dior that Ivory might be mad at Big Red too for him treating her the same way he was treating Dior but Lillian bit her tongue and Dior went on with airing more *dirty memoirs*.

II

Dior recalled with exact detail what she wore ten years before on the sunny but bone-chilling Friday morning she entered the doors of Four One Five.

She dressed semi-casual in her favorite pair of acid-washed jeans with a sleeveless top.

The jeans had lost color richness from years of washing but they were the right type of snug fit over her round butt and thick thighs. Her mint green shirt was old but not as old as her jeans and it was still cute. It stopped above her gold belly ring and hugged her D-cups enough to distract from the two gold words CITY MADE that were decoratively fading and peeling off the front.

The one thing that was making Dior's outfit look compliment worthy was the island-white double-breasted blazer she found hanging amongst her aunt's belongings in the living room closet.

From the expensive price tag still attached to the inside Dior knew her aunt had likely stolen it and was planning to sell it but she was not around the house for Dior to ask. She had been there the previous day but she had not been back

Dior mentally weighed the consequence of sporting her aunt's blazer without permission but when she faced her aunt's full-length mirror to see herself in the final product with her gold dangling earrings and all, any fear of consequence went adrift to never-never-land.

The blazer was her shot at looking pulled together.

She would only get to make one first impression to snag the job and she intended for the bosses to see her as someone to keep beyond a meager winter season.

Dior walked through the door of Four One Five unintentionally noisy with each step.

The store had just opened and was still empty and Lillian was bringing the attention to the too sexy shoes she also borrowed from her aunt's closet without her aunt's permission.

Big Red was standing off to the side of the cashier counter and Dior did not even say hello or good morning before she asked was Four One Five still hiring temporary seasonal positions. She told Big Red she had come to speak with the hiring manager because she really needed a job and heard they did same day interviews.

Big Red asked who did she hear they were hiring from and Dior said actually she overheard it. She stuttered to say she overheard it from passing strangers on the street because who she overheard it from was not a stranger.

Big Red told Dior she was speaking to the owner. He said the only reason he was onsite to open the store was because the opening manager and the sales associate both called out sick.

Dior smiled with a twinkle in her eye and came closer to the glass store counter.
She finger combed through her long braids and she pulled them from hanging over one shoulder to hanging over the other shoulder.
She leaned into the counter and told Big Red it was clearly fate for her to have walked into his store on that day of all days.

Big Red told Dior to tell him a little about herself and

Dior skipped the small talk.

She jumped right into her mom dying earlier that year. She said with her father being in jail out of state she had to take care of her eight-year-old brother and their aunt who she said was maybe fifty-years-old or something.

Big Red questioned her having to care for an adult and Dior was not willing to speak ill about her aunt but she was not willing to lie. She said her aunt being her guardian in the beginning was fine and only recently she started drinking too much and popping a pill for everything and if she made it home she was sleeping for days at a time.

Big Red asked Dior what was wrong with drinking, popping pills and sleeping and Dior said nothing if the person who did things like that worked to afford that lifestyle and did not have kids depending on them.

Dior said she knew better than to think of their aunt's behavior as normal but she could not say the same for what her little brother was going to think. They did not have parents to set them straight and her little brother needed to be in school and around his peers not drinking, popping pills and sleeping for days.

Big Red continued to ask Dior questions and she continued to answer them even as customers started to trickle in. When customer demands went beyond what Big Red could do at the register like a price check or purchase he had to tend to the sales floor. He asked Dior could they reschedule their conversation and Dior asked when. She thought he was going to say a time after the weekend like on Monday morning but he was thinking sooner like when his staff coverage came in the next hour.

Big Red asked if Dior was familiar with the San Fran Cake & Pie Factory and she said she knew of it but she had never been. He told her to walk a couple of blocks up Market Street to the Powell Street Trolley turnaround and from the turnaround go a couple of blocks up Powell Street to the Geary Street Department Store on her right side before the stoplight. The restaurant was at the top floor and inside the store entrance was the elevator to take her to the rooftop.

Big Red said soon as his staff arrived to cover the store he would meet her to continue her interview and he gave Dior specific directives for when she came off the elevator at Cake & Pie.

She was told to add her name on the waiting list for a table for two and wait in the waiting area. If her name was called before he arrived he told her to take the table and he would find her. He told her to go ahead and order what she wanted if she was ready to eat and he would settle the tab when he got there.

III

Big Red entered the Cake & Pie Factory about an hour later.

Dior had eaten her meal and she was filling her mouth with double size bites of a slice of Lemon Meringue Pie.

Big Red sat down and did not need to look at the menu to place his order. He knew what he wanted and soon as his appetizers came he devoured them and guzzled down two and a half apple martinis. Half of his third drink he shared discreetly with Dior and he was careful not to get caught slipping his vodka to her.

Big Red was calling their time together an interview but they were laughing and talking about Dior's dreams and their discussion became about more than her skills and work experience.

Big Red flagged their server to order them both something to keep warm as Dior continued telling him where she saw herself in ten years. He ordered himself a hot coffee with warm cream and brown sugar and he ordered Dior a hot chocolate how she said she wanted it with extra whip cream and chocolate sauce.

Dior was saying she saw herself as a dancer, a children's book writer, a pediatrician and as a wife with two children by the age of thirty-five.

She and Big Red shared some laughter talking about her plans for achieving her three dreams before getting married and starting a family at age thirty.

Big Red raised his cup when the server sat their beverages on the table and he told Dior to raise her cup for a toast to forever dreaming big. He said holidays were for making wishes and having dreams come true and as their cups tapped he told Dior she should make a wish before she took her first sip.

Dior asked was he going to make a wish too and he said he already had.

The cold midday air around their small patio table for two was bearable but the talking between them naturally began to dull down. They had marveled enough at the sight of the colorfully decorated giant Union Square Christmas Tree across the street and Big Red insisted Dior let him take her home.

During their ride Big Red asked if Dior would meet him for a second interview but before Dior nodded her okay she asked was that his wish and Big Red asked her what did she think.

At Dior's drop off Big Red bid her a good weekend and he told her to expect a car to pick her up the following Monday afternoon then at the end of lunch on Monday Big Red asked could a car pick her up Tuesday for dinner and Dior again nodded her okay.

For weeks Dior said yes every time Big Red asked to send a car to pick her up for dinner or to a different jaunt of his choice.

Sometimes Big Red brought her home afterward and sometimes he sent her home in a car but the Friday of their third week dating he took her home and he made a detour. He parked them not far from Dior's house near the water basin at the Candlestick Park shoreline and he rolled a blunt of weed on his lap.

Big Red offered Dior the first toke but she declined.

He asked had she ever smoked weed and yes she had once with her aunt but she did not like the feeling of being high.

Dior asked why he liked to get high and Big Red took a long slow hit of his blunt then he cracked his car window to blow his smoke out.

He hit the weed again and as he reached behind Dior's seat he said he came up in a smoking household and the first person he ever smoked weed with was his mom and his brother.

Dion held up a sealed white letter size envelope and he handed Dior the envelope after he blew his second drag of smoke out the window.

Dior accepted the envelope and Big Red told her plainly if she wanted to be his, he would take care of her, her little brother and her aunt.

Dior could feel the envelope stuffed full of money and she asked skeptically what she had to do for the money.

Big Red said she did not have to do nothing and it was up to her however she wanted them to be.

Dior looked at the envelope. She squeezed it and held it at different slants and she was tempted not to let the envelope go but some sass came out her ass from where she did not know.
She aggressively threw the thick paper covered wad of cash at Big Red's chest catching Big Red off guard and he choked up the weed smoke he had just dragged into his lungs.
He was not expecting that to be Dior's reaction and he was not quick enough to block the envelope from hitting him.

Dior had never saw so much money in her life and she had to swallow her drool to speak but she amicably told Big Red her being fifteen did not mean she was game-goofy. Not his money or the twenty years he had on her could sway what she did with her body.
She said real love blocked his way of getting to that delight and if by some strange circumstance she were about that life, her pussy was priced at way more than he could fit in any size envelope.

IV

Richie Laurent Rich was born eighteen months from the day Dior walked into Four One Five.

Dior completed her freshman year of high school and half the tenth grade but she kept only to herself.

She dropped out after she got too big to hide her pregnancy and no one missed her.

She did not have anyone asking where she went when she returned from an out of town trip and it was nobody's topic how she afforded a nice car with no driver's license and nice clothes and shoes and jewelry with no job.

The money Big Red had her living on she could not get working for the hourly wage a teenager with no high school diploma could land and without any friends no one inquired who her baby-daddy was.

Her and Big Red were in agreement that show and tell was for kids. She had no problem keeping their relationship top secret and she fancied only those she loved. For them, she prepared savory meals day and night to bring them joy and she let no one but immediate family lounge inside of her house of fine interior.

Chapter 5

A PERFECT FAMILY

Dior was home with Dion the night she went into labor. He was the one to call Big Red who came right away to take them to the hospital.

Both Dion and Big Red stayed in the delivery room for Richie's birth and they were the only two that knew Big Red was the father of Dior's child.

Big Red was by Dior's side during delivery but she told medical staff her baby-daddy was murdered. The lie kept the lid on Big Red being the one to impregnate her as a minor and Big Red wearing scrubs helping to hold one of her thighs wide screaming for her to push gave medical staff the notion he was the grieving grandfather standing in for his son.

Roderick Lowell Rich was the person Dior implied she was pregnant by. She would not have said his actual name but a nurse who was trying to be sympathetic said for her to say her baby-daddy's name out loud to honor his spirit.

Lillian had the itch again to say something at Dior's mention of Roderick.

It was the same itch she had at Dior's mention of Ivory but same as with Ivory she did not know how Dior would take what she had to say. There was the risk Dior would clam up hearing Roderick was her older boy crush when she was eleven-years-old and he made her stay shushed about their romance but his last morning alive she had given her virginity to him.

I

Roderick was Big Red's baby boy he kept under his wing.

He frequently spoke of him even around Dior and she knew of him to that end but she was a year older from a different part of the city and had never met him. It was unforeseen for her to associate herself with him the way she did in the hospital and it made Big Red distressed.

He got teary eyed and chocked up but he set his triggered emotions aside and he kept wiping Dior's face. His voice stayed calm as he soothingly told her in her ear to breathe she was doing great.

Dior knew she was wrong not to get Big Red's permission to speak on Roderick but he was too grief stricken by his murder for her to get his permission beforehand.

Big Red had to lower his son's body into a grave right after throwing him a big fifteenth birthday bash and he blamed himself.

His son was shot outside a basketball tournament coming to see him play and he was the one left holding Roderick as he died in his arms of multiple bullets tearing through his body.

There were no good times in the six months between Roderick's death and Richie's birth for Dior to approach any topic about Roderick and she had also not found a fitting time to mention to Big Red she knew his eldest son.

Reddy Lawrence Rich Jr. attended Jo D. Byron High School the same year Dior did.

They shared a zodiac sign but he was a few weeks younger.

He transferred to JDB High the first semester of their freshman year and he became an annoying pest to Dior in one of her classes.

She purposefully avoided him and never gave him the time of day but her rejecting him did not stop his advances.

II

Reddy drove a flashy car and thought he was too fine looking to be turned down by any girl.

He bragged about his family's money for the attention and to get friends but he was not the brightest light bulb in the box and he had behavioral issues.

He had already been kicked out of a top private school and he refused homeschooling but a transfer to JDB High put him at the premier placement for the city's public school system.

Dior was not hiding that she knew Reddy but Big Red had never asked and she never had a reason come up to disclose it.

Until she shared her secret with Lillian no one knew it was Reddy blabbing in class about Four One Five being his family store that he could get anyone a job at.

Dior pretended she was not listening to Reddy gassing the job up to a classmate.

He was saying Four One Five had a partnership with the city to hire seasonal youth workers. He said the youth got what the adults got like the same high wages, discounts and free shit and trips out of town for meetings and the next day instead of Dior going to class she walked into Four One Five.

Dior returned to high school for her second semester of freshman year and she was back in class with Reddy but being rude as could be like it was not because of him she met his daddy.

She muted his aura by ignoring him if he said anything but simultaneously she was creeping into position to be his daddy's Side Chick.

III

Dior carried a disdain for Reddy that did not end with her dropping out of high school.

It meandered the back of her mind even during labor.

She sat at the bottom edge of the upright hospital bed with her legs wide and her baby coming out with blood and shit spilling from her insides and still she had space in her mind to dread the day her son entered the Rich family.

Like any little brother he would put his big brother on a pedestal.

He would be gung-ho to look up to him and follow him and he would want his mother to see the good in him but Dior would only ever look at Reddy and see a world-class clown.

IV

Years passed and not once did it become necessary to make Dior known to Reddy.

When Richie brought up his mom he did not call her Dior and both Big Red and Reddy would cleverly steer him into talking about something else.

It was without any significant detail being disclosed about Dior that Reddy and Richie formed their bond together with their father.

Reddy hated that his parent's constantly fought but he took a position on his dad playing around on his mom and that was the mention of other women was off limits while he and his mom remained married.

Reddy was as close to his mom as he was to his dad but he did not condone his dad cheating on his mom and he did not condone the fights his mom started with his dad.

Their fights would get loud and violent and two months before Richie's sixth birthday their fight got as bad as it had ever gotten.

Reddy had to standby and witness the police handcuff and take Big Red away for domestic violence but Reddy did not take his mom's side and against her wishes he attended his father's court dates.

He watched the court sentence Big Red to serve ninety-days in county jail but he did not see his father freed for two years.

V

Every night until Big Red's arrest he was home to tuck Richie in bed and every Friday afternoon he was one of the parent volunteers in Richie's kindergarten classroom.

He and Richie spent their Friday evening's afterschool with Reddy and every other week their Friday evening involved the barber chair.

Richie's sixth birthday was his first birthday with his dad behind bars and for the first time since he was two-years-old Big Red would not be there to take him for a haircut.

It was on Dior to take him but Reddy was his barber and chances were he might identify his little brother's mom as the girl he pursued to no avail at JDB High.

VI

Sucka Free Cutz was known as Reddy's barbershop. He was the top barber and he ran the place but he was not an owner. He was a high school dropout at sixteen same as Dior but he was gifted at cutting hair and his uncle recognized his talent.

Maxim Gene Gilman V was Ivory's baby brother. He made Reddy enroll in a dual program at the San Fran Barbering College and at almost twenty-years-old Reddy obtained his barber license with a General Education Diploma.

Reddy was put in charge of the brand new barbershop Sucka Free Cutz as a graduation gift and Maxim was one of the three co-owners. He coughed up more than half the money to acquire the business and he ran business operations with Ivory. She was a substantial investor at thirty-three percent and Big Red was a silent partner. His share of the business was less than ten percent but he made the bank deposits for the shop, restocked shop supplies and he oversaw the shop upkeep.

VII

Dior missed three of Richie's haircut appointments because she did not want to encounter Reddy and for those six weeks Richie talked about nothing but his big brother giving him a design cut for his birthday. He came home everyday from school having the same conversation about getting the freshest haircut on the planet because his big brother was the illest barber in the Bay.

Richie had never celebrated his birthday close enough to San Fran to have a party and invite guests so he did not know how to act. He was more excited about getting a haircut to show off than he was about his actual birthday party.

Dior knew she had to take Richie to get his haircut but she waited for the Friday before his party when all she could do was pick him up from school, drive to the barbershop and be a walk-in.

VIII

The night before Richie's haircut he was sitting at his desk in his bedroom and Dior asked him had he found a picture of what he was going to ask his brother to design in his scalp.

Richie showed Dior a picture he started to cut out from the cover of his coloring and activity storybook and the picture was of a Superheroine with her crime fighting family.

Cipher Black was the story of an average run-of-the-mill Black woman turned badass.

The Spirit Kingdom's Guardian of Humanity saw her fit to carry his son Mega from heaven to earth and Mega was being created to defend humankind against three of The Spirit Kingdom's fallen angels. They had come to earth on a mission to destroy humanity and Mega was to grow up and lead an army to stop them.

Cipher Black was a reclusive emotional quirky type beyond an age for having children but she was the Spirit Kingdom's cherry-picked vessel and one night a baby arrived inside her.

She was using her parent's bathroom that adjoined their bedroom to the TV room and on her parent's bathroom floor she went from being childless to delivering a superhuman son and inheriting his superhuman gifts.

Cipher Black's parents were home. She had a parent on the other side of each bathroom door but they could not hear her screaming out for them.

They were in a deep sleep having the same dream about the Guardian of Humanity. He had visited them to give them the special resources and protections to achieve their new purpose in life and that was to help their daughter and new grandson combat evil.

The picture Richie chose had Cipher Black's parents standing side by side.

Their raised hands were clasped in the air forming an upside down V between them and Cipher Black's mother had her left arm around Cipher Black's shoulder.

Cipher Black's right arm was held up pointed straight parallel to the ground with her elbow locked and her hand balled in a clenched fist.

Her left hand rested by her hip and was holding Mega's child size hand.

The Guardian of Humanity was perched above the family with outstretched arms holding the four of them together on both sides. He held his son's left hand in his left hand and he held Mega's grandfather's right hand in his right hand.

The five characters appeared as one beneath their storybook title One Force and Dior asked Richie why did he pick the cover image.

Richie said because he saw himself as Mega. He saw Dior as Cipher Black. His big brother Roderick he saw as the Guardian of Humanity. He saw Big Red in place of Cipher Black's mom and Reddy he saw in place of Cipher Black's dad because to him his family was One Force.

Dior was in awe of Richie's imagination and she smooched on his chubby cheeks a bunch of times after he finished elaborating on his haircut design. She told him he was amazing and should always cherish his creativity and she said his father and brothers would be as proud of him as she was.

IX

Dior and Richie arrived at Sucka Free Cutz and it was packed to the door with old and young men and mommas with their sons waiting to be next for any open barber.

The six barber chairs were full and when Dior and Richie entered the shop Reddy did not look up from the head he was working on.

Dior did not go further than the crowded waiting area but Richie animatedly took off in his brother's direction.

Reddy was in the first station from the storefront and in the second station was the shop's female barber.

She was an average height brown skinned woman with hair hanging almost to her thighs.

She wore an oversize pair of beautiful feather earrings and her body was covered in a long Aztec print Kaftan with splits up both sides. She gathered the Kaftan at her midsection with a gold belt she tightened to fit her thirty-six inch waist and the belt matched her flat gold sandals laced from her ankle to her knee.

Her barber station featured framed Native American pride sayings and drawings and art pieces and before Richie reached his brother he stopped at her station to hug her affectionately.

The lady kissed Richie's forehead asking why had she not seen his angel-face in so long and Richie smiled but he shrugged his shoulders to signify he did not know why. She asked did the tooth fairy pay him double for his two missing front teeth but he shrugged again then ran to his big brother.

Reddy was unfastening a black customized SFC cape for his customer to rise from his barber chair and he saw Richie come in his station. He had no free hands with the SFC cape in one hand and his clippers in the other hand but he bent down anyway to give his little brother an elbow bump with a few extra theatrics that made Richie laugh.

Richie stood mid-thigh to Reddy and he remained at his side while Reddy wrapped up with his customer.

Reddy's customer needed a tad of Reddy's assistance getting to his feet and he hardly checked the mirror for satisfaction. He paid for his haircut and said goodbye and Reddy did not have to tell Richie to bypass the waiting customers. He already knew the drill and like any natural born Very Important Person he simply climbed his VIP butt into Reddy's newly open chair.

Richie pulled the picture for his design out his backpack and he held it while he waited.

Reddy hung up the adult cape and he had Richie stand a moment for him to wipe down his barber chair. He used a mini broom and dustpan to clean his floor area then he dropped his clippers inside a clear jar of disinfectant and he went to go use the bathroom.
He returned to his barber station and draped Richie with a black kid size SFC cape and he asked who had brought him to the barbershop.

Richie pointed to the crowded waiting area and did not use his words but Reddy was using a towel to finish cleaning his clippers. He was not looking at Richie until he glanced up from his clippers a few seconds later and he followed Richie's finger but Dior quickly turned another direction.
She looked down into her purse for something, anything and after she decided on a piece of gum she looked back towards Richie to find him and Reddy focused on the picture for his haircut.

It was a little over an hour before Richie came excitedly crashing into Dior's body and she accidently caught Reddy's eye. She had not seen Reddy for more than six years but he gave her a head nod to let her know he saw her and Dior flashed him a side smirk lip curl. She was hopeful he did not know who she was and she had no reason to go over to his barber station. There was no money to exchange for Richie's haircut and in case Reddy felt beholden to speak out of courtesy Dior gently gripped Richie's hand and pulled him hurriedly out the revolving door of Sucka Free Cutz.

In the car ride back home Dior asked Richie if he liked his haircut and his response was he loved his haircut more than anything in the world.

Dior asked kiddingly would he say it was bomb and Richie said it was for sure bomb and he blew up his hands with an explosive sound.

Dior asked Richie about the woman who kissed him and he said his brother told him he could call her Auntie.

Saba Yazzie was Maxim's girlfriend and Richie said he first met her in what he described to his mom as that humongous house like the size of his school.

Dior asked had he been going to the big house a lot and Richie said not a lot only sometimes for him and his dad to get his brother.

Dior's next question was what did him and his brother talk about during his haircut and it was just what Dior was afraid of.

Richie had invited his big brother to his birthday party. He said he begged and begged during his haircut for Reddy to please come and he even said with their daddy in jail it was his job as a big brother to come in their dad's place.

Dior told Richie she could not believe he went that far and she asked how he got that idea in his head.

Dior was driving and she could not turn around to see why Richie was not answering her but she cocked the rear-view mirror to see him holding his shoulders shrugged with an upside down grin on his face. She repeated her question and Richie said the idea just popped out his mouth to get his brother to come to his birthday party but it did not work. His brother was booked with clients and Dior fixed her mirror back for Richie to not see her face expressed happiness that Reddy would not be able to make his party.

Dior knew Richie wanted his big brother at his party more than he wanted any of the other guests. She knew before going into Sucka Free Cutz how badly Richie wanted his brother to be invited but Dior chose not to converse with Reddy on any details of the party. She did not want to see him the next day under any circumstances.

She had long dreaded Reddy knowing of her romantic involvement with his father because him finding out actualized her choice to bed the one man married to his mom. His father was old enough to be her father and Big Red had not only committed adultery with her he had produced living breathing walking proof of his adultery.

Dior felt it was despicable to face Reddy with what she had taken from him. He was a reflection of the wrong she had done to secure the perfect life and to keep him at bay let her remain in the bubble that protected her delusion of *a perfect family.*

Inside Dior's bubble her and Big Red kept to themselves and eventually they were going to prepare for the day they could no longer hide what they had but Dior could in no way prepare for Richie's sixth birthday to be the day.

On all Richie's previous birthdays Big Red packed him and Dior up in a nice roomy rented vehicle and the three of them hit the road. By the time Richie was five-years-old, he had been to the Monterey Bay Aquarium, San Diego Zoo, Disneyland, Knott's Berry Farm and Magic Mountain.

X

Richie was allowed to decide where he wanted to have his sixth birthday party and he picked the Discovery Kingdom in Vallejo California. He and seven of his friends rode elephants, fed tigers and kissed dolphins. They got their faces painted and their hands and arms tattooed and they screamed their lungs out on several rollercoasters and water rides.

As the sun began to drop, a nice warm breeze started blowing in and Reddy made a grandstand of an appearance with a big-boob girl on his arm.
She wore a swimsuit beneath a thin colorful sarong and her hair matched her attire. It was three-toned with black at the root, blonde in the middle and fuchsia at the tip and she carried Richie's big gift bag in her hand.

Reddy came close to Dior compelling her to take two steps away to keep a respectful gap. He told his date to hand

Dior the gift and his date handed Dior the bag but before Dior could say thank you Reddy said she was welcome. He called her Hot Chocolate like that was her name then he said oops she was a Hot Chocolate Mama now and he asked did she remember him but Dior pretended to be occupied with a parent.

She had just let parents know the party would be ending soon and she had given Richie permission for him and his friends to get in line for their last ride.

The one parent Dior was trying to engage was trying to return to their kid.

They had not walked away yet because of Dior not letting them but once they eased away Reddy asked Dior again if she remembered him from JDB High.

Dior said her memory was bad and high school was so long ago but Reddy asked if she knew Hot Chocolate was her name around the boy's locker room and Dior ignored him. She busied herself with opening Cipher Black themed napkins and bowls for the Cipher Black themed cake and vanilla ice cream but that did not stop Reddy from talking and for Dior it was high school all over again.

Reddy said he was genuinely surprised to see her bring Richie for his haircut. He asked his date was it a dream or a nightmare his pops was the reason nobody including him could smell Dior's panties back in the day.

Reddy's date smiled knowing he was being silly and he was facing her admitting he and some other fellas ranked Dior the finest girl in high school. He faced Dior's direction to tell her a couple of his boys bet they could get her number but they reported back to him she was ice cold.

Reddy began to laugh. He said he was laughing that the gossip whispers were true about Dior having a rich sugar daddy spoiling her making it impossible for the dudes their age. He asked was the joke on him though her sugar daddy was his real daddy but Dior did not answer. She repositioned the party table favors around the cake and repositioned them again to stay busy.

Reddy said he never would have thought his pops had it in him to snag a young cutie like Dior and Dior glanced towards Reddy's date but she was checking her phone.

Dior grinned and told Reddy his reminiscent schoolboy tales were flattering and she thanked him to get him to stop talking but that did not work.

Reddy went on and on about Dior knowing all the schoolboys wanted her fine ass and he commenced to recall the most memorable stories of boy locker room talk.

Dior swore to Reddy what he was saying was news to her. She said she had no idea she was that popular, which was a lie. She had every guy in school even the ones with girlfriends making a pass at her anytime they ran into her alone but Dior was never interested in any of them or anything else.
Her high school days were only a few months after she was the one to discover her mother at home dead from a heroin overdose.

Dior descended into a dark place and was full of melancholy and her going to high school was her Aunt Emerald's doing. When Aunt Emerald stepped into her and Dion's life clean and sober she was constructive and caring but she guilt-tripped Dior into getting an education by saying her mother's wishes were for her to get an education.

Dior was not trying to be around people.

She learned from her mom if she stayed away from people there would be no one to ask her questions but she went to high school to satisfy her mother's wishes and what helped her cope with her grief was keeping to a routine similar to when her mom was alive.

She went to and from school and home and nowhere in between and she did quit her youth dance troupe but she continued the physical conditioning required by her dance instructor.

Every troupe member had to do pushups, sit-ups, squats, jumping jacks and planks before bed. There was no food after seven at night for the first four nights of the week beginning on Sunday and there was no breakfast before seven in the morning Monday thru Thursday. She had to run an hour three times per week and no matter what time she went to sleep she got up every morning to meditate at sunrise and thank God for another day.

Dior's routine worked as her therapy but her pregnancy made it hard for her to stick to it.

Being with child she fed every craving and ate anytime she wanted and after Richie was born she ate anytime she could.

She was never exercising and she went up two dress sizes to show for it.

The weight gain had changed her appearance but not in the worst way and she dressed her bigger body just as sexy as the smaller one.

Receiving regular compliments on her style motivated her to keep dressing fly but Reddy and his kinky remarks made her wish she could be invisible around him.

He had brought a long skinny babe with him to Richie's birthday party but his eyes were not on her. His eyes were on Dior and his comments were mainly about her thickness.

Dior asked Reddy had no one taught him it was rude to call a woman fat and he said he was not calling her fat but Dior felt fat.

She had reached the limit for what looked firm and good on her frame. She had started weekend workouts to keep her dress size from growing to a size sixteen and she carved herself a three-hour gym slot on both Saturday and Sunday mornings.

Most weekend mornings she made it to the gym but what usually happened was what happened the morning of Richie's sixth birthday.

Richie had his life setup to where he was served breakfast in bed on weekends same like Dior did for his dad but Richie had to have his breakfast ready for his morning cartoon time.

Dior's gym routine was supposed to be ninety minutes on cardio and weightlifting then sixty minutes going from the whirlpool to the steam room to the sauna to the shower leaving her thirty minutes to dress and get home to make Richie his breakfast.

The morning of Richie's birthday Dior made it to the gym but she was late.

She could have finished her workout and went back home to Richie without the whirlpool, steam room, sauna and shower but she cut the cardio and weightlifting short.

Her cutting cardio and weightlifting to fit into Richie's world was why she could not comfortably fit into the size fourteen's she was steadily buying and stretching to the max.

Thankfully Richie's party area inside Discovery Kingdom was in line with the summer sun. She was getting away with the fat creases and the extra skin showing and most of what Reddy was saying about her size was harmless.

He said he would not use the word fat to describe her and he leaned close to her ear to say if he called her anything it would be sexier than a Clydesdale but if she wanted him to keep it PG he could not say much more than that.

It was a few seconds later Reddy tested the waters saying Dior's weight had gone to the right places but then he crossed the line. He said her pound cakes looked double baked and were sure worth a triple taste and Dior was done with playing nice.

Reddy's voice had been made her want to puke on his brand-spanking-new shoes and on his bitch pretty airbrushed painted toenails.

Dior could see his Black fuchsia Blondie did not give a fuck about anything. She had left it on Dior to deal with Reddy but were Dior to slap the shit out of Reddy's face old girl would be trying to give a fuck about that and Dior did not want to start a fight at her son's birthday party.

Her alternative to violence was to turn Reddy into a helper. Her rationale was if she gave him tasks she would not have to listen to him talk and she curtly asked him to gather Richie and his friends together for the cake cutting.

Richie begged for Reddy to be at his side during his cake

cutting but Dior said no. She pulled Reddy from the kid cir-cle to video everyone signing happy birthday and she tasked him with taking plenty of action pictures of Richie with his friends having their cake and ice cream.

Reddy was given a final task to usher the combined dozen plus children and their parent chaperones to the VIP parking. Three black suburban trucks were awaiting them and Dior clashed with Richie loading him into their truck telling him no, no, no and no.

No his brother could not ride in the truck with them.

No his brother was not coming to the hotel for his slum-ber party.

No she was not taking him to his brother's house the next day to show him his presents and no he could not use her phone to call Reddy right that second to thank him for coming to his party.

Chapter 6

HER WAY IN LIFE

Richie's sixth birthday was two years and four months prior to Royal's born day.

On many mornings following Dior and Lillian's bonding moment they tossed around baby names while Dior cooked breakfast. She told Lillian she was praying for a niece. A niece would be the next best thing to the daughter she never had and she asked Lillian to keep it between them she prayed for a girl. The name she picked out for if she had a daughter was Richie and when she came up with the name Royal for Lillian's baby she said that name too was unisex.

Lillian loved the name for a girl but unlike Dior she did not have a gender preference. She was okay with if she delivered a boy but if she did have a son she said she was naming him Dion Jacob Hayes Jr.

Dior got to the hospital before Lillian delivered Royal but the delivery was in progress.

She told a nurse she was the aunt and she belonged in the delivery room but the nurse said too many people were already crowded inside.

The doctor had requested anyone else wait until medical staff came out.

Dior had her phone off for Friday's were her pamper day of the week and she got Dion's message late about Lillian going into labor.

She tried to fight back the tears for missing the birth of her brother's first baby but she did not win the fight.

Big Red held her in his arms as she bawled her eyes out and they waited for the nurse more than an hour to escort them to the room where Lillian had been moved.

Dior let Big Red enter Lillian's room first so he could hold the door open for her. She walked in front of him and he trailed her closely with Richie and Reddy trailing him.

There was a large whiteboard in the room that Dior noticed because it had her first and last name written terribly in Dion's handwriting. She then lost all equanimity realizing what was written was for her namesake.

Dior squealed and jumped and kissed Dion and Lillian raspily said surprise to them having a girl.

Lillian said she was sorry but she needed to close her eyes and rest them a minute and Dior told Lillian her body should be taxed pushing out eight pounds and she could give it the recharge it was demanding her baby was in good hands.

Dior went to look at her niece in Grandma Dah's arms and she was bewitched. She could not look away from her and she did not stop hogging her once Grandma Dah handed her over.

The baby was hers for the time being and anyone who came in Lillian's room had to look at Royal in Dior's arms.

Royal squirmed and was a little fussy but Dior just patted her swaddled two-hour-old bum without raising her head to notice Lillian or anyone else.

I

Lillian awakened from her powernap and could see everyone in her room without raising her head from her pillow.

She wanted Dion to get her some water for her dry throat but he seemed bewitched by Big Red. The two of them were shoulder-to-shoulder leaned against the footboard and Big Red was speaking at a tone only Dion could hear or not hear from the way Dion's eyes were locked on Big Red's mouth. He was hanging on every word to plumb what was being said.

Reddy brushed by Dion and his dad coming back in Lillian's room from using the hallway bathroom and he did not take a peak at Lillian but she was looking at him.

Lillian had never seen Reddy and Dion in a conversation. She had never seen Reddy and Big Red in a conversation and she knew Dior did not fool with him. She watched him thinking how did he get to be someone at her child's birth and she might have said something were he not sucking up Kamber's time in one of the four corners of Lillian's room.

Reddy had Kamber giddy and giving him her most sensual body language. He was pasted to her arm and was in her ear and he must have been whispering saccharine nothings to which she was reacting like a lust-stricken schoolgirl.

Only the lord knew what story Kamber told Reddy about her scrapes and bruises and Lillian wanted to know what they had got started during the length of her nap but she was more curious about what Big Red was saying to have Dion's undivided attention.

The one person sitting nearest Dion and Big Red was Eliza. She could have probably heard some of what they were mouthing but too bad she was having her own conversation through her headphones with the earpieces in both ears.

II

Eliza arrived at the hospital after Kamber.

When Eliza first showed up and removed her trench coat Lillian told her she would have easily felt overdressed for the hospital and too cold to wear what she was wearing but Eliza said she was dressed-down. She wanted to be there for the giving birth part so she ran out the house makeup free and spent no time getting ready.

Kamber told Lillian with Eliza standing there that Eliza was a liar. She said her outfit was not dressed down nor would she call her overdressed. If anything that ass was underdeessed waltzing out the house getting rained on and shit knowing damn fucking well the Bay had the coldest nights ever.

Eliza laughed and told Kamber to stop being the fashion

police. She had worn the outfit more than once. Her rule of thumb was it did not matter where she wore old shit and she asked did Kamber not see her outerwear. She put her coat back on over her shoulders and she told Kamber to go ahead and put her hands on it. She said she wanted her to know the feel of a real expensive gift that kept an underdressed ass dry and real warm.

⟡

Eliza was seated at the bottom corner of Lillian's hospital bed.

She was bent over with her elbow dug into her thigh supporting her fist under her chin.

Her long shapely legs were crossed and she was holding her cellphone in one hand.

Her top leg bounced up and down slowly and Lillian could see the red-bottomed soles of her shoes.

The shoes matched her red one-piece romper shorts and Lillian was childish enough to ask were her red-bottomed shoes also dressed-down but she did not ask because she did not want to start her and Kamber back going at it.

Eliza's free hand ran her long almond-shaped fingernails through her long dark brown hair and she thought she was using her inside voice but she was not.

She was loud enough for Lillian to hear her whine disingenuously about being sorry and begging for the person on the other end of the call not to be mad at her.

Eliza said yes she did take the Skylark without asking but soon as she left the hospital she was bringing it back and she asked did the person not care Lillian had the baby.

Lillian knew who the caller was soon as she heard Skylark.

Mali Montgomery was Eliza's dude. He owned a pearl painted old-school Skylark with a black convertible top and Eliza referenced him for the longest time as her manfriend. She never said his name and every time she came around sporting a conspicuous new trinket it was her manfriend who gave it to her or it was her manfriend who gave her the gift card she purchased the new trinket with.

It was years before Eliza gave up her manfriend's true identity and when she eventually introduced him to Lillian he introduced himself as Monty.

Monty was his nickname from family and close friends but Eliza never called him Monty and once their courtship went public she referred to him as Mali.

Eliza met Mali the first time she ran away from home at twelve-years-old.

She walked out her front door barefoot in a cotton floral nighty and she walked through the night unconsciously making several twists and turns ending up on the mountaintop of Twin Peaks.

Twin Peaks was a place for tourists and lovers but Eliza had showed up before the tourists. They would be arriving to snap pictures and wait in line to see the city through telescopes but it was still the time of morning for lovers to be rocking the backseats of their cars.

Two parked cars were not far enough away to miss Eliza

collapse. If they were watching the skyline in her direction they would have seen her crumple to the ground and curl in a ball at the base of the four-foot cement safety barrier where Mali later ran up and discovered her.

Lillian was thirsty but she was not ready to draw the room's attention.

Eliza's apologetic phone convo with Mali had gone sideways from something he said about her being spoiled and unappreciative. She repeated spoiled and unappreciative back to him and she asked was she not supposed to be spoiled by her man.

She further asked what was it she was supposed to be more appreciative about when he was the one being unappreciative complaining his girlfriend did not ask to drive his car knowing damn well he did not want her asking someone else for a ride.

If Eliza would have looked to her right side she would have seen Lillian's eyes on her and Lillian would have said something but effort was what Lillian could not muster and with Eliza being heavy into her call it would have taken effort to get Eliza.

Lillian could have used her leg to prod Eliza in the back but her legs were weak. Her throat was too dry to go above a whisper and her being awake had gone unnoticed by every adult in her hospital room.

She thought the two children seated on the floor had noticed her.

One child glanced up while her eyes were on him but in a couple of seconds his eyes went back to the phone in his hand.

The other child raised his head as if he felt Lillian watching but his eye contact lasted less time than the other boy.

It was like they both looked through her searching their tiny minds for something they found while looking through Lillian.

III

Richie had one of his arms pressed to Dior's leg. One of Richie's feet was almost touching the knee of Eliza's little brother who was seated crossed-legged on the floor beside him.

David Daniel Duncan Jr. came into Eliza's life as a newborn baby and if anyone asked David his name he said Three-D because that was all anyone ever called him.

Three-D's parents were deceased and no one knew Three-D was not Eliza's blood relative including Three-D.

Eliza and her mom were the only family Three-D had and he and Eliza were as close as any siblings could be.

On any occasion Eliza was around she was his nurturer and she brought him everywhere she went that was appropriate. She took him to and from preschool until he was age five and now she was taking him to and from elementary school.

She was the one to help him with his homework and play with him and reward him with sweets and tickles to keep him happy and she gave him overflowing kisses and hugs to show him love.

Three-D was two years younger than Richie but they were about the same size.

Both boys had earpieces stuck in both ears with their earpieces connected to the phones they held in their hands and their eyes were cemented to the phone.

With how overprotective Dior was of her son, Richie was surely on his phone playing a spelling game or a counting game but Eliza was too busy in her own conversation to notice what Three-D was watching or playing.

Everyone in the hospital room other than the kids and Eliza were preoccupied with someone else in the room.

Kamber was glossy-eyed gazing into Reddy's equally glossy eyes and next to them were Lillian's other two best friends talking to each other.

CoCo Marie Butler and **Jonny-London Lois Jones** had arrived during Lillian's post-labor nap.

They were over by the window seat where Grandma Dah was sitting and they were both smiling in good spirits holding each other close arm in arm like it had been forever.

Jonny-London and Kamber called themselves same-age-besties because they were the same age but Jonny-London's bond was stronger with CoCo.

Jonny-London was two years younger than CoCo but the two of them liked to party Friday and Saturday nights and they were likely together as recent as the previous weekend.

Lillian tensed her neck to lift her head a bit to peer

through the middle of CoCo and Jonny-London. She figured their bodies standing so close together hid her grandma's tiny self but Grandma Dah was not there and neither was her stuff.

Lillian remembered before her eyes forcefully closed Grandma Dah handed her baby to Dior and was talking to the nurse that showed Lillian how to latch Royal on her breast nipple to feed.

Lillian relaxed her neck seeing Grandma Dah and the nurse had gone but she continued to stare towards CoCo and Jonny-London.

Their two oversized bags were in the window seat but when CoCo moved to prop her body on the wall Jonny-London moved their bags to take the seat and the window became a big mirror.

Lillian's well-lit room contrasted with the outside darkness reflecting her room back to her.

She was drawn to the rain streaming the window and as she watched the raindrops in the reflection she roamed her memory for the last time she and her four best friends were together.

They were once joined at the hips growing up encountering one another daily but it had been nearly two years since they were in the same room and each had branched off to find *her way in life*.

IV

Jonny-London was doing the college thing and she had won a two-year academic scholarship for graduating Alamo

Park High School as her class valedictorian.

She walked the stage earlier that year with her Associates Degree and everyone thought she was finished with college including her but in preparing for graduation she had a meeting with a guidance counselor. The counselor told her if she attended summer school fulltime she would be eligible to transfer to San Fran University for the fall semester.

Jonny-London had not considered continuing her education until the counselor said in only two more years she could get a higher degree and her financial aid would follow.

Jonny-London became the first in her family to go to college but after she finished her final summer semester at junior college she became the only one from the neighborhood to make it to a university.

She was currently two months into her first semester at SFU and her financial aid had afforded her a car to commute to school from where she lived and it also covered other major purchases like her laptop, schoolbooks and her printer.

The small stuff like food, gas, clothes and shoes, hygiene products, notebooks, pens, printer paper and ink she bought with money she made selling weed on and off campus for her mom's boyfriend.

V

CoCo lived forty-five minutes outside San Fran in her condo in Benicia and she was juggling three jobs to afford her lifestyle.

During the week she was a fulltime ferryboat ticket agent and two nights per week she was a part-time driver.

On weekends she was a food and beverage cashier for

stadium baseball games and concerts but no one knew by looking at CoCo what she did for her money.

She had been in her fulltime job for five years since graduating high school and her position as a ferry ticket agent was uniformed but she went to and from and around outside of work dressed as if she was a six-figure plus-size runway supermodel.

CoCo commuted to San Fran six days per week to chase her paper but on day seven she commuted to the city to pick up her foster mom for church.

Gilda Lee George stepped into CoCo's life when CoCo was a pre-tween in need of a mother.

Gilda instantaneously made CoCo the focus of her life and once the adoption was final Gilda retired early from her nursing job at the Veteran's Hospital. She told her boss who pleaded with her to stay that the job was too demanding and she needed more control of her schedule.

Gilda became a fulltime mobile beauty consultant and with selling beauty products she was her own boss. She could be at every school fieldtrip, every school event and she was able to participate in every school fundraiser.

VI

Some of Lillian's best memories as a young girl were with Gilda.

Gilda was always driving out of town for the weekend and she liked to stay in costly amenity-rich hotels. She would be visiting a city to vend her beauty products and services at a local fair, festival or conference but she split her time making money with relaxing, sightseeing and eating good food.

Usually it was just Gilda and CoCo taking the out of town drives but a couple of times she allowed CoCo to bring Lillian, Kamber and Jonny-London. She called them her Junior Beauty Associates. She drove them to Monterey and Pismo Beach California and Reno and Lake Tahoe Nevada but on the three and four-day weekend trips she only took CoCo.

They went as far as San Diego California, Las Vegas Nevada, Portland Oregon, Seattle Washington, Salt Lake City Utah and Tucson Arizona until Gilda got into a bad car accident.

Right before Eliza joined their crew Gilda's mini vacations came to a halt but because the accident was not Gilda's fault she was awarded a settlement.

The amount was generous enough to afford her and CoCo a vacation wherever they wanted to go but she developed severe anxiety being behind the steering wheel. She could afford to fly to her destination or take a train but when she had to sit more than an hour or two at a time she suffered back and neck pain.

CoCo inherited the keys to her Momma Gilda's Cadillac at age fifteen. She was allowed to drive freely by herself without a license but when she asked to trade the Cadillac for a newer model Gilda said not until she got her license and a fulltime job.

No sooner than CoCo turned eighteen she got a job flipping burgers at a fast food restaurant. The day she cashed her first paycheck she scheduled her driving test and Gilda scheduled them for an appointment at the car dealer that same afternoon.

At midnight the morning of CoCo's test day her and Gilda sat in the Cadillac playing music drinking wine coolers and saying their goodbyes.

CoCo passed her test with flying colors and on the way to the dealer she and Gilda shared a packed lunch in the car for old time sake.

They were at the dealer a couple of hours and Gilda let CoCo choose their new vehicle.

Gilda was happy with the price and size of CoCo's choice and she hyped CoCo up about using her good sense and being mature pennywise but CoCo felt insulted. She did not want praise for being basic and in two years she returned to the car dealer without Gilda present.

CoCo had started earning more money working two jobs and she traded their new car for a newer car with a higher price and custom features.

Two more years later CoCo traded their new car again for something even newer and Gilda accused her of thinking she was too good to drive a car more than two years old.

CoCo said she certainly was too good. She then asked Gilda was every two years too basic but CoCo answered herself saying yes it was too basic and that a trade-in every year would be the better look.

Part II

CHOICES

Chapter 7

HER LIFE TO LIVE

Lillian Aroya Webster was waiting for someone to notice her.

She had observed everyone in her hospital room but after no one looked her way she called out to Dion to get her some water.

Dion had moments ago sealed Big Red's blunt with his saliva but he was still holding the blunt in his hands. He was that wrapped around whatever Big Red was saying but at the sound of Lillian's voice Dion passed the blunt so fast it dropped and Big Red had to catch it.

The blunt was probably dry but Big Red habitually struck fire from his lighter and drew the flame quickly along the seal of the blunt between both ends before he placed the blunt in his shirt pocket.

Dion forgot the water he heard Lillian ask for but he came to her bedside.

He kissed her lips and all around her face and he kissed the hand he was holding and Lillian appeared pleased. She asked was he trying to show sympathy for what she had just went through to have his child and she pushed his mouth away. She playfully insisted he keep his kisses and bring her some water but he kept kissing on her.

Big Red watched Lillian and Dion a moment then he looked at Dior. She, like everyone else in the room but for the kids, was looking at Dion love on Lillian.
Their expressions of fondness made Big Red gaze over Dior and she saw him watching her.

She motioned for his eyes to follow hers and Dior nodded with her had for him to look at the plastic oversized hospital issued water cup and he got it that Dior was nodding for him to bring Lillian the cup.

Lillian thanked Big Red and he said there was no need to thank him but she said yes there was. For paying attention enough to give her what she asked for instead of some dry ass kisses and Dion did not take offense to Lillian being snide but he agreed Big Red better not be giving his girl no kisses.

Dior came to the side of Lillian's bed next to Big Red and he stepped out of her way to let her get closer to Lillian to hand her the baby.

Dior kissed Lillian's cheek sweetly without a word and Lillian embraced Royal but she did not immediately stop eyeing Dior.
She was secretly in awe of how Dior enlivened her soft demeanor.
Merely by the way she packaged her classic beauty she could go undetected in a room until the moment she was

noticed she became the most entrancing sight.

Dion flooded Lillian with more kisses to get Lillian's eyes on him then he switched his affection to their daughter. He kissed Royal slow and gentle on the forehead, the nose, the lips and both cheeks and in between kisses he told Lillian he was about to leave with his sister and Big Red.

Lillian gave Dion a look. She needed not say a word to ask why he would be leaving her and their baby but Dion put the blame on his sister. He said Big Red was with Richie and Reddy when Dior called them to bring her to the hospital but she had asked for Dion to give her and Richie a ride home. She wanted to let Big Red go about his preexisting plans with Reddy and Lillian could not be too mad.

Dion's car was really a present to Dior from Big Red and if Dior needed a ride Dion had two choices. Give his sister the ride or give her the car.

Dion tried sugarcoating his announcement by saying it would give Lillian time with her homegirls. He promised to call and check on her and Royal when he got home but Lillian said calling when he got home was not good enough and he had to promise to return.

Big Red summoned Richie off the floor and told him to say his goodbyes.

Dior followed her man and son out of the hospital room and Dion followed behind his sister.

Reddy was the last in their group to leave.
He clearly did not want to quit his conversation with

Kamber and it seemed she had to walk him to the hospital room door before he collected the gall to pull out his phone and deposit her phone number.

I

Those four and a half people cleared space in Lillian's room and the thought crossed her mind again that the face she most cared to see was her grandmother. She had gone without saying goodbye and Lillian asked those around her where she was at.

Eliza said Grandma Dah's boyfriend came and picked her up twenty or so minutes prior, give or take a few minutes and Lillian reached for her phone. She remembered it lying on her side table but it was not there anymore and she asked where was her phone.

Eliza again was the one to answer. She said she let Three-D use it to keep him occupied but Lillian asked Eliza why give Three-D her phone and the reason was Eliza wanted to stay on her call with Mali.

Lillian told Eliza to give her call a break and let Three-D have her phone but Eliza said no because Three-D did not pay nobody phone bill and the whole room had to listen to Three-D beg for Eliza not to take Lillian's phone from him.

Eliza had a short tug of war with Three-D to pry Lillian's phone from his hands and he whined about it not being fair to mess up his game in the middle of playing.

Three-D wanted her to wait and let him finish but she gave Lillian back her phone and told him to stop being a big ass baby but he steadily grumbled about Eliza being mean and him wanting to go home to play his neighbors game.

Mali must have asked Eliza what was going on in the room because instead of Eliza shutting Three-D's grumbling up she recounted to Mali what was happening.

Lillian told Eliza she might as well put Mali's nosy ass on speakerphone but Eliza ignored Lillian. She pretended she was going to keep babbling to Mali about not giving in to Three-D's rotten behavior and she threatened to spank him and toss him in the bathroom for a time out but she caved.
She ended her call with Mali and gave Three-D her phone.

Lillian started dialing as she thanked Eliza for letting her call her Grandma Dah in peace.

Grandma Dah's phone number was in Lillian's recent call history and it was stored in her phone under Mom-Mom. She did not need to dial the phone number to reach her grandmother but Lillian liked dialing the one of very few phone numbers she knew by heart.

Lillian let the phone ring and go to voicemail two times and she was ready to call a fourth time when Grandma Dah answered the third call on the last ring and Lillian forgot her manners.
She skipped the hello how are you and accused her grandma of ignoring the danger in getting a ride from a drunk senior citizen and Grandma Dah said she was fine. She said Lillian sounded foolish but Lillian said foolish was her taking back her cigarette chain-smoking heavy beer-drinking potbellied twit of a boyfriend and Grandma Dah

told Lillian to mind her own business.

She said sorry she did not say bye before she left the hospital but she did not see the point in waking her. She had been with her a lot of time already and she complained about her own need for rest before starting her nightshift.

She tried to rush Lillian off the phone saying in the morning after work she would be back to see her and the baby but Lillian did not let her go.

She asked her grandmother had she made it home and Grandma Dah said yes she was about to shower, get in her uniform and rest her eyes on the couch a minute.

Lillian asked was her boyfriend still with her and was he staying the night at her place and Grandma Dah told her yes and yes and to stop asking questions but Lillian asked another one.

In a disgusted tone she asked why her grandma at her age was settling for a lame. He made her cry and he lied for nothing, he claimed he was broke and never offered to help with any bills and he never gave her more than two's and few's but Grandma Dah told Lillian enough with her talking about any of that.

Lillian told her to please not claim old age made her forget her old man's last debacle. Not after having her pregnant ass driving the both of them around the streets of Oaktown and San Fran looking for a reason to dump him.

Grandma Dah laughed and Lillian said it was sad not funny she knew where to find her man on the blade and Lillian asked did her grandma need to see again what her nasty boy was made of. She said she still had the video saved on her phone of him in his car getting his ding-a-ling sucked by a mature woman of the night but Grandma Dah went silent.

Her silence made Lillian rudely say hello and Grandma Dah replied calmly asking Lillian how she was feeling.

Lillian replied calmly asking Grandma Dah did she plan to use a condom and Grandma Dah scoffed.
She told Lillian she had to get off the phone but she went silent again and did not end the call.

Lillian sketchily heard a man's voice then she heard nothing like Grandma Dah covered the phone so Lillian could not hear what the man's voice was saying but she came back on the phone with a message for Lillian.

Bally Grier Manning had congratulated Lillian and Dion on their baby girl and he commented on how beautiful Royal was from a picture Grandma Dah showed him on her phone.

Lillian did not thank Bally but Bally thought she did because Grandma Dah lied and put two on the ten. She said Lillian thanked him and very much appreciated his compliment and hoped he was doing well.

Lillian told Grandma Dah that a lie through false teeth was still a lie and she asked what happened to her no longer letting the devil in.

Grandma Dah said I love you to Lillian as was customary to end every call between them no matter the nature of the call good or bad and when Lillian said I love you too she was met with the dial tone.

II

Lillian returned her cellphone to her side table and looked down at her sleeping daughter cradled in her left arm. She adjusted the knit cap on Royal's head and handed her to Jonny-London.

Jonny-London had walked over and was pressed into the side of Lillian's hospital bed with her hands out.

She accepted Royal by carefully scooping her with both her arms and she walked over to take the chair Dior freed up next to Lillian's bed.

Once Jonny-London got comfortable she asked for everybody's attention. She had some news to share that was important to her.

Eliza did not have to move but from one foot of Lillian's bed to the other and Kamber had to end the text war being waged against her by her abusive boyfriend. She zipped her phone inside the zipper area of her purse and CoCo finished the last sentence of the paragraph she was reading. She closed the fiction novel she had just seconds ago pulled from her purse and the four of them including Lillian were now looking Jonny-London's way.

Lillian blurted Oh My God Jonny-London was pregnant and Jonny-London screeched and almost woke Royal with her melodramatics. She clarified no bun was in her oven and would not be any time soon if ever and she said her big news was she had been invited to pledge a Black Greek sorority.

Eliza was first to ask what that was but Lillian did not wait for Jonny-London to answer Eliza. She questioned if

Jonny-London was talking about sororities as portrayed in the movie about Stomping The Yard and Jonny-London said yes. Movies like that and the classics about being Dazed by School or A college World being Different showed black Greek sorority life.

Kamber asked if joining a sorority meant Jonny-London was going to change but Kamber's question went unanswered due to CoCo walking over to Jonny-London and saying she was very happy for her.

CoCo could not give Jonny-London a full hug without smashing Royal so she gave her a half hug around her neck. The top of their heads touched together and Jonny-London said thanks.

CoCo asked was she excited about the invitation and had she already accepted and Jonny-London admitted she was both excited and scared and she said yes she had accepted.

Jonny-London acknowledged Kamber's question saying honestly she did not know if pledging would change her. She did know it was going to be a time commitment and with homework and sorority life, she was not going to have much time for other stuff.

Kamber restated the words other stuff and she asked the follow up question they were all thinking. Was Jonny-London calling them the other stuff and picking the sorority over them and Jonny-London said that question was not fair.

They never asked was Eliza picking Mali over them or was CoCo picking her however many jobs over them or was Lillian picking her new family over them or was Kamber being in a new nigga face all night her picking yet another boyfriend over them.

Jonny-London revealed that on the coming Monday at noon she was going to an Invitational and it would be her first official pledge club event with the others on her pledge line.

The women who could make them into sorority sisters would be interviewing them and after the Invitational she would know more of what to expect but the four of them would not know more because she was joining a secret society.

She asked could they be okay with that or did they forget how to be her ride or die bitches. Her day-ones were supposed to support decisions that were hers to make and if necessary lend her their ear to listen and give her their shoulder to cry on.

Kamber said Jonny-London sounded like she was joining some cult shit and Jonny-London said no it was not some cult shit but she would not be telling them every single thing anymore because those days were officially over.

She reminded them that her saying a word about pledging was a courtesy to them as her best friends and they should need no explanation. She said for them to miss her with their shit talking and let a bitch live since it was *her life to live.*

Eliza asked Jonny-London had she finished sharing her news and yes Jonny-London was finished so Eliza shared with them her surprise from Mali. He added her name as his plus one to the VIP guest list for the annual invite-only Mayor's Ball and Eliza put deep emphasis on VIP and invite-only. She then explained the Mayor's Ball was the only night of the year where the Shadow Criminals who were above the law commingled with the political, academic and social elite.

Jonny-London questioned why Eliza was so turned up for an event someone almost every year got shot at or around or because of but Eliza did not get to say why.

Kamber blurted she was done-done. She said not another nigga was about to beat on her and no matter how much he could do for her she was worth far more.

Lillian responded to Kamber that she was happy she was done-done being abused but she doubted it Kamber truly knew her worth.

Kamber asked Lillian to explain what she was suggesting and Lillian said she did not think she knew her worth. She asked that Kamber allow her to point out her saying the shit seemed influenced by the newest pussy-hound chasing her panties.

CoCo jumped in saying she had something important to say and they looked at CoCo before Kamber could go off on Lillian for calling her disingenuous.

CoCo told them she had grown bored with her work. She wanted what was recently explained to her as a career.
She heard a guest union representative share a story at a recent union meeting about how he decided on a career path. He set a simple career goal but he had big ambition and he spent his days eagerly unionizing jobs for hardworking people. He negotiated the best contracts to improve the quality of life for individuals working in the blue-collar industries and he went so far as to ensure their blue-collar

families shared in a great employee experience.

Kamber interrupted CoCo to say they could see she was very passionate about the union dude but they were up close and in a small space. She could totally bring down her energy a level or two and they would still feel her but to please continue.

CoCo more calmly picked up where she left off saying unionizing was how her union rep planned to make his mark on the world and he decided thirty years ago when he was in his early forties.

CoCo pointed out her being only twenty-three but she asked if she lived thirty, forty or even fifty or sixty more years was she okay being a ticket agent or a delivery driver or a seasonal cashier in her sixties or seventies.

CoCo sank the room into thoughts of aging until Lillian caught them off guard revealing that Dion was cheating. He had been sneaking around for months with some older hot looking bitch and ears stood at attention listening for Lillian to continue.

She admitted to being on some detective shit and following Dion on a couple separate instances. She got a glimpse of him talking with a woman she did not know but she recognized the residence where she followed him.

It was the ritzy townhome of Big Red's other baby-momma and Lillian could not remember her name but she knew the shoe museum where she worked. She had been to the museum with her son Roderick and Eliza elbowed Kamber to verify Roderick was that piece Lillian messed around with who got knocked off.

Lillian said she knew the shoe place from Roderick

taking her there to design a pair of sneakers he bought her but she never got to wear them and CoCo said she remembered that. He ordered the shoes to be delivered to his address and Jonny-London said she remembered that too because of Lillian telling them of his murder before the shoes could arrive.

Lillian said she had to stalk the shoe museum to find the woman she seen Dion with.

She figured the woman was a neighbor or friend or co-worker of Roderick's mom that Dion had likely met being around Big Red and she was right on the money.

On two occasions after watching the shoe museum she tailed Roderick's mom home and she saw the woman that resembled the one she got a glimpse of with Dion.

CoCo queried for more details and Lillian said she did not have hard proof like Dion in the act of sex but she was not a fool. His was suddenly into foreplay sucking toes and giving foot rubs. It was no coincidence he was behaving like a better man and it was no coincidence he was at the housing complex of Big Red's baby-momma with some fine ass older woman she saw with Big Red's baby-momma.

CoCo asked what was she going to do and Lillian said she had her reasons for not confronting Dion or doing anything about her suspicions.

Kamber asked for her to tell them one reason and Lillian said the main reason was she felt her place with Dion was secured.

She lived with him. She was in good with his sister and now she had his baby, his firstborn.

Kamber asked that Lillian allow her to point out she was sounding like a weak ass bitch and she was letting Dior's side-chick mentality be her guide.

Lillian reiterated what Jonny-London said about them supporting the decisions that were hers to make and she said being silent about her baby-daddy cheating was one of those decision.

Chapter 8

THE FOLLOWING NIGHT

Royal was asleep wrapped tightly in a nursery blanket and she was lying in a clear plastic rollaway baby box next to Lillian's bed.

Lillian allowed more than an hour to pass before she or anyone in her hospital room looked at the time. They would not have looked at the time was it not for the nagging nurse who continually entered the room to remind them of the no child policy outside visiting hours.

Eliza was first to leave after the nurse's last interruption and not because of hospital policy. She wanted to tell the nurse to shove the policy where the sun did not shine but Three-D was in the window seat sleep. The poor boy had his head propped against the crease where the window met the wall and Eliza knew it was past time to get him home and in bed.

Jonny-London left the room next.
Every fourth Saturday of the month the sorority she was joining did community service.

They hosted breakfast for a volunteer-run street out-reach organization, Church In the Park and in several hours Jonny-London would be helping prepare food and serve the homeless in Tent City.

Kamber knew an ass whipping was waiting for her right where she left it if she went back home to her abusive boy-friend so she was going home with CoCo but CoCo was too tired to safely drive the stretch to Benicia.

CoCo called her momma Gilda to ask if her and Kamber could sleep on her couch and leave at dawn and Gilda said she did not mind so long as they could deal with her full house.
She was hosting her mother's group that had run over and she did not know how late their confab would go.

CoCo asked Lillian could she and Kamber sleep there a few hours before getting on the road and Kamber offered to drive them home but CoCo squeezed beside Lillian in her twin size hospital bed.

Kamber asked CoCo what about her offer to drive and CoCo said she heard her.

Kamber asked CoCo was there a problem and was she trying to hate on her driving and CoCo said no but that Kamber knew better than to think she was driving her car on a suspended license.

Lillian texted Dion to tell him Kamber and CoCo needed to stay the night and Dion replied he would see her and the baby in the morning. He sent a second message to ask did she want her usual for breakfast and Lillian's reply was a symbol of a red heart, a smiley face blowing a kiss and the word yes.

I

Dion was with Big Red when he received Lillian's text message.

He and Big Red had been together since leaving the hospital.

It was half past nine o'clock when they were in the hospital parking lot walking to their vehicles and Dior spoke on dinner.

She said it was too late for her to go home and cook and Dion gave his sister his car key for her to go get her and Richie some food.

Dion said he was going to go burn with Big Red and Reddy and would catch a ride home with them.

Dior took the car key but she checked with Richie on what he had a taste for and she asked did anyone else care to join them for Chinese food.

Reddy said he was hungry enough to eat a bear and he had healthy food waiting at home but something salty, greasy and fried sounded like right now to him.

Dion said he was cool off the hospital food menu and had not eaten all day worrying about Lillian so he was game and Big Red said he could always eat Chinese and had been craving some wor won ton soup.

Big Red gave Reddy the keys to his truck and said he was going to ride with Dior and he told Richie to go with his brother and uncle.

Richie asked why he could not go with his mom and Big Red said because he was not allowed to be around them smoking.

Richie said his momma did not smoke and Big Red asked his son what his point was in saying that. He wanted Richie to answer why he thought it was cool to speak on his grown-up momma but Dion told Richie to be quiet and get in his dad's truck.

Reddy said for Richie to get in fast before he wrote a check his ass could not cash and Richie got in the truck asking his brother how was his ass going to cash a check.

II

Reddy followed Dior's car to the restaurant.

The restaurant was busy but mostly with to-go orders and parking was bad but once they got seated their order came quick and by eleven o'clock Big Red had paid the tab and their party of five was heading for the door.

They walked together to the car and said goodbye to Dior and Richie then they walked to the truck and Big Red went towards the driver door but he had been drinking.
He was already walking around to the passenger door when he asked his son was he sobered up enough to drive and Reddy had been drinking too but he said he was good and since he drove the truck to the restaurant he had the key.

Dion jumped in the seat behind Big Red.

He fired up the blunt to let Reddy choke on it before taking off and in nearly ten minutes flat from where they ate dinner, Reddy was turning the rap music down on their car stereo to enter his residential Sir Francis Woods's community.

He slowly came upon his street and navigated around the circular white porcelain water fountain at the traffic circle.

He coasted up his ashy-red-checkered cobblestone driveway to his home until he pressed his foot down on the break and stopped.

He shifted into park about six feet from the fenced foyer that led to the main doubled-door entrance marked Gilman Mansion.

Reddy shared his multi-level twenty-two hundred square foot home with family members and non-family members.

Mr. Maxim Gene IV and Mrs. Malone Gilman owned the Gilman Mansion and they were the aging patriarch and matriarch who controlled the family's wealth.

Their daughter Ivory catered to them and in return she was the boss of them and the mansion and her brother Maxim occupied an entire floor of the home to himself.

Maxim's finished basement area had a private entrance, four bedrooms, two bathrooms, a gym and a living room and he shared it with his girlfriend Saba, her daughter and son, **Morningstar** and **Eagle Johnson** and Maxim's daughter, **Mona Mia Gilman**.

Mona lost her mother in childbirth and during Mona's delivery right before her mom died Mona's brain was crushed coming through the birth canal.

Mona was born completely blind with a medical diagnosis of mental retardation and she was rendered unable to think for herself or speak sentences.

She was a teenager in a pre-teen child's body and she slouched and kept her head down with her eyes squinted but she was not without her late mother's striking beauty.

The only time she might show her beauty was if she raised her head in the direction where she heard a sound or a person speaking or moving.

Mona required round the clock care but she was nocturnal and was allowed to do pretty much whatever she wanted that did not cause her harm.

Her favorite thing to do was roam the foyer entrance at all times of the night holding her portable compact disc player in her hand and listening to Stomp, Beat It and Hammertime on repeat.

She talked to herself and laughed and she sang and danced to her own rhythm and no one bothered Mona or tried to silence her joy.

Mona's voice could be heard from the foyer more clearly when Reddy turned off Big Red's truck engine and the brief clinking and clanking beneath the hood came to complete quiet.

Dion asked if anybody else heard what he was hearing and yes they could all faintly hear Mona's incoherent singing echoing from behind the foyer gate.

Reddy asked his pops was he and Dion coming in and Big Red said no. It was best he came around when his mom was not in an angry mood, an arguing mood or a silent treatment mood and that morning before he left home she was in the silent treatment mood.

Dion was grateful to be in the darkness of the backseat where Big Red and Reddy could not see that being at the Gilman Mansion gave him emotional starry eyes.

Never would he have ever met the type of people someone from a century ago loved so much they planned for them to never go hungry or homeless.

It was only because of Big Red he had stepped his foot in an environment of a rich family living off generational wealth when his reality was generational poverty. The public housing projects was home to his mom and dad, their mom and dad and their mom and dad and what stimulated Dion's emotions was he wished in his lifetime, not in another lifetime and not only in his dreams, his people were the people with money long as the Gilman's money.

III

Big Red had not made a habit of bringing Dion to his wife's home but he had brought him a couple of times.

Dion's first time at Gilman Mansion he met Ivory and Big Red introduced him by just his name then he went to do what he came to do and Dion was around Ivory a few minutes alone.

She was nice, polite and hospitable but Dion said nothing after he said hello.

It was not his place to say who he was and how he knew Big Red and when him and Big Red left he felt no need to bring up Ivory but Big Red did.

Before they cleared the mansion driveway Big Red was

explaining to Dion his relationship with Dior was different from what he had with Ivory.

Big Red first knocked his wife's looks and made a wise-crack saying Dion's eyes were young but even a blind man could see his wife was a hard sight and Dion laughed with him but then Big Red grew serious. He gave Ivory props and said she had class and style. She always had his back and she had her ways he did not care for but her loyalty was priceless and the ample supply of resources she kept at her disposal made up for her deficits.

Big Red asked Dion could he have passed up on a piece like Ivory and Dion did not say yes or no. He respectfully recognized Ivory sounded like she got the party started with a few drinks, a few lines and a few laughs and Big Red agreed that a good bitch was exactly what she was.

He began to entrust Dion with him and Ivory's marriage story but he had to stop to admit to being fucked up towards Ivory from the beginning. He said when he graduated from juvenile to jail he needed her money and her time and she gave of both willingly after they met by phone.

The boy he shared a juvenile cell with had a girlfriend he talked to nightly by phone and one night his celly's girl told him to give Big Red the phone she had a friend for him.

His celly's girl was playing matchmaker and gave her phone to Ivory and their phone introduction was long enough for the celly's girlfriend to nudge Ivory to not be shy and give Big Red her number.

Big Red had not been talking to her for many weeks but as his days grew shorter for him to go to the penitentiary and serve the rest of his time as an adult he asked Ivory to marry him and she said yes.

They had a jailhouse marriage that Mr. and Mrs. Gilman attended to witness and support their daughter but within a year Big Red asked for an annulment after Ivory missed one visit with him to attend the birth of her baby brother.

Maxim was conceived by a miracle with Mrs. Gilman's in her late forties approaching menopause. She had long given up on having her own child but the pregnancy and Maxim's birth made her deathly sick and Ivory's father needed Ivory's help with her mother and the baby.

Ivory wrote Big Red a letter to tell him about Maxim and his mom. She thought he would be happy for her family but on her next visit with him he said all a young nigga in prison cared about was money over bitches and what he read between the lines of her letter was she had a well that was about to run dry.

Ivory asked was he going to spend his visit talking to his wife like she did not mean shit and Big Red put it in her head who she did not mean shit to was the Gilman's. She was the adopted charity case for a wealthy White man to give his once barren Black wife an heir and now they had their own child, a rightful heir.

Big Red said if she was about to lose it all why should he keep a wife that could not take care of him while he was down.

Ivory knew her and Big Red had an arrangement that would not work if her wealth got cut off but she was able to keep his financial support flowing and a divorce was never filed.

IV

The money Ivory sent Big Red was significantly reduced from what she had him accustomed to but it was more than what any other person was doing for him and she stayed down with him the remainder of his years in lock-up.

The day of Big Red's release Ivory was waiting for him. He walked out the penitentiary to find a stretch vehicle and a chauffeur who addressed him as Mr. Rich when he opened his car door.

Ivory was naked in the back seat and she told Big Red get in she was about to give him a proper welcome home.

Big Red got situated for Ivory to pass him one of the two double shots of vodka she already had poured but she did not wait for him. She threw her shot down the hatch and chased it with a few gulps of chilled orange juice then she passed Big Red the chaser to chase his shot.
She poured them both a second double-shot but when she fired up a blunt of some purple mixed with green bud he was first to down his second drink.

Ivory passed the weed to Big Red and she drank her second double-shot slow going between sipping the vodka and sipping the orange juice.

Big Red put the weed to Ivory's lips when she finished her drink and she took a long hit. She held the smoke then she blew the smoke in Big Red's face and as she put the weed to his lips she coughed a little before she put his dick to her lips. She gave him sloppy wet head on their scenic drive to Gilman Mansion and they consummated their marriage before arriving home but arriving home did not stop the party.

Ivory kept the celebration going for months and Big Red had stayed away from powder growing up but Ivory introduced him to the good stuff.

They were both high as kites fucking all day everyday until she got pregnant with Reddy and she quit celebrating cold turkey.

Reddy was incessantly texting during dinner at the Chinese restaurant to solidify his Friday night plans. Except for when actively bringing his chopsticks to his mouth he was glued to his phone arranging a date that included an overnight staycation and a convertible whip to paint the town in.

No one was really talking to Reddy over dinner except Richie. He could not shut up about his upcoming fieldtrip with his science class to the Exploratorium Public Learning Laboratory and Dion, Dior and Big Red showed interest in the field trip but not Reddy.

They asked Richie questions to have him share more of what he was excited about but Reddy would not get off his phone. It was bad to the point of him being on his phone while driving Big Red and Dion from the restaurant in the Mission District to the Gilman Mansion in Sir Francis Woods. It would have usually taken closer to fifteen minutes by freeway in zero traffic but it took Reddy only ten minutes in medium traffic because of him speeding. It was a wonder they made it to their destination with no car accidents and Big Red and Dion said nothing not even when Reddy had to swerve more than once to dodge a close encounter.

V

Reddy was anxious to jump out his father's truck soon as they got to his home entrance.

He had to take a dump and refresh before he went about his merry way but after his father said him and Dion were not coming in Richie's attempt to immediately exit his father's vehicle failed.

Big Red instructed him to close the driver door for the two of them and Dion to have a conversation. He said he wanted Reddy to confirm what he was supposed to do and where he was supposed to be *the following night.*

Reddy made a slick comment asking was more discussion really necessary right at that moment because he had other shit to do and Big Red asked was he saying he had no doubts or fears or issues with the job.

Reddy said nah but Big Red did not like the way he said nah and Big Red asked was he saying he was ready and clear on everything and Reddy said yea.

Big Red felt Reddy's nah and yea were shaky and rushed and he was not convinced so out of nowhere and with the quickness Big Red grabbed Reddy by the back of the neck with a vice grip.

Dion had unbuckled his seatbelt and slid to the edge of the middle seat when Big Red told Reddy to slow up for them to discuss the following night. He was between Big Red and Reddy to be part of the conversation but he was close enough to sense the rage in Reddy's bent but stiff posture and the side of Reddy's face got flush from how hard his father grabbed him.

Big Red spoke low and crisp to Reddy saying he was his muthafuckin son and his muthafuckin son could make no mistakes on something that big. The risks were too high for him to be on some stupid unsure kid shit and he chose him because he was the one nigga he trusted to get the job done right.

Dion was not about to get into no father and son quarrel and Reddy was not about to do much with his neck in a vice grip but someway he found the courage to say he was doing his dad the favor not the other way around and putting hands on him was not necessary.

Big Red brought Reddy in because they were a man short and this was no secret to Reddy. His dad already told him he was being brought in on a job last minute and the only details he would be given were out of necessity but Big Red must have forgot saying this and he raised his voice higher not to the point of yelling but to an intense enough tone to be taken seriously. He asked his son again if he was ready and clear on what he needed to do the following night and Reddy this time said a sharp militant style yes sir.

Big Red released the squeeze and he pulled his son towards him into the bend of his forearm. He kissed the top of Reddy's head before he pushed him to go ahead and get out the car but Reddy did not rush off.

Dion had said nothing but Reddy included him in the eye contact as he confirmed the part he played in the following night and he told them both not to worry. He said he would do what he had to do and be where he was supposed to be at the time he was supposed to be there and he got out the car.

Big Red remained seated and being as though the car was not going to start driving itself Dion climbed from the backseat into the driver seat. He knew where they were going next but Big Red told him anyway to drive to the spot.

VI

Reddy had been texting with his uncle Maxim about the hotel hookup and borrowing his sports car solely for showing off to Kamber and he had been texting with her trying to get back to the hospital to pick her up.

Lillian and CoCo had at different times fallen asleep listening to Kamber. She had gone on and on about leaving her old boyfriend to make Reddy her new boyfriend and finally she stopped talking long enough to realize her two best friends were out like a light.

Kamber was dozing off and on but she could not get comfortable in her seat and her phone kept waking her up. Between texting with Reddy she broke things off with her abusive boyfriend once he swore he would burn her wigs, her make up and her clothes and shoes if she did not come home then he said he would burn her ass up if she did come home.

Kamber's grandma made wigs so they were easy to

replace and she did not want to have to start over again with make up and clothes and shoes but she was not about to go be around a nigga threatening to burn her up. She knew it was over at that point but she had to have the last word and she texted him one long paragraph.

She bet he would not burn the wigs he liked wearing when he was calling her daddy during role-play and she said he did not have to pick a fight to graduate from her strap-on to the real thing. He had her blessing and she was happy for him he was moving on to becoming somebody else's bitch.

Kamber hit send then blocked him so he could not call or text a reply and she put her cell phone in her bag.

Her phone started vibrating but she ignored it thinking it was her ex-boyfriend calling from a different number trying to go bad on her.

She sank into a good nap until her bladder ended it and she grabbed her phone as she got up from her chair. She woozily went to the bathroom thinking of the many repulsive messages her ex had left her and when she sat on the toilet to look at her phone the text messages were from Reddy. His most recent message was him asking could he be on his way.

Kamber had forgotten she was supposed to text him a time to come and get her but she still had not made up her mind to leave the hospital with him.

Kamber flushed the toilet, washed her hands and she was headed back to her hospital chair when her phone vibrated in her hand. It was Reddy again so she answered but she kept it brief over the phone and said she would text him.

Her text message questioned his intentions with it approaching midnight and she asked where did he have in mind to take her during booty-call hours.

Reddy's reply offered her a comfortable hotel bed to spend the rest of her night no strings attached and depending on when she woke up, breakfast, lunch or dinner served in bed overlooking a view of the Bay.

Kamber sat in her hospital chair staring at Reddy's reply.
She pulled her makeup case from her purse and she stood up.
She took a second look at the hospital chair on her way back inside the bathroom and she put her phone on the bathroom sink counter with the text message open.
She stared at herself in the bathroom mirror and she stared at the text message and she concluded a hotel bed would be more relaxing and better for her neck.

Kamber picked up her phone and texted Reddy he could be on his way and she came out the bathroom lightly perfumed with her makeup touched up.
She skedaddled without waking anyone but she did leave a note on top of CoCo's purse.
The note let CoCo know Kamber would see her in Benicia late the next day but that if CoCo was not home yet Kamber knew where to find the spare key.

Chapter 9

GROUPIES

Big Red and Dion finished smoking the rest of Dion's blunt while driving from the Gilman Mansion. No one talked until they reached the Fillmore District Townhomes and Big Red told Dion where to park outside 908 Williams Lane.

Dion was first out the truck and at separate strides he and Big Red walked a short plant-lined footpath to a black door with 908 in shiny gold numbering nailed to the door side.

The door was set in a row of individual but identically made homes attached one to the next with every front lawn exceptionally groomed.

Dion knew not to ring the doorbell due to the hour so he fell back behind Big Red who stepped forward with his cellphone in his hand.

Big Red unconsciously cleared his throat, adjusted his clothes and stood tall with his best pose and then and only then did he text his baby-momma to say he and Dion were waiting for her outside her front door.

I

Bashan Mya Scott met Big Red when she was in the second grade and he was in the fourth.

Their moms both drove for the public bus company during odd shifts and became coworker-friends. They were both single parents raising young kids in San Fran so they started helping each other with the baby-sitting and sharing the cost to hire babysitters.

Long before Bashan became baby-momma number two she was Big Red's elementary school and middle school best friend and by high school they were sweethearts at the zenith of their relationship.

Bashan came to Big Red's high school two year's behind him. Some of the female students did not like her because of him but others hated on her because she was confident.

For the last two years of middle school Bashan either stared or co-stared in every leading role the drama club offered and she even landed a non-talking part in a cereal commercial.

She got to high school and landed the lead role in the first play of the school year and she became enemy number one to a group of girls that auditioned.

Bashan also became enemy number one to a group of classmates. She was uninterested in their extracurricular activities and they were bitter she always said no to going with them but she was mostly focused on her path and her time outside of schoolwork and acting went to Big Red.

She hung out with him, his teammates and with the other junior classmates. She was with them from in the morning before school when Big Red picked her up to being with them for off campus lunch and again after school for the school dances and football games.

Big Red was one of the stars on the football team. His student stardom made him the face of student life for every high school student publication and his prominence came with an entourage. Seven girls from the junior and senior class flocked to his crew for status and attention and Big Red introduced Bashan to the girls.

Initially they were lining up to be her friend. They smiled in her face and had invited her into their circle until they seen she had the real thing with Big Red. Their circle turned rancid from the way he adored her and anytime she was around boiled the jealously in his *groupies*.

They travelled two or more from classes together but Bashan would go from class to class alone and they were always bullying her. They would bump her without saying excuse me or without saying an apology and they tried to trouble her mental with chatter of their involvement with her man.

One groupie said Big Red had come to her house and another said he bought her gifts. A third groupie said she got more than one ride out of Big Red and she accused Bashan of not knowing her man as well as she thought.

The things the groupies said bothered Bashan but she was not bringing it back to Big Red. She was telling her mom and her auntie who was telling her to be smarter than them messy bitches. They were trying to get her to fuck up her relationship. Their messiness was taking stabs at her to get her to confront Big Red but Bashan did not give the groupies what they wanted thanks to her mom and her auntie and the groupies got more desperate.

Five of them on separate occasions upped their ante with graphic sexual accounts and Groupie One caught Bashan in the stairwell. She talked about how Big Red picked her up, slid her down on his dick and fucked her while standing and she asked Bashan had she experienced that with her man or any man at her size but Bashan told Groupie One to try and go fuck herself while standing.

Groupie Two caught Bashan leaving out of class. She said Big Red moaned for her to bite his chest and suck his chest nipples to make him cum. She asked Bashan did her man ask her to do anything to make him cum and Bashan told that bitch what her man asked her to do was come get some money. She was on her way to get enough to pay for her hair, nails and eyebrows and Bashan asked Groupie Two did Big Red ask her to do that.

Groupie Three caught Bashan coming from the auditorium. She told Bashan Big Red liked her to play with his balls when he was hammering her backside but she claimed she cut him off to respect their relationship. She asked Bashan was she not able to satisfy her man and was that why her man was still calling her phone and Bashan asked Groupie Three to show her. Let her see the phone records of Big Red calling her phone but Groupie Three walked her donkey ass away saying she did not have to show Bashan a damn thing.

Groupie Four caught Bashan at the nurse's office getting a Band-Aid for a hangnail she ripped off. The groupie said she gave Big Red pleasure in exchange for pain and she liked him to hit her ass repeatedly with the wooden handle of a mini lasso. She did not let him stop until her ass puffed from swelling and at times her skin would break and bleed. She said for Big Red splitting her ass she let him fuck her in the mouth and leave his semen on her face and Bashan told Groupie Four to get the fuck away from her and go to see the school therapist about that sick shit.

Groupie Five caught Bashan near the science lab. She asked Bashan did she want to know how Big Red got her asshole ready for anal and Bashan said no but the groupie continued to say he stretched her hole with his fingers while he fucked her lying on her side. She asked Bashan could she take dick up the ass then she answered for Bashan saying hell nah. She could look at Bashan and see she was a missionary bitch.

Bashan rolled her eyes at Groupie Five but she kept her lips tight. She was right Bashan could not take dick up the ass and she was a missionary bitch but so what. So what Groupie Two knew her man moaned for his chest to be bit and for his nipples to be sucked for him to cum and so what she was not the size of a girl her man could toss up like Groupie One.

Bashan refused to let the groupies fret her. Everything they spoke of could have been true but she did not care. She was in a league of her own with Big Red and their intimacy came after years of courting. He had only ever been gentle and sweet and romantic and they had only ever made slow love in a bed with Bashan on the bottom and him on top and no groupie could tell her what she had with him was puny. She knew Big Red loved her and a day came when three of the groupies caught Bashan during her time of the month.

Groupie One, Groupie Three and Groupie Five were

passing Bashan's hallway locker mean-mugging and sizing her up.

Bashan was cramping so bad putting her fist through her locker would have felt better and Groupie Three said something fucked up to the other two groupies but what she said was for Bashan to hear.

Bashan's norm was to brush it off her shoulders and turn the other cheek but she was fed up with them speaking on Big Red like it was their place. She cut Groupie Three off asking was she and the other minions mad Big Red was still her man then she yelled oh fucking well. He was going to stay her man because their relationship was too full of purpose to be mad her man had run-thru a group of hoes.

Groupie Three got her fists ready but she did not throw a punch and each groupie in her own words dared Bashan to repeat herself.

Groupie One asked did Bashan think she would not get knocked the fuck out for calling her a prostitute and Bashan clarified she had called them hoes not prostitutes and she explained the difference. A prostitute had value and her pussy did not come free but they were a group of hoes that had no value and like trash their pussy did come free.

Bashan had to block a couple punches from Groupie Three and Groupie Five and Bashan threw a couple punches back that landed on Groupie Five before strangers got them apart warning them of the school police.

Later that day Bashan threw a couple punches with Groupie One that got broken up too but the following morning she fought Groupie Three with no interference and she beat her prettier skinnier longer-weave wearing ass until that bitch ran away screaming.

Groupies were a downside for Bashan dating a popular schoolboy but she was a student celebrity by the end of her freshman year because she was Big Red's girlfriend.

Big Red was the junior prom king and Bashan was chauffeured to junior prom with Big Red and the rest of the junior class student elite. That got her written about in the student yearbook as the first freshman to be nominated junior prom queen from the floor. Her nomination was from Big Red and she did not win because a freshman was ineligible to run but she did make school history.

In the summer after Bashan's ninth grade year Big Red was in the wrong place at the wrong time with the wrong people and he went to jail.

Bashan carried on her relationship with him the rest of the year through his court appearances and into the earlier part of the following year but when he was sentenced he told her she deserved better and to forget about him.

II

Bashan had a moment of weakness four years after she graduated high school.
She reconnected with Big Red when he was fresh out and they shared one night she thought she could keep on the low but she became pregnant.

Fifteen years later their son's life came to a tragic end

but in the days leading up to his death he came home with a baby.

Bashan walked in her apartment from a typical day at work. Like she did five to six days out the workweek she got home late, took off her blazer jacket and kicked off her kitten heels at the front door. She went further into her home to find that Roderick was not alone. He had brought a daughter and a baby-momma to live with them.

Guillermina Guadalupe De La Cruz was glued to Roderick's side and their baby **Roe Vera Rich** was cradled in her arms.

Roderick calmly introduced them and expected his mom to say something but Bashan was too in shock to have a kneejerk reaction. She had never heard of Guillermina and because she knew nothing of her pregnancy she had no time to prepare for being a thirty-seven-year-old grandma.

Roderick could see his mom about to break bad and he asked that she let him explain.

Roderick repeated Roe was his daughter and Guillermina was his daughter's mom and they had come to stay with him but as he was speaking Bashan told him to stop with who Guillermina was.

She said his two-piece was his problem but his ass was still hers and he should be explaining who in the world he thought he was to spring a baby on her. She asked was he giving her a whole ass human life to say what, welcome fucking home, but Roderick could say nothing before Bashan slapped him across the face.

She told her son he had her all the way fucked up and

she turned to Guillermina who stepped back protectively and held Roe tighter in her arms.

She told Guillermina she did not know if she spoke English and understood what she was saying but she was sure she understood that slap across her son's face meant goodbye.

Bashan walked to her front door and opened it for Guillermina and Roe to leave but Guillermina did not move.

Roderick rushed over to the front door pleading for his mom's forgiveness.

He said they needed her help and that she knew him bringing Guillermina home was the right thing to do but Bashan was immovable.

She struggled with Roderick trying to shut the front door but Bashan was not letting him close it. She told him to take Guillermina back to where they fucked up on that baby at in the first place and there was a pause.

Bashan looked at Roderick and he looked at Guillermina and the two of them looked at each other and then to the floor.

Bashan took a deep breath.

She threatened to slap fire from Roderick's face again if he dared say he had fucked up on that baby in her home when she was at work putting in ten and twelve hours per day to feed his funky Black ass.

Bashan took another deep breath. She asked dryly why Roderick would think it was okay not to involve her at any point prior to making an entire new family he thought he could bring into her life without her say-so.

Roderick's defense was for Bashan to look at how she was reacting. He asked his mom if she thought he would be begging for her help if he could avoid dealing with her embarrassing him in front of his girl and their baby.

Roderick effectively made Bashan feel like shit on a stick and when he saw he weakened her he asked again for Bashan to please have a seat on the couch for him and Guillermina to get a word in.

Bashan slowly closed the door looking at Guillermina who kept her head down to avoid eye contact.

Bashan took a seat like her son asked but she told him before he plopped his ass on her couch and started talking he needed to bring her a drink and a joint and she told Guillermina if she had a problem with whisky and weed she could go and sit some place else.

Roderick presented his mom a stiff libation and a barely burned preroll joint from her bedroom ashtray and he joined Guillermina on the larger of two couches.
He comforted Guillermina and Roe with affectionate touches and kisses as he waited for his mom to settle into sipping and smoking and when he felt she was ready to listen he began telling her about Guillermina.

III

Guillermina's parents came to San Fran from Mexico before she was born.
The building where they raised her in the Mission District was one of many burned down in a series of arson attacks.

The attacks were being investigated and attributed to malice and fraud but meanwhile Guillermina's family was without a home.

Guillermina's father had been with his employer several years and his employer was gracious enough to offer her home for his family to reside however long they needed.

Nora Ann Cane was a wealthy novelist. She was known to the publishing world as N. A. Cane but she answered to AC and close family called her Ann.

Guillermina's family called her Ms. Nora.
From the success of her debut novel she bought herself a Hillsdale mountainside estate in San Mateo County located twenty-five minutes outside San Fran and she hired Guillermina's father as her fulltime groundkeepers and handyman.

Nora had two children of which both were grown and married with children of their own but they did not come around her and they did not bring her grandchildren to see her.
Neither her son nor her daughter tried to hide they were much closer to their religious zealot of a dad who did not approve of Nora's life choices before or after their divorce and he had turned their children against her.

IV

Nora and her ex-husband were raised in an all White family with all White friends in an all White community.
She stayed home to raise their two children while her husband worked fulltime and eventually finished college.

By the time he snagged a handsome paying job at a firm with all White partners their son and daughter had became teenaged and were attending a predominately all White high school.

They became typical self-absorbed little adults and every morning if they did not skip breakfast they took a couple bites and got on the road and they did not return home until after dinner was stored in the fridge for leftovers the next day.

Nora being void of children enrolled in community college and when Nora's husband questioned her not going to a school closer to their Southbay neighborhood she said San Fran Community College had the best sewing program.

Her choosing a course of study that was domestic gave him nothing else to question but Nora got to college and let her curiosity take over.

She enrolled in a racial and economic justice class with the help of a stranger on campus and she engulfed herself in an abundance of conscious matters.

Nora's lunch buddy became a Black classmate who only ordered vegetarian meals.

They had lunch together sometimes as many as three times in a week and slowly Nora too started ordering vegetarian but she did not stop there.

She became an animal rights activist and with that she became pro earth and started recycling at home and encouraging her family to go green.

Nora's vegetarian Black classmate was a professional hair braider at an African hair studio in Oakland and Nora asked for an appointment to get her hair styled.

Nora went to the African hair shop for braids but after she sifted through the pages of a Black hair magazine she changed her mind and had her straight brunette hair cut short above her ears close to her scalp with short bangs.

What caused Nora's husband to file for a divorce was he remained the male chauvinist she married and she became a community organizer.

She was a voice for Black and Brown lives and women's rights and her husband was using his voice to fight against any diversity in civic engagement.

He was a registered gun carrier who was against stricter gun laws and she was participating in inner-city neighborhood actions to get handguns off the city streets and while she was pro immigration fighting against boarders and aldutnapping he was anti-abortion, anti-gay and anti-immigration.

The mental and physical transformation of Nora came from two semesters in college and she did not return to school for the second year. She was too busy divorcing her husband and writing her first bestselling novel.

She wrote a fictional account of her life that took her almost three years to write but <u>The Lie In The White Lullaby</u> sold over one million copies in the first six months.

Within that initial year of success Nora bought her Hillsdale home and she wanted to grow marijuana in her backyard greenhouse for medicinal purpose but she needed someone to manage her newly acquired land.

It was by chance on a weekly hair care visit to the African hair studio Guillermina's father had been hired by the studio to install a new toilet and Nora asked him if he had other qualifications.

Guillermina's father said he was skilled in landscaping, scaffolding, painting, ironwork, plumbing and general repair of appliances and on the spot Nora offered to pay him a generous salary to maintain the inside and outside of her new home and he accepted.

For her interior designing Nora had someone in mind she met in her racial and economic justice class.

Meadow Constance Harris was a flamboyant Black guy full of feminine energy.

He embraced his metrosexuality and flaunted a fantastic sense of style and Nora had a number for him in her phone from a group assignment.

She called him not thinking after so many years she would reach him but she did.

She reached his voicemail and offered him the job as her Interior Decorator and he called her back later to accept. She knew Meadow would give her home the perfect touch and she gave him creative control to design every inch from top to bottom.

Meadow was more than half Nora's age but before he completed her home improvement project she bedded him, moved him in and made him front-page tabloid news as her handsome much younger boytoy.

V

Nora was in her late forties when she met Guillermina's father and he was a little more than five years her younger. He worked for her almost a decade before the fire and he carried his entire family of six on the salary she paid him.

She had been part of their family from Guillermina's

earliest memories of being enrolled as a five-year-old into a small Burlingame charter school Nora was a major donor of.

She was active in the education of Guillermina and her sibling's and she gave contributions to the school sizable enough to cover their four tuitions through graduation.

Guillermina's mom was a homemaker.

She was the most devastated when the years of splendor she put into their home went up in smoke.

The night the fire happened Guillermina's father told his wife they would not have to get a room at a hotel but his wife was uncomfortable with taking more of Nora's charity. She felt they had the money to stand on their own and she asked her husband did he not feel Nora had done enough.

Guillermina's father insisted them staying with Nora was standing on their own. They were not running to family or friends with their hand out. They were not going to live in one room or sleep at a shelter. They could be comfortable staying with Nora at the same time saving their money but his wife insisted otherwise.

Guillermina's father tried to make his wife understand it was just temporary but his wife was being stubborn about not living under Nora's roof. She did not care how big and nice the house was and the night of the fire she stipulated they sleep in their van if her husband was refusing to take them to a hotel.

Guillermina's parents argued more than an hour outside of Nora's house in their van and their children had fallen asleep including Guillermina.

Guillermina's father brought up Guillermina was

nearing nine months pregnant about to deliver a baby and their other three young children were not use to sleeping in the back of a mini van.

Guillermina's mother finally told her husband her pride would not allow it. No other woman would take care of her family as long as she had breath in her body. It would shame her. It was enough Nora was her husband's boss and had paid for her children's education but that was where she drew a hard line.

Guillermina's mom asked her husband was there more to him and Nora's relationship he was not telling her about and Guillermina's father was appalled at the question.

Guillermina's mom said she was defending her one job and Nora was not taking her one job of being his wife and their children's mother.

She echoed they were her children and she echoed he was her husband.

She said her children would be bathed in a tub only she cleaned and only she would iron the clothes for her husband to go to work and for her kids to go to school and she would be the one to cook for them, read to them before bed, comb and brush their hair and pray with them before they went to sleep. These were things she took pride in and she would continue to do them with no other woman to confuse her family on who they listen to.

Guillermina's father held his wife's hand and guaranteed her no other woman could take her place in their family. He and their children loved her immeasurably and she had not a thing to fret over ever and he begged his wife to have faith in him as her husband and follow him. Allow them to just stay at Nora's house for the night and he would find them somewhere to live.

Guillermina's mom finally said okay to one night but one night turned to many nights and it put a strain on their marriage.

For weeks Guillermina's family slept safe and sound in more than one of Nora's many warm bedrooms but Guillermina's father did not know what to do.

He did not sleep those many nights stressed and worried and thinking about what he could afford to buy. His wife did not want them to be renters anymore. She wanted them to own their next home and his money was good but not the sort of money that could buy within the fifty mile vicinity of Hillsdale where he worked or Burlingame where his kids went to school.

Guillermina's father finally fell asleep from the exhaustion of not being able to sleep and he dreamed of when he and his wife first came together from Mexico. They stayed with a family in Chula Vista California who had made a trailer park community their home and his wife seemed fine living in that temporary arrangement. He was the one who complained about being cramped and sleeping almost on top of each other not being able to move around but his wife never complained.

Guillermina's father woke the next day and knew exactly what to do. He grabbed his savings that he had hidden in Nora's basement and he had Meadow drive him to find his wife a place of her own.

Guillermina's father returned to Nora's home hours

later and he drove inside her estate in a twenty-eight foot long luxury motorhome RV and he parked it behind his work truck.

The motorhome was state of the art brand new with a master bedroom, a living room, kitchen and bathroom and it slept six comfortably.

Guillermina's mom did not know what to say except where would they park their new home and Guillermina's father said everything was already worked out.

He had rented them space for the month at the San Fran Candlestick RV Park.

Roe was born the night Guillermina's father drove their new motorhome up Nora's driveway and Nora had an ambulance take Guillermina and her mom to the hospital.

Nora came to see Guillermina after Roe was born and she was strident about Guillermina coming back to her home when she got discharged.

She said her home in her opinion was best for a newborn baby and not to say anything was wrong with a motorhome or a trailer park but from her perspective it was just too public of an environment for an infant.

Guillermina's mom was sitting right there when Nora got mouthy about wanting Guillermina to choose her home over her parent's motorhome and Guillermina asked her mom what was best.

Guillermina's mom said as her mother she would support her either way but it was her baby and what to do with her baby was up to her.

Guillermina chose to stay in one of Nora's king size bedrooms and Nora catered to Guillermina hand and foot for a little over a month until one morning Meadow could not wake Nora from her sleep.

She had died during the night.

Within the first two months of Roe being born, Guillermina's father went from making money and having access to Nora's amenities and connections, to having no job and living six and a half deep in a motorhome.

VI

Guillermina met Bashan only hours after leaving Nora's burial site. She was afraid and insecure and she sat the whole time next to Roderick on Bashan's couch like a statue.

Bashan called her a groupie out of nowhere trying to squat in her home and Guillermina spoke in defense of herself seeing Roderick was not speaking up for her.

Guillermina asked Bashan to pump her breaks and not say she came out of nowhere and Bashan stood up and looked around her living room. She sat back down and looked at Roderick before she said surprise-surprise. His little chica could talk and with a fucking attitude and she asked Guillermina how come she did not respect her enough to acquaint herself before popping up on her doorstep with a baby by her only son.

Guillermina declared she was Roderick's girlfriend for two years and she said she met Bashan on more than one occasion. Once at the shoe museum where she worked which

Bashan shrugged off and said she came across too many everyday faces to recall Guillermina's face.

Guillermina said fair enough. She told Bashan of a second time they met at Roderick's fourteenth birthday party which Bashan shrugged off and said there were too many of Roderick's friend's faces for her to remember anyone.

Guillermina said fine Bashan could say whatever but she was not a girl out of nowhere.

Roderick leaned into Guillermina and whispered for her to let it go but Guillermina asked Bashan would a girl out of nowhere be invited to her last birthday cruise to the Caribbean Islands. She said she would have been there with Roderick were she not too pregnant to fly to Puerto Rico and disembark.

Guillermina included details to prove her relationship with Roderick was real but naïvely she had given Bashan ammunition to discredit the relationship.

Roderick brought a date to Bashan's birthday cruise.
He shared a cabin with a girl he introduced to the family as his girlfriend but she was not several months pregnant.

Bashan huffed and postured her body to fire off some truth about her precious Roderick.
She got ready to tell Guillermina that her not being able to travel did not mean a thing. Her son took after his father and like Big Red at his age he kept a litter of groupies. The only difference between her and the others Roderick brought home was that she was dumb enough or unlucky enough to become the big-bellied one.

Bashan opened her mouth to call Guillermina a fool but she saw tears appear on Guillermina's face and she wondered was it something she already said because she was about to say something a lot worse.

The tears could have been crocodile tears but they looked to be coming from a painful place deep in Guillermina as she told Bashan she was not ready to leave her family. She wanted to be with her mom and dad and her sisters and brother but their home burning down and Nora dying left her parents doing bad. They did not know from day to day how they were going to survive and Guillermina could see no way for her parents to take care of her and Roe and her siblings.

She did not want to be begging Bashan to take her in but she belonged with Roderick. She had created a family with him and that was now the family that mattered the most.

Guillermina admitted to being young and foolish and making a mistake. She had brought a baby in the world she could not yet take care of but that was not a mistake she had made alone and she asked was Bashan about to try and deny that too.

Chapter 10

THE PRICE

Bashan's insurance policy on Roderick covered his burial expenses and left her with enough to relocate after his murder. She took the leap from renting a two-bedroom single level apartment to becoming the owner of a newly built three-bedroom two-story townhome.

Bashan lived only two miles from her previous apartment but her new community was impressive and offered resident amenities.

There was twenty-four hour surveillance and maintenance service, an indoor lap pool and small heated whirlpool, a full service clubhouse with a fitness center and an area for resident social events and a kid park attached to a court for basketball or tennis.

Bashan's townhome was built on a steep hill.

Her main entry door was on the second level facing the street and her first level had a patio door facing the backside of the home.

Bashan's patio opened onto a tenant-shared flower

garden with plants and palm trees that formed a perimeter around the other shared amenities.

Her second floor main entry level had two bedrooms and one and a half bathrooms and the patio level had the kitchen, living room, a storage area and a full bathroom that connected to the third bedroom Guillermina shared with Roe.

Guillermina came and went through the patio entrance from where she and Roe parked in guest parking near the clubhouse.

Bashan came and went through the home's main entrance from her enclosed carport that was accessible only from the street.

Her master bedroom had the master bathroom inside and across from her bedroom was an inlet with a washer and dryer for laundry.

Down the hall from the inlet near the main entrance was a half bathroom with a toilet and sink for guest usage and across from the main entrance was where the top of Bashan's staircase ended right next to Roderick's shrine.

Bashan kept her son's full-page size obituary inside a gold frame fastened to a wide column facing her front door.

The shrine was center distance between the half bathroom and the second bedroom and the location of the shrine made it impossible to walk in the front door without seeing Roderick's smiling face.

You could not walk from the second bedroom to the half bathroom nor could you walk from Bashan's bedroom to any other part of the house without being reminded of her son.

The obituary hung inches above an eyelevel mantel where Bashan kept a scented candle aflame to illuminate Roderick's smiling face in a cropped oval shaped picture.

Roderick's honey brown complexion was shades lighter than his mother and equal shades darker than his father and the dimple in his right cheek was identical to the dimple in his mother's right cheek.

According to the sunset date printed on the obituary he would be turning twenty-three years old in two months and eleven days.

—⸺((◉))⸺—

Bashan was in her bathroom when the text came through her phone saying Big Red and Dion were waiting for her outside her front door.

She started to leave her bathroom but she heard Guillermina and Roe roughhousing on the other side of her bedroom door and she called out for Guillermina to let Big Red and Dion in.

Guillermina had just hoisted Roe's lengthy almost nine-year-old body up on her back for a horsey-back ride down the stairs. This was apart of their laundry routine so when Guillermina opened the front door for Big Red and Dion she had Roe on her back.

Guillermina welcomed Big Red and Dion inside and Roe leaped off her mother and into her grandfather's open arms. She hugged and kissed him not acknowledging Dion and she reported on her day at school and her weekend plans with her mom and grandma.

Roe then happily pleaded for her grandpa to give her a horsey-back ride down to the bottom of the stairs and back up.

She asked her mom to stay at the top of the stairs and wait to give her another horsey ride back down and Guillermina told Roe hell no which was opposite of what Roe wanted to hear.

Roe started to pout and Guillermina told her she had asked for too much. She was now going to walk down the stairs because neither she nor her grandpa was about to carry her down.

Roe's bottom lip dropped and she went into full brat mode. She was moaning and asking why they could not both do what she wanted and Guillermina threatened to spank her ass and give her something to cry about if she was about to cry about nothing.

Roe begged to remain upstairs with her grandpa and Guillermina again said opposite of what Roe wanted to hear and she reminded her it was way past her bedtime.

Roe held her arms around her grandpa's neck and whined about it being a Friday night and Guillermina told her she did not care.

Guillermina started to make her way down the stairs and she warned Roe that if she wanted the ice cream sandwich for helping clean up their bedroom and sort the laundry she had better beat her to the bottom of the stairs.

Roe kissed her grandfather's cheek and slid down her grandfather's body to her feet. She started racing Guillermina who started moving faster pretending she was going to out run Roe.

Roe screamed in laughter and gripped the stair railing as tight as she could to move her skinny legs fast as possible.

She jumped the final three stairs and landed on her toes and palms and she excitedly rolled onto her back.

She called out to her mom she won she had beat her to the bottom of the stairs and she said she should get two ice cream sandwiches instead of one.

Guillermina asked why two and Roe said one for the bedroom and one for the laundry and Guillermina said fine but two was it.

I

Big Red told Dion to go ahead to the guestroom without him he was going to check on Bashan and Big Red walked to the right of the stairs and Dion walked to the left.

Bashan had set up her spacious square shaped guestroom like a cozy studio.

Guests could rest easily or watch a flick and pop a bag of popcorn or heat a frozen burrito and make it a meal with a drink and some chips.

The room had a mini refrigerator, a microwave, a coffee maker and an electric teapot and the microwave sat on top of the mini fridge.

Bashan kept the fridge full of mini bottled waters and

soft drinks and she kept the freezer full of fruit juice bars and frozen snacks.

Dry goods like chips, bread, peanut butter, nuts, fruit, granola bars, cup of noodles and seasonings she kept inside a three-foot glass double-door caddy beside the mini fridge and the coffee maker and teapot were on top of the caddy.

Bashan's kitchenette stretched half of the bedroom from the guestroom door to the back wall.

Up against the back wall there was a minibar and a tall two-door cabinet.

The cabinet had things like paper towels, trash bags and cleaning supplies and between the cabinet and the minibar were the trash and recycle receptacles.

The minibar had a couple of swivel chairs and on the wall above the minibar were mounted shelves stocked full of top shelf liquor, mixers and red wine.

The room had one large window that provided the fresh air and sunlight to the Desert Rose and the Bird of Paradise and the two houseplants each sat on a single-legged table at each side of the window.

In the center of the room more nearer to the window than the door was a loveseat that converted to a double size bed and faced the television.

There was a small dining table pressed to the back of the loveseat with a pair of cushioned high-back chairs at opposite ends of the table facing each other.

The television was mounted on the front wall in the center of a four-piece entertainment console.

Neatly placed inside the console were family pictures, books, Black beauty and lifestyle magazines, a cable box, a phone docking station with a speaker, a multiplayer videogame system and at the bottom of the console were two drawers with sheets, blankets and pillows.

The left side of the loveseat was Dion's side for no other reason than he sat there the first night he came to Bashan's and had sat there ever since.

Azra Esmeray Harpuzon liked the right side of the loveseat.

Every time Dion entered the guestroom Azra was there but saying hi and greeting him was not her thing.

She was icy and if she felt like being bothered she did something like snatch his snack or his drink and down it then suggest he get himself another.

Bashan and Big Red always came to the guestroom loud and engulfed in their own jolly world.

They had not found it suspicious that in the latter two of the four months Dion and Big Red had been coming over, Azra and Dion could almost always be found in the same position.

Azra's face was always in a book or magazine she pulled from Bashan's small display.

Her bottom legs would be bent back on the loveseat with her feet barely inches from Dion's thigh.

She would be covered with a throw from her mid thigh to her toes and Dion's eyes would be closed with his head resting on the seatback like he was sleep.

Being in the same position every time was part of a game

Azra and Dion were playing and they were amused that it went unnoticed every time.

Bashan even once pointed out Azra holding a magazine upside down and she turned it right side up for her like it was not a strange thing.

If Bashan and Big Red were not always so loud coming from Bashan's room, Azra and Dion would not have had the time to stop fooling around and Dion might have been caught with either his dick in his hand or Azra's long toes in his mouth.

II

The first night Dion met Azra he asked what was her relationship to Bashan.

His thirst would have been quenched with her saying her uncle was Bashan's boss end of story. He was not the type to meddle in people's private lives but Azra willingly outed herself as a Hospitality Consultant.

Dion questioned did she work for a hotel and Azra told him not exactly.

She said Hospitality Consultant was a title her uncle preferred to label her rather than a call girl or date or escort and he said it was because when selling her services to rich customers it sounded better rolling off his tongue.

Nefon Harpuzon was the sole owner of Harpuzon Shoe Museum where Bashan had worked her way up to management.

Bashan was first hired as a Welcome Attendant and her job was to greet customers as they entered the Shoe Museum.

She stood at the Please Wait To Be Greeted sign passing out small company swag items for keepsakes and inviting customers to stop by the Welcome Bar anytime for complimentary espresso, tea, water and mini pastries while shopping.

Bashan was next promoted to an Experience Concierge and her job was to guide customers from the welcome area into the store. She assessed their shoe needs on a walk-thru of how to enjoy their Museum experience then she matched them to an appropriate Shoe Designer.

Because of Bashan's customer satisfaction survey ratings she was invited to apply for the Management Trainee Program and she was accepted.

As a Trainee she shadowed store Shoe Designer's briefly and observed Shoe Makers offsite at the store warehouse to learn their functions.

It was without being hands-on the Trainees learned the Shoe Designer's process of assisting customers in either choosing their one-off sneaker from the shoe displays or from the in-store computer software system used to customize a shoe.

At the shoe warehouse Trainees observed how the Shoe Makers made the shoes for the Customer Care Agent in the warehouse Shipping Center to pick up, package and send out to the customer.

Bashan's current position was Assistant Museum Director and she was now the mastermind behind daily Museum Operations and Security.

Azra's uncle discouraged fraternizing amongst his employees and his consultants but Bashan and Azra had met and bonded without his knowledge.

Over years and right under his nose Bashan grew to love Azra like a little sister and Azra knew Bashan was her one true friend. She knew she could tell Bashan anything and not be judged by her but Bashan had loyalty to Nefon as her boss.

Until that loyalty was severed Azra could not undoubtedly trust Bashan to destroy her uncle when the time came to put an end to the torture she endured by his hands for so long.

Azra needed to twist Bashan into feeling hate for her uncle and when her uncle sent her on a Hospitality Consultation with a high paying regular sadist, Azra saw her chance to reveal the truth.

She ran to Bashan balling her eyes out with redness around her neck, wrists and ankles and she had swelling on both sets of her cheeks.

Bashan examined the bruising from Azra's client violently fucking, chocking, hogtying and smacking her around during his consultation and seeing Azra banged up made Bashan cry for revenge on who had brutalized her and Azra pointed the finger at her uncle Nefon.

Bashan wanted to confront Nefon but she asked Azra for another way to get revenge.

She was in favor of a plan that did not piss off her boss and cost her the fattest paycheck ever and she mentioned the mortgage she had to pay and her granddaughter she had in private school.

Azra knew the abuse Bashan was looking at on her face and body had her anxious to strike so she offhandedly hinted at robbing her uncle and the idea took shape.

The two of them started devising a scheme to rob Harpuzon Shoe Museum and they spent more than a year thinking, plotting and planning until the both of them came to the conclusion they could not pull the robbery off alone.

Bashan admitted to there being one person she trusted with her life and she proposed they bring Big Red in on their plan to help them further along.

Big Red and Bashan had not been in contact for any reason.

One would catch sight of the other when Big Red was picking up or dropping off his granddaughter Roe but those visits went directly through Guillermina.

Bashan did not know if Big Red would respond to her unsolicited call and he did not answer her two back-to-back attempts to connect.

She accepted her and Azra were shit out of luck and she left Big Red a voicemail she thought was a long shot but an hour later he was at her townhome door.

Big Red had been a customer of Harpuzon's Shoe Museum and he listened carefully to what Bashan and Azra were planning.

He thought the bank from the business came legally from the high ass shoe prices ranging hundreds to thousands per pair but he learned from Azra how her uncle really got down.

For certain Museum clientele their purchase had nothing to do with a shoe. Their money was for purchasing dope and or sex and for those transactions the shoes were a front.

Bashan and Azra gave Big Red the details of their

thinking. They had him convinced the job would be easy money and Big Red told them that him sitting down for those couple of recent years had put a triple dent in his pocket. He said he would of course do anything for Bashan but he was all in for the money and an inside job was just the type of quick lick he needed.

III

Their initial meeting about the robbery went on for hours.

Big Red concluded they would need more than the three of them to pull the robbery off clean and Bashan and Azra agreed.

They asked did he have anyone in mind and Dion was the person Big Red thought of.

Dion previously said to Big Red he wished for a cool come up. With a baby on the way he wanted to get his own place to move his family out from living in a living room and so Big Red mentioned to Dion he had a beneficial opportunity to meet with him about on the quiet tip.

Dion agreed to the meeting. He knew nothing but where Big Red was picking him up and that the meeting was about some money but before they got to where they were going Big Red told Dion to start thinking of another one maybe two nigga's he could trust and Dion asked why.

Big Red said he just wanted for him to put some thought to it but then he admitted that asking him might have omitted a step. He said any nigga he could think of that he could trust besides Dion was dead or in jail or gone in the head with his brain on drugs but he told Dion he would be clearer on things after the meeting they were headed to.

Big Red could have told Dion they were going to a meeting with Bashan but he was on edge about it.

He had kept his second baby-momma and Dion separate partly because of Dion being the little brother of his third baby-momma but mostly because when he got around Bashan he could not hide that his affection for her ran deep, eternal and unparalleled.

Bashan and Big Red had agreed it was a must to keep a respectful distance around Dion.

She more than him wanted their newly rekindled seventy-two hour old intimacy to remain quiet because it did not change a thing.

She fucked him the night he responded to her call but they were still just friends and the two of them along with Azra had settled on how their first night of planning with Dion would go.

The agreement was that after a few drinks, some chips and dip and homemade appetizers, Big Red would explain the job to Dion and tell him why Bashan of all people was involved.

Big Red was going to say that since Bashan brought him in on the opportunity her involvement was necessary. He was not being disrespectful to Dior in any way by having dealings with Bashan but for everyone's benefit it was no way around bringing Dion and Bashan together.

Big Red would then be quiet after he asked Dion if that was a problem.

IV

The night of Dion and Bashan's first encounter he came inside her front door. He followed behind Big Red who did not say who Bashan was but he explained Roderick's shrine and his explanation gave it away without saying the home belonged to the mother of his late son.

Bashan offered to take Dion's jacket as they entered her guestroom but he said he was good with it on and before any drinks were poured, before Dion could take a seat and have a bite to eat and before Bashan could introduce him to Azra, Big Red went off script

He shared some history of how he met and grew up with Bashan and Bashan let him tell the cute story of their childhood but his tone was borderline rude and in Bashan's opinion, uncalled for.

She felt he was being extra especially when he referred to her as his best friend saying she was someone special in his life and would always be.

He went too far left saying if Dion felt some type of way because of Dior they could chalk it up like nothing happened and he offered to take Dion back home but before Dion could react Bashan interjected.

She asked him to please hold his response and allow her to make him a drink.

Bashan did not know Dion or care a thing about him but from what Big Red said of Dion they needed him so Bashan shifted the energy.

She turned on a soulful harmony to lighten the mood and she brought out two bottles of Pure White she purchased on her annual trip to the Caribbean.

She poured twelve shots for everyone to take three and she said their meeting was a special enough occasion to warrant a toast with her exclusive cognac.

Dion asked what was so exclusive about her liquor and Bashan said it might not be exclusive to other people. She lifted her first shot glass saying it was exclusive to her because it was not sold in the United States and she was of those select few to return to the States with a case of bottles from overseas.

She asked Dion did he want to lift his first shot and have a toast to them being of the select few and Dion lifted his shot but asked what were they the select few of.

Bashan told him to wait for it and she instructed them each to take their three shots together one after the other and when the twelfth empty shot glass slammed upside down against the table Bashan gave her reason for having them drink their shots back to back.

She said the single shot represented the number one. Having the three shot glasses in front of them represented the number three.
Taking the three shots together represented three sequential zeros and drinking all three the way they did was symbolic.

Dion asked what was the symbolism of the one, the three, and three zeros and Bashan got animated and said it was symbolic of what the fuck he just said. Thirteen-thousand-dollars was the minimum they each stood to make knocking off the Harpuzon Shoe Museum.

No amount had yet to be mentioned nor had the job and location been said and Azra, Bashan and Big Red each stole unnoticeable glances at each other.

Bashan could sense Dion's curiosity swell and she added a few more details about the robbery.

Dion asked a couple of questions to express his interest and he did not say he was in but Bashan knew she had refocused the meeting on where it should have been from the beginning.

Not on what Big Red said about his stalwart feelings for her but on the job and *the price*.

With the evening back on the right track Bashan invited Big Red to help her with something downstairs in the kitchen. She promised Azra and Dion that she and Big Red would not be too long. She directly addressed Dion to say she was aware Big Red had a curfew to return home and she was sure Dion had a curfew too.

Bashan leaving the room after dropping the thirteen thousand dollar bomb and overtly inferring respect for Big Red's home life was her being strategic.

She was giving Dion time to think could he really turn down an inside job for his sister's honor that no one was trying to threaten.

Bashan and Big Red's exit was code for Azra to play her small but critical role.

She had been assigned to turn on her charisma to sweeten the deal. This was her expertise. She was good at being alluring with her perfect smile, her seductive gaze, her hypnotizing voice and her sensual charm.

She was always in total control of herself and her prey. She kept her true intentions locked away and only she ever knew what the truth of the matter really was.

Azra's misbehavior towards Dion before Bashan took Big Red out the room was also according to the master plan.

After introducing herself at the beginning of their sit down she laughed a time or two but did not say a word.

Her place was next to Dion on the loveseat and not once did she acknowledge him even with a looksee.

She was mildly offensive making her disinterest with Dion palpable but the moment she was alone with him, she asked him if she could get him another drink or did he want water or some coffee.

Dion told her he thought she was either one of very few words or she just disliked him for no reason. He said he knew she could hear and comprehend because her movements were on cue. She handed Bashan the remote for the music when Bashan mentioned the need for some mood music. She laughed when appropriate. She opened the window when Big Red asked for some air but Dion said he heard crickets when he asked her to repeat her name and when he made the remark about her good-smelling perfume. He asked did whoever raise her not teach her to say thank you and Azra's reply was that she was having coffee and would make him a cup too.

Dion wanted to ask Azra was she really about to ignore him again but he just said okay to the coffee and he started from scratch. He asked Azra as she walked towards the kitchenette where she got her accent.

Azra filled the electric teakettle with an open liter of

bottled water and she plugged the teakettle into the electric outlet.

She pulled two coffee mugs from hooks screwed in the wall and she sat them on top of the microwave.

Dion watched her put teaspoons of instant coffee, brown sugar and nondairy creamer into the coffee cups but he was waiting for her to acknowledge he had asked her another question she was again ignoring like he had not said anything.

Azra walked to Dion's arm on the arm of the loveseat. She remained standing as her fingertips drew up and down the top of his forearm.

She told him her homeland was a coastline village she did not care to speak of nestled in a country she would not be returned to and Dion swallowed whatever he was going to say as Azra's mouth came towards his face.

She pressed her wet lips into his softening any apprehension and he closed his eyes for those seconds she parted his lips and danced with his tongue.

Azra pulled back and thanked Dion.

She said him asking her something personal meant he cared to know her and Dion told her it was nothing but Azra said what was something was him.

She altered the focus to it being about him being a dutiful brother and she dispassionately expressed knowing not one person who would turn down the type of money he was being offered.

She claimed to only have come across those willing to do a lot more for much less but Dion told Azra he had not turned anything down and she really did not know him.

He said he was one of those people who had done a lot

more for much less and as if Dion gave the right answer to the riddle nobody else could solve, Azra's gut instinct told her he was the one. She took the risk on being able to further tempt him to help her destroy her uncle Nefon and she asked Dion would he do more for her.

Dion looked confused so Azra clarified. She asked was he willing to do something more on the Harpuzon Shoe Museum job for her and only her if she paid him the money to do so. She then asked how did ten thousand dollars sound on top of his thirteen-thousand-dollar split.

Azra crossed the room to the coat rack and reached into her purse.
She pulled out two bands and each band had one hundred fifty-dollar bills secured in a brown and white wrapper to keep the five thousand dollars bound tightly together.

She tossed one band into Dion's lap and told him if he took that five-thousand-dollars he was accepting her side job.

Dion tucked the five thousand dollars in his jacket sleeve and asked Azra what more on the Harpuzon job she wanted him to do.

The teakettle started whistling and Azra dropped her other band of five thousand back into her purse.
She walked to the kitchen table and added the hot water to their two coffee cups.

She came back over to Dion and in passing him his cup she said they had the next four months to discuss what she had just paid him half of ten thousand dollars to do.

Chapter 11

SWEET REVENGE

Dion and Azra had finished their coffee by the time Bashan and Big Red returned to the guestroom.

Right before Bashan twisted the doorknob to enter Dion asked Azra was their anything about her side job she could tell him and other than not to tell Bashan or Big Red she said in due time more detail would come.

Dion did not wait to be asked was he in or was he out. He looked at Bashan directly to say he saw no problem in them getting money together.

He turned to Big Red to say Dior was his woman he had never disrespected verbally or physically and his affair with her had nothing to do with him. His sister was grown and as a brother he had more love for her than anything or anybody but he said Big Red had given no cause for a brother's interference.

Bashan acknowledged a deal had been struck.

She paraphrased for Dion what Azra had told her and Big Red about the ways her uncle trafficked females and dope in plain sight and just when they thought they had wrapped up the night Dion let the team know he would need to see things for himself.

Neither Bashan nor Azra agreed with his need to do that.
They contended with the value in him seeing Azra's uncle do his dirty business and Bashan asked what were the things he needed to see to rob the store.

Dion said anything he did was for a reason and if he revealed something of value cool but if not, no harm no foul and he told them to not be worried about his covert missions.

Dion entered Harpuzon Shoe Museum more than once in disguise and after he acquired pertinent information to planning the robbery Bashan and Azra did not contest him again.

I

Dion and Big Red had robbery planning meetings three sometimes four times per week but their meetings were during timeframes not too late to be offensive to Dior or Lillian.
Both women were being fed the same reused excuses about where their men were going for two to three hours every other night. The excuse would be either for making a run to the store, picking up a package or shipping something, seeing about some money, grabbing drinks or smoking with the homeboys and because Dion and Big Red backed each other Lillian did not confess to Dior she had her suspicions her brother and Big Red were selling them wolf tickets.

Dion arrived at Bashan's sometimes separately from Big Red but usually they arrived together and their meeting flow was the same.

Business got called to order after Bashan and Big Red gave priority to each other.

She was always needing him to help her with whatever or Big Red would need her help with whatever but usually in the privacy of Bashan's bedroom.

Dion and Azra were left by themselves and the inevitable happened.

They started with the flattering. They flattered each other on the littlest things like his newest scent or her hair game or his ever-changing creative ensemble of urban fashion or her newest pair of earrings she matched to the ever-changing colors of her manicure and pedicure.

In front of Bashan and Big Red they acted as unattached accomplices and they kept up their façade to avert any mistrust and protect their hidden agenda.

Night after night after night after night after night during their alone time, they flirted and kissed a lot and they held hands cuddled together on the couch.

Dion got as far as his fingers and tongue up the front and up the rear of Azra's love zone but he hit the wall at foreplay.

Azra went as far as spitting on his dick a time or two or three but only for a hand job and it was not that he did not ask for Azra to suck his dick.

He asked but every time she said love was free pussy was not. He could never afford her lips on his dick and each time he finished in her hand she jokingly reminded him he was the only man she rendered a hand job for free.

Dion asked what a nigga had to do to get some head and she said to get free head it would have to be the end of the world with them as the last two people on earth and he had made it his dying wish.

Dion said there had to be another way and Azra said yes the other way he would get the best head on earth was if he was her husband.

II

The Tuesday night before the robbery of Harpuzon's, Azra picked her pair of stilettos carefully.

It was not that she doubted Dion's loyalty from the moment he took her down payment for the side job but giving him some pussy wearing just a pair of stilettos was the kind of extra motivation that could not hurt.

This much she had learned from three of her uncle's special high profile clients.

His lawyer, his banker and his accountant were amongst some of the first to rape Azra.

In exchange for payment for services they provided to her uncle they repeatedly requested sex with her as a child and extra motivation in their cases went a long way.

Azra kindly but legitimately threatened to expose their private behaviors and they could not face the possibility of being found out about.

With everything they stood to lose the lawyer, the banker and the accountant chose to serve Azra's best interest by each helping to prepare her uncle's affairs for in the event of his untimely death she would benefit.

Earlier on Azra had indirectly let Dion know the side job

entailed her uncle and his two security guards. She said they were a problem in such a manner for Dion to make a determination without her using the words she wanted the three men permanently out of her way.

Azra had waited more than a decade planning and meditating day in and day out to be absolved of her uncle's control and she had learned the virtue of patience.

She thought recruiting Bashan was the definitive step in destroying her uncle but Bashan knew another side of him. He was her employer. He had given her opportunity and a professional identity and Azra had gotten Bashan to go as far as robbing him but Azra could not rely on Bashan to go further.

In meeting Dion, Azra knew he was the definitive step and Dion was powerless that Tuesday night she decided to unzip his jeans and disappear his dick inside her.

Dion and his dick were lounging on his side of the loveseat with Azra next to him.

He did not notice her get up but he noticed her lock the guestroom door and that was something she had not done before.

Azra made her way back over to Dion while unwrapping her kimono. It was white silk with an array of giant black orchids outlined in gold and she let it slide to the floor.

Dion's eyes went from Azra's sexy shoes up to the top of her pretty brown body and back down twice to be sure his sight was not playing tricks.

Azra came onto him and aggressively snaked her bare

upper body between his legs.

His dick went from being limp to being a log as she snaked her way up from his crotch at an easy pace and started sucking his tongue.

She licked and bit his neck and earlobes and kissed on his chest and Dion mumbled something about a condom but Azra was in a trance.

Before he could put up any resistance she was vehemently galloping in his lap with his hands lifted over his head and she had a tight grip on his wrists like he was her bitch.

Dion was so satiated he wanted to scream like he was her bitch and the idea of safe sex crossed his mind hazily but he did not want her to stop.

Even when Azra released his hands and clung to his shoulders to pull him on top of her he could not stop.

His hands were free to push Azra away and pull out the condom he had in his pocket but instead he used his large palms to grip her ample ass and push his dick inside her.

Azra focused each of her pelvic thrust on Dion's dick hitting her spot and she kept slowing him down to feel his entire dick inch by inch but Dion could not go slow for too long.

He kept losing control and speeding back up to maximum passion and he would catch himself and get his stroke under control but not because Azra whimpered for him to pull back or stop. He had mashed her pussy to the floor and she did not complain. She let him go so deep he felt tempted to let her know how good it felt to be inside her but he stayed silent.

They got in sync and were fucking at a steady hastened rhythm and Azra reached her hilltop but after she came

Dion paused to hold his nut. He was not ready for it to be over but he could not stop his release and he should have pulled out but he did not.

Azra's soft skin had melted him and her scent had intoxicated him and her beauty had his heart fluttering.

With his eyes closed he could still see her face and when he finished he opened his eyes to look down and she was looking up at him. Her sad brown eyes took hold of his soul but she turned away to break their gaze and she told him to get up.

Azra went to take her a wash-up in the second floor bathroom and when she came out for Dion to go in she was fiending for a cigarette.

Bashan did not allow smoking cigarettes in the house but instead of Azra going straight outside to smoke she stood at the bathroom door.

She listened to Dion wash their sex off his dick in the sink but because she let her mind go to another place she did not hear him turn the sink water off.

Dion opened the bathroom door and was bugged out by Azra standing there but she said she was only waiting to ask him to join her in the tenant-shared courtyard.

Few people knew Azra smoked because she always went to smoke alone.

She did not want Dion to know she smoked but she needed a cigarette as much as she needed him out of the house. She could not risk being heard for what she was about to tell him.

Azra was finally going to say more about her side job than just her uncle and his two security guards were a problem.

Dion followed Azra down the stairs to the lower level of Bashan's townhome and out the patio door to the courtyard.

She waited until they reached the courtyard bench to fire up and Dion told her that he hated cigarettes.

He took a seat while saying he knew others that closet smoked but he said if anyone else had fired up a cig in front of him including his dead mom he would have walked away.

Azra sat as far from Dion as the small bench allowed but she was still close enough for him to smell the smoke.

She thought she was at least blowing the smoke the other way after every drag until Dion asked had she brought him outside just to kill him with secondhand smoke and Azra said no. She brought him outside to tell him a secret.

Dion said he wanted her to first help him gauge the real on her relationship to Bashan and how was her safe place Bashan's guestroom and Bashan was the one hiding her from her uncle Nefon but they were not close enough to share secrets.

Azra said she could see where Dion was going saying a thing like that but she assured him that her relationship with Bashan was not a fake. She confided in her about her childhood and her family but only the glimpses of her life not overshadowed by misery.

She said her story of coming to America fourteen years ago was an unhappy story she had shared with no one but she told Dion he needed to know for him to grasp fully what her uncle did to her and her three sisters.

III

Elif, **Zehra**, **Safi** and Azra journeyed together to America and they were chaperoned by their mother's widowed aunt.

Great Aunt Nehru had been educated in America and she knew their father's eldest brother Nefon from when he was a boy.

Aunt Nehru brought Azra and her sister's to come to live with their uncle Nefon based on the stories of how fortunate of a life he had made for himself in the American shoe business.

The life Azra left behind in her homeland was not much by way of material things but she and her sisters were not deprived.
They lived in a loving nurturing household with a mother who cooked and made their clothes, a father who worked in the hospital and provided for their family and an older brother who was studying medicine and preparing to become a doctor.

One evening, Azra's parents and her brother did not return home from a welcome reception at the school where their brother had been accepted on a full scholarship.

Azra and her sisters waited weeks before they were advised to flee their county for their own safety and Uncle Nefon lured them to America with the promise of safety, an education and a good life.

When the sisters arrived in San Fran none were older

than fifteen and Azra was the youngest at age eleven.

Aunt Nehru's ninety-two year old heart gave out six days after they landed and their uncle Nefon beat them and starved them into obedience. He then forced them into sexual slavery and he auctioned the virginity of Elif, Zehra and Azra to different wealthy male associates.

Their uncle told the eldest sister Safi he did not consider her pretty enough to sell but he raped her and took her virginity for himself. He made her answer to the names Darky and Little Ugly and his statements to her were cruel anytime he came around. He stopped raping her after the third time Safi's body would not respond to birth control and he had to pay an exorbitant under the table fee to a doctor to perform an illegal late-term abortion on her.

Uncle Nefon left Safi alone physically but he still verbally abused her and made her do household labor as the overnight caregiver for his wife, **Kamu Harpuzon**.

On Safi's first night alone with Aunt Kamu, Elif and Zehra made her swear to poison the midnight snack she served their aunt with medication.
They wanted their aunt to pay for what she allowed her husband to do to them and Safi swore to her sister's she would administer the poison but after Safi saw their aunt had completely checked out of life she could not do it.

Aunt Kamu did not know which way was up to know what was happening in her own house.
She needed Safi's help with feeding, bathing and grooming.
She was pitiful and she kept repeating the same things

to Safi. Mainly about once being a vibrant businesswoman but her metamorphosis into a depressed homebody began after her fifth miscarriage. The reality settled in at age fifty-one she would never bring a child into the world and she wished to waste away and die.

Safi had to tell her sisters killing their aunt would be doing her a favor and would not make their uncle pay for what he was doing.

The sisters started spending every waking second trying to figure another way out their situation but then thirteen-year-old Zehra went missing.

Uncle Nefon told them Zehra was dead but Zehra had told her sister's of a rich old man in the country temporarily on business. He was obsessed with having her as his lunch-time appointment everyday and she was scared he was going to take her away.

Uncle Nefon told Azra, Elif and Safi he killed their sister but they did not believe him. They knew their uncle's greed and they attacked him and accused him of selling Zehra to the obsessed man but their uncle fought them off.
He choked Safi near death and he threatened to kill her and sell Elif and Azra if they ever defied him or his well-paying customers ever again.

That same night their uncle made the threat on their lives, Elif told Azra and Safi maybe Zehra had made it out.
She said Zehra told her the old man was kind. Maybe Zehra was lucky and where she went was better and Safi told her to put the drinking down. She said she knew Zehra would choose death over being some old man's sex slave in

some far off place where she might never see them again but Elif cried that at least Zehra had gotten out of there and she was going to get out too.

Elif asked Azra would she not take being dead over being their uncle's prisoner and Azra thought it was the booze talking.

Elif was taking swigs of scotch from Aunt Kamu's untouched liquor stash but Azra and Safi had not seen how many of Aunt Kamu's sleeping pills their sister took.

The following morning Safi found Elif lifeless with no pulse on the floor beside the bed they all shared.

After Elif's suicide, Azra and Safi vowed to not lose each other.

They knew they had to survive and fight their way out but getting out was not sufficient.

The only way to fill the holes Zehra and Elif left in their hearts were their regular thoughts and their tightlipped talks of *sweet revenge*.

Safi focused on their aunt.

She had been the architect behind Uncle Nefon's business from his early beginnings and she had claim to all his assets.

Uncle Nefon was distant from his wife but he gave her anything she wanted to keep her from his dealings and when their aunt demanded Safi be the round the clock person instead of having a different day and nighttime nurse, Uncle Nefon did not put up a fight.

He fired the day nurse and Safi secured her position. She

could now go and come from their home as she pleased all in the name of meeting her aunt's needs.

Safi read to Aunt Kamu and she made her read for herself and their reading was always about business and economics or communications and technology.

Safi baked and fed their aunt familiar authentic family recipes from their home and she made her help with the cooking.

She also made her exercise and get fresh air and as a way for Safi to visit the library they walked the long way around their neighborhood on their way to the park.

Azra told Dion she and Safi lost their two sisters within the first three years of coming to America and the darkness came over her eyes as she ended her story snappishly saying outright her uncle Nefon was the devil. She and Safi had long ago sentenced him to death and she owed it to Elif and Zehra to ensure his execution.

Dion felt rage for what Azra's uncle did to her and her sisters but also for the thought of it happening to the child he had on the way.

He and Lillian were waiting for the birth of their baby to learn the sex but were they to have a daughter she would grow into an innocent pubescent eleven-year-old Azra.

The thought of men like Azra's uncle wanting to rape and sell his child to be raped by other men had Dion ripe to offer to kill Azra's uncle and his goons for free but he did not say that to Azra.

The words out his mouth were she could consider her uncle and his two goons already dead and the money she was paying him was more than enough.

Dion remained in the tenant-shared courtyard with Azra discussing a plan divergent from what Big Red and Bashan thought the plan to be but they were outside long enough for Azra to have chain-smoked almost a half of her pack of cigarettes.

Azra divulged to Dion they would be getting her uncle for much more than money. He had a crawlspace behind a short two-drawer file cabinet inside the Harpuzon Shoe Museum basement office where he had hidden a bag of rare gems, artifacts and jewelry and a dozen or so keys to houses and commercial space, safety deposit boxes and storage units all over the San Fran Bay Area.

IV

It was late for a weeknight and Bashan's living room was quite but quiet as Dion and Azra tried to walk through and up Bashan's stairs they made a loud creak with every other step.

Azra reached the top of Bashan's staircase first before Dion.
She walked left to go to the bathroom to wash the cigarette smell off and Dion walked to the right to the guestroom and for the first time Big Red and Bashan were the two waiting.

Dion started to talk business stat and not that nothing was obvious. He did not come into the guestroom with Azra. Technically he could have come from someplace without her but he got to naming who he was bringing to the team to hopefully distract from he and Azra being outside the guestroom at the same time.

Bashan said it was good Dion finally had his men ready. She was starting to get worried being at the five-day mark and not being able to go over the seven roles involved.

Her and Big Red were a pair for what they had to do and Reddy and Azra were on their own but Dion had two people that would be by his side.

Dion was jawsin while he was thinking of someone he could care less lived or died but who could get the job done.

Prior to Dion just confirming the stipulations of Azra's side job he was going to involve two of his closest Fillmoe Kings but no way was he about to ask real friends to step in the line of fire. He had to search a couple networks in his mind to turn up the one person he told Bashan and Big Red about and he said that person came with his own second in command.

Big Red and Bashan were skeptical of who Dion had chosen due to him being a Mobson for the notorious street gang Lake View Mob.

LVM had been in San Fran for generations and was the city's oldest and wealthiest organized crime syndicate.

Mobsons and Mobdaughters were judges, fireman, nurses, journeyman, longshoreman and government employees and they protected their clan by any means.

They held grudges and were known for waiting twenty or thirty years to retaliate and many of the shot callers were doing life sentences for murder.

They lived by a mob aphorism take the heart for an eye, aim at the head for a tooth, play fair get played the fool, a mob trigger finger will not wound.

Not even cops got in the middle of their vigilante justice and Bashan's concern was if something went wrong. Say the person from LVM got hurt or God forbid, killed. It happening in Fillmoe might cause the blowback to land on Fillmoe.

Dion respectfully disagreed with Bashan. He said Fillmoe would be the last to be suspected because Harpuzon Shoe Museum was located in Fillmoe. It was loved and cherished by the community and if anything it would look like the two security guards were involved.

Bashan was trying to object but Dion spoke over her to say he put his feelers out around town and found out Nefon's security guards were father and stepson from two of Fillmoe's rival turf gangs. The father was a shot caller with the Geneva Tower Savages and his stepson was raised Army Street Posse.

Dion's point was if LVM retaliated it would likely be against the Savages or the Posse.

Bashan reminded Dion of the truce and said perhaps he was too young to know about it and Azra asked Bashan to tell them what truce she was speaking of.

Bashan explained the security guards being from rival turfs and being staffed in Fillmoe was tactical and part of a near decade old citywide anti-violence campaign known as One Frisco.

Before Azra had to ask Bashan told her One Frisco signified the truce and it was formed in the wake of a video arcade shooting at the city's Fisherman's Wharf.

The shooting was a drive-by assault at the hands of two siblings.

The sister was the driver of the vehicle and the brother was the shooter who opened fire on the arcade entrance in broad daylight.

Both siblings were from LVM and were after a boy from Hunter's Point and the boy ran into the arcade but he was not one of the dozen near the entrance to be killed or shot.

The horrific incident left a handful of different San Fran turfs mourning the loss of a dozen teens and children.

The affected families together with the city attorney's office formed the One Frisco collaboration to ceasefire and end gun violence.

The LVM refused to be formally apart of One Frisco but the Mob shot callers did agree to honor the ceasefire on the turf's that formed One Frisco under two conditions.

One condition was for the city attorney to take the death penalty off the table for the minors being prosecuted in the arcade shooting and offer them life with the possibility of parole.

The other condition was LVM was untouchable by any turf that formed the truce.

Army Street, Geneva Tower and Fillmoe were truce forefathers and for that reason Bashan told Dion his logic about how retaliation would happen and to who was wrong wrong wrong.

Any harm to a Mobson meant a war would be waged on One Frisco and Bashan asked was Big Red not going to say anything.

Big Red said whether they brought in old boy from LVM

or not, the potential for starting a turf war was still there. If one or both of the guards got dropped trying to get in the way, Army Street Posse and Geneva Tower Savages would be looking for blood too and Big Red made them envision the robbery going wrong. Going wrong meant people ended up dead with One Frisco dying with them and Big Red asked could they all live with that.

Bashan's face froze as if she saw a ghost and she shook her head no. She could not live with that.

Azra and Dion both said they could live with it and Big Red said he did not want to be the reason the truce was broken but his reality told him bad shit happened when you robbed a muthafucka.

Chapter 12

NOW OR NEVER

Nefon cleaned the bulk of his dirty profits regularly through the Harpuzon Shoe Museum but on the fourth weekend of the month he kept enough cash stashed in his basement office for the re-up on his dope the following week.

Once Nefon hid his money he partied his Saturday night away with his two security guards and the Corporate Retreat account paid the bill.

Bashan and the rest of her band of thieves were set to rob Harpuzon while Nefon and his guards were inside the VIP Suite drunk off gin, doped up on pills and powder and preoccupied by the generously paid adult entertainment.

I

Bashan was still training to be the Museum Manager but she had begun assuming managerial duties. One of those duties was ordering adult entertainment for the monthly Security Team Retreats and Bashan had placed the order once before but the weekend of the robbery was the first time she placed the order without a supervisor's approval.

Her supervisor had already submitted her six-week notice to resign. She was one foot out the door when she told Bashan the range of the luscious appetites of the three security team members and she told her to decide what to order and get used to making the decisions.

For the night of the robbery Bashan ordered the adult entertainment services of her childhood best friend.

Augustina Grace was an exotic performer in high demand in her prime but had for the most part aged out of the life. She was looking for what to do next but at the age of forty-eight she still had her flawless beauty and poise to woo any man from his conventional ways.

Bashan did not tell the others involved in the robbery she was placing eyes inside the VIP Suite. She was counting on Augustina as her best-kept secret to help ensure they got away scot-free with no hiccups and she assigned Augustina three simple tasks. To satisfy, distract and keep the door to the VIP Suite closed.

The one thing Bashan said for Augustina to worry about was that after the Museum closed Saturday evening it did not open until Monday morning and the Security Team Retreats could go until Sunday night.

Augustina did not know what she agreed to take on for Bashan's undercover assignment.

She always wore a purse recorder for her own protection and insurance but at Bashan's request she was asked to videotape her boss getting some of her delectable mango cocktail.

Bashan let on that the kind of dirt she was asking Augustina to record might come in handy but she kept her in the dark about the robbery.

Augustina told Bashan that in exchange for her complicity a bitch was going to need to be offered a retirement plan and Bashan promised Augustina a salaried career with full benefits working at Harpuzon's.

⟫⟫⟫«⟨◉⟩»⟪⟪⟪

The Friday night before the robbery was the shortest meeting of the entire planning process. All bases had been covered and Bashan assured the team Nefon would not know he had been robbed until he returned to his office on Monday.

Dion left Bashan's guestroom and went out her front door but Big Red heard Roe and Guillermina still awake and he walked downstairs to the living room.

They were on the couch under a blanket watching a movie and he took only a second to say goodnight.

Dion was in Big Red's truck seated behind the wheel waiting with the truck running but Big Red came to the driver side door and opened it.

He told Dion to scoot over he was good to drive and on their ride home he asked Dion why did he not mention his daughter was born that evening.

Big Red admitted he wanted to say something. He felt modifications to their plan could have at least been discussed but since Dion kept it on the hush he did the same.

Dion said he felt there was no need to mention his daughter's birth because it would make no difference. Tomorrow night was the night they had planned months for so everything was locked in and had to go according to plan.

Dion reiterated that the heist, Azra and Bashan was business and his daughter Royal was personal and he told Big Red he knew how seriously he treated a job and he asked was his work ethic not the reason Big Red chose him.

Big Red answered yes with a head nod without saying yes and Dion continued to say they decided on the fourth Saturday of October for very specific reasons and it was too late to change anything.

The owner and his goons would be distracted and according to Bashan the cash on hand for the re-up would be close to sixty grand.

Dion threw up the peace sign to say they had two options.

Follow through with the robbery as planned or wait another month until November, which was really not an option with the Thanksgiving holiday.

If they waited until December that was Christmas and New Years and at that point it might never happen and Dion said candidly it was *now or never*.

Big Red quietly let what Dion said sink in as he coasted the dreary gated streets of the Double Rock public housing community where Dion and Dior lived.

The housing complex was circular with one way in and one way out and Big Red bent the short curvy streets contemplating was he going to park his truck and stay with Dior or drop Dion off and keep it moving.

Big Red wanted to go back to Bashan and spend the rest of his night into the morning and afternoon into the big night with her but he heard her voice in his head telling him not to fuck everything up. He would already be at Dior's house to bring Dion home it made no sense not to give the rest of his night, the morning and the afternoon to her and Richie.

Big Red decided to listen to his inner Bashan.

He parked his truck outside Dior's place and he followed Dion inside.

Dion stepped quietly into his home with Big Red stepping in just as quietly behind him.

Big Red went up the stairs to Dior's bedroom and Dion took a seat on his futon couch.
His eyelids felt like bricks and for a couple of seconds at a time they shut but he forced them back open and continued to try his hardest not to fall asleep.

Dion did not know his eyes closed again until he jolted awake in what seemed like a few seconds later.
He wiped his eyes and looked at his watch and he could not believe hours had passed.

To keep from falling back to sleep he went upstairs and jumped in a cool shower for about thirty minutes and when he came down to the living room and got dressed it was almost dawn.

Dion sat down to put on his shoes but he knew if he stayed seated he would be sleep and he was tired enough to sleep through any alarm.

The diner where he was going to pick up Lillian's breakfast had not yet opened but sleep was bound to happen if he
sat at home waiting for them to open.

Dion got in his car and turned the air conditioning up to
full blast.

He was sitting with his head against the headrest but the
AC was not helping him stay awake so he shifted into gear
and he drove off.

Two minutes later he pulled inside the small parking lot
of a box-shaped dive with windows for two of the four walls.

He parked beneath the lighted Bee & Jay's Diner sign
but he had to get out the car and he walked to the front of
the diner entrance to wait for them to flip the window sign
from closed to open.

The lights were on inside with two diner staff working to
get the diner open and the waitress could see Dion pacing
the entrance.

She already had a pot of coffee brewed and decided to
open the diner doors a few minutes early to let him come in
out of the cold.

Dion thanked the waitress as he took the first stool at the
long sit-down counter.

He watched the short shapely middle-aged Latina grab
her black apron, tie it around her waist and come towards
him holding the handle of a steaming pot of coffee.

Without having to ask she poured Dion a fresh cup and
she added just enough cream and the right amount of sugar.

The cook emerged from a back room carrying the final

additions to his cooking area.

He slid the loaves of bread over next to the olive oil and a tub of butter to make room for the diced peppers and sliced onions he had freshly prepared.

He stepped to the stove that he already had heating and stuck his muscular tattooed arm out over it to determine if he could feel the heat.

The cook then gave the waitress a look.

The look seemingly conveyed the stove was hot and ready because the waitress pulled a pen and pad from her apron and asked Dion if he was ready to place his order.

Dion ordered the chicken fried steak special and the waitress did not have to ask how he wanted his eggs or if he wanted the special with grits, rice or potatoes.

He told the waitress what he wanted off top.

Dion knew Lillian liked her eggs easy and her potatoes smothered and he added to her order a sweet tea mixed with orange juice.

The waitress asked what type of toast he wanted and he said wheat toast without thinking but had to scratch that.

He got Lillian lightly buttered sourdough toast and after the waitress ripped his completed order from her writing pad he remembered to tell her to make his order to go.

The waitress walked to the stove to clip the order in front of the cook's eyes then she walked over to the cash register. She tallied Dion's order and printed his receipt and as she handed his receipt to him she walked into the back room.

Soft rock music started to play from the ceiling speakers above Dion's head and the waitress was gone about six minutes but when she come from the back room she walked over to the hot pot of coffee.

She returned to where Dion was seated to pour him a refill and she made it again with just enough cream and the right amount of sugar.

Dion threw her a twenty-dollar bill and a five-dollar bill for a sixteen dollar and ninety-nine cent tab and he told her to keep the change.

While he waited for Lillian's food he sipped his second cup of coffee slower than the first cup because he did not want the waitress to pour him a third.

II

Dion entered Lillian's hospital room. He was carrying her breakfast and her drink and CoCo was rocking his baby but she looked at him with a look of fright.

She said it was a good thing Royal could not see her father looking like the walking dead and she asked Dion had he not slept in more days than just one.

Dion told CoCo to save the drama for her momma but CoCo kept running her mouth and said he did not scare her. She told him she cared more for her girl than being afraid of him and that he should be grateful for her. She was someone speaking truth he needed to hear for his benefit but Dion told CoCo not even. He said the only truth that should matter to her was that her girl was in love with his walking-dead-looking-ass and to benefit him and her girl, she needed to say less.

He placed Lillian's food down on Lillian's side table and

CoCo said to not wake her she had just fallen asleep from being up most of the night.

Dion did not say he would not wake her but he went to use the bathroom and when he came out CoCo was handing him his baby.

She was eager to see what he brought Lillian to eat and the smell of gravy woke Lillian soon as CoCo cracked opened the brown compostable food container.

CoCo told Lillian to sit back and be served and she slit the container down the middle and handed Lillian a half portion of her food inside the container lid.

CoCo sat next to Lillian with the other half of the food and she took in a couple of bites to calm her growling stomach before she started talking about her recent scandal at work.

Lillian could hear CoCo uttering words but she had not given her full attention.

She was eating hungrily and when her eyes were not on the plastic fork going back and forth to her mouth they were on Dion nodding in and out of sleep while comforting their baby.

Lillian stopped eating to wash her food down with her drink and she asked CoCo if she wanted to taste how good OJ mixed with sweet tea was.

CoCo took the drink from Lillian and kept talking but she still did not have Lillian's attention.

Lillian's thoughts had been hijacked by the beautiful

image of her man holding their baby's swaddled body to his chest. Her head rested in the crease of his neck and her thick black curly hair was playing peekaboo from the small hospital issued knit hat.

His grip on her was gentle and they were a set too precious to look away from.

Lillian watched her baby peacefully sleeping in her father's arms and she realized her new reality as it began to settle into her mind and her body and her spirit.

Across the room was her prince charming holding their little princess and she felt so lucky to be in a world that felt fairytale.

The bursting sensation in her chest pulsating through to her fingers and toes she thought must have been her heart rupturing and her mind magnifying to conceive the emotional depth of having just created a family.

When Lillian heard CoCo say, got caught, she thought CoCo was saying she got caught and Lillian told her to rewind her story. Start from where her supervisor pulled her from working outside crowd control duty to inside the box office to sell tickets.

CoCo asked if Lillian heard the part of the story about her co-worker walking off the job and never coming back. The part right before CoCo asked could Lillian believe the dumb nigga got caught and Lillian said she had not heard that part either and she asked what dumb nigga.

CoCo came nearer to Lillian's bed.

She whispered that she would start her story again if Lillian was ready to stop staring off in lah-lah-land telling herself her black ass baby-daddy was some prince charming.

CoCo teased about Royal being a perfect little bundled up biscuit but she said too bad she was her momma's child she could not stay that way. Purely for all the shit Lillian put Grandma Dah through when they were young she should expect the same head and heartache from Royal.

III

Grandma Dah walked into Lillian's hospital room slowly and Lillian exclaimed Grandma Dah was going to live a long time. She always said this to her grandma for walking in or calling at the moment she was mentioned.

Grandma Dah's response was always for Lillian to stop believing that make-believe stuff.

She came to Lillian's bedside and pressed her wrinkled petite hands into Lillian's bed to lift herself on the tip of her toes and kiss Lillian's cheek.

As she kissed Lillian she reminded her that just because she thought or talked about somebody and they happened to show up or call at that same time did not mean their life would be any longer than before she thought about them and they showed up or called.

Grandma Dah scanned the room looking for Royal and she let Lillian know not to expect her to stay long. She was telling Lillian she had just got off work and Bally was waiting but Lillian interrupted to say her grandma meant to call Bally a beer-belly chain-smoked-out ass old man but Grandma Dah swatted at Lillian's mouth and finished saying Bally was waiting for her outside the hospital. She was working a double for the extra money and he was taking her home to rest before taking her back to work.

Lillian asked Grandma Dah if she at least used a condom with Bally and Grandma Dah did not bother answering Lillian's intrusiveness. It was like the question died in the air and did not reach her ears and she swatted her hand at Lillian's mouth again but this time she plucked Lillian's shoulder hard twice with the flick of her right middle finger.

Lillian rubbed her shoulder to stop the sting where she had been plucked and her and CoCo laughed at how red a reference to sex made Grandma Dah's face.

Grandma Dah went over to look at her great grandbaby becoming squeamish with Dion.

Dion had started rocking his knee side to side to create a soothing movement for the baby with his eyes still closed but when Grandma Dah started pulling the baby from his grip she accidently woke him.

He was back sleep seconds after Royal was secure in her great grandmother's arms but Grandma Dah did not hold the baby for too long. She kissed Royal and passed her to Lillian for a breastfeeding then she said her goodbyes. She did not get fully outside Lillian's hospital door before she looked back at Lillian. She watched her cup Royal's tiny body so perfectly and adjust her in the way the nurse had taught her to get the baby to latch correctly onto her nipple and Lillian moved exactly as her mother did.

The image took Grandma Dah's mind back twenty years to the moments she spent in the hospital with her daughter after her daughter had gone through labor and delivery.

Celestine Leilani Mendoza was Grandma Dah's only child and her and Celestine's father met and fell in love in their early twenties.

She was from Asia by way of the Philippines and Celestine's father was from Europe by way of Spain.

They were each living in San Fran with roommates working multiple odd jobs scraping to get by and they met while attending night school to improve their English as a second language.

One was shy to talk to the other but they both loved the city's nightlife. Every weekend they got together with friends and classmates to party at the same nightclubs and bars for drinks and dinner and the two of them always ended up dancing for hours until one or the other had to get to work.

For about a year they did the friendly-dating thing but on a friend's birthday road trip to Reno they avowed their love and eloped.

They moved in together and for nearly twenty years they continued to work hard and save money towards their dreams.

Finally they invested their savings in a struggling neighborhood pub and in the midst of Grandma Dah's husband becoming a co-owner Celestine was conceived. She was unquestionably planned and prayed for and wanted but she was not expected.

Grandma Dah was no longer charting her ovulation and scheduling extra sex on those days to get a baby but surprisingly on her thirty-ninth birthday Celestine was born natural and healthy with no complications.

Celestine was a few nights old when her father did not

make it home and Grandma Dah took Celestine with her to his pub to find him. She got there and was told he had tried to intervene in an altercation and became a murder-victim of a hate crime.

Grandma Dah was left widowed and penniless with an infant to care for and according to the pub's co-owner the business was only breaking even.

She was obligated to take on a fulltime job for her and her baby to have food and for her to cover the rent but all she could find for the type pay she needed was a graveyard shift in the housekeeping department at the San Fran County Psychiatric Hospital.

Neighbors were kind enough to watch Celestine through the night when Grandma Dah was at work but as Celestine got older, by the time Grandma Dah realized something was wrong Celestine was far-gone. She was drug-addicted, wild, young and too naïve to outsmart the streets but she was fearless and she fought, she begged, she stole, she lied, she cheated and she conned to buy her drugs.

Celestine was only thirteen when she became pregnant and she was fourteen when she delivered Lillian and her younger twin brother almost a full two minutes later.

IV

Lillian had no memory of Celestine. She could not know how much she resembled her but Grandma Dah saw Celestine in Lillian's manner and even her gestures.

With Lillian's face angled down watching Royal feed Grandma Dah saw her baby girl Celestine in that hospital bed and she was holding Lillian all over again.

Lillian had Celestine's long neck and her defined broad shoulders and Grandma Dah had not seen Celestine for longer than she had seen her in life. It had been so long Grandma Dah wanted to rewind time and freeze the last morning she returned home to see Celestine alive.

Grandma Dah came in her front door from working her graveyard shift at her usual time and she went straight to the bathroom. She was delighted to have Celestine and the twins staying with her but she did not want to disturb the three of them asleep in Celestine's twin bed.

Celestine had gone to stay with the family of her baby-daddy after the twins were born but before the twins turned a year old Celestine had come running to her mom for help.

Grandma Dah let Celestine bring her twins back to their studio apartment home and Grandma Dah had no regrets with them being there but she was left with only her mornings after work for some me-time.

In the bathroom Grandma Dah liked to listen to talk radio while she pinned up her hair for her shower but before stepping inside her shower she turned the radio to music and the music played until after she oiled her skin and got into her nightgown.

Grandma Dah did not believe in going to bed on an empty stomach but she had to pass through the living area to get to the short hall leading to the kitchen. She succeeded at walking quietly by her full-size bed adjacent to the foot of Celestine's bed but all she could do to not disturb her sleeping beauties was close the kitchen door to muffle her making sounds.

Grandma Dah ran some water in a pot and put the pot on the stove on high heat to boil.

She cracked a couple eggs in the skillet and scrambled them in butter with some left over steamed rice, fresh garlic, diced green onions and a little sea salt with ground pepper.

She waited for her eggs to be half done to put her two slices of wheat bread in the toaster then she added shredded cheese to her egg rice scramble and she turned the heat down low to let the cheese melt.

She poured the boiling hot water over her green tea and she put a plate next to her teacup.

She slid her eggs with the spatula onto her plate while her tea sifted and she grabbed her toast.

She sat down to spread butter and grape jelly on her toast and when her tea was ready she added two lumps of brown sugar and two tablespoons of honey and she ate her breakfast reading a magazine article.

Grandma Dah could not get to bed until she cleared her sink full of dishes and put them away but she finally closed her eyes to Celestine and the twins sleeping serenely.

She woke around four hours later to use the bathroom and the twins had crawled from their bed. They had quietly and contently gotten into everything they could get their small hands on but Celestine was gone.

Many weeks later there was still no mention of Celestine on the news, no calls from neighbors or no contact by police then finally a construction crew discovered a body and called the authorities.

Grandma Dah was asked to come identify the body and after she made a positive ID she was told her daughter had been raped, beaten, murdered and left for dead beneath the rubble of a demolished San Fran freeway onramp.

Chapter 13

NO WITNESSES
NO MISTAKES

Saturday night had finally come. It was twenty minutes after midnight and everyone was in position to break-in Harpuzon's Shoe Museum.

The Museum security system was disarmed for the adult entertainment to come and go so Bashan and Big Red were able to come through the service door from the street with no alarm sounding.

Their role was to secure the premise and unlock the back door access from the side alley for everyone else to enter.

There was a trapdoor in the floor of the Harpuzon Shoe Museum entrance covered by a large decorative rug that led a backup security room.

The backup security room was created after Nefon bought the Museum and the knowledge that it existed was known to less than a handful.

Bashan only knew Nefon installed backup security

because Bashan's boss was told to settle the final invoice for the installation from the petty cash box but Bashan's boss reassigned that task to Bashan.

Prior to paying and shredding the final invoice as Bashan was told to do she called the vendor to verify all services had been rendered and a small slipup from the vendor told Bashan exactly were he installed the additional security.

I

Big Red stood lookout while Bashan entered the trapdoor near the entrance. She tampered with the backup security system to erase their break-in then they crept downstairs to the basement server closet for Bashan to do the same with the main surveillance.

Bashan and Big Red discreetly came out the backdoor into the alley disguised indistinguishable from the others except for size.

They all wore black clothes and shoes, black caps, black curly wigs and black scarves over their face and dark shades over their eyes and no one showed their body markings or piercings.

Big Red gave Azra and Dion the green light and Dion signaled to his hired muscle they were about to rush the backdoor.

Dion was in the lead and his two gunmen got behind Azra and Dion led them downstairs.

Azra went one direction and Dion pointed for his the two men to go the other direction towards the VIP Suite.

Azra's role was to get the stash from her uncle's office and clear the contents of his crawlspace while Dion and the two gunmen guarded the door to the VIP Suite. They were to stand guard and make sure Nefon and his Security Guards did not interfere with Azra cleaning house.

II

Reddy was waiting where he was supposed to be in a rented maroon Odyssey. He had the mini van running and Bashan and Big Red were first to get in the van.

Ten minutes later, five minutes behind schedule, Azra made it to the van.

She had the merchandise from her uncle's crawlspace in a small area separated from what she emptied out her uncle's lockbox but everything was in the thin nylon drawstring sack on her back.

Five minutes later. Ten minutes behind schedule, Dion arrived at the van and told Reddy to take the fuck off.

Bashan yelled wait and asked where were the other two niggas that were with him and Dion blurted **Boscoe** and **Bam Bam** were dead.

Bashan wanted to know before they drove off how the fuck that happened and was anybody else dead and Azra said quietly everybody was dead and she insisted they get a move on.

Reddy drove the speed limit honoring all rules of the road as Dion told what went wrong.

He said the four of them got downstairs to the basement

level and Azra went to the business office to do her job. He along with Boscoe and Bam Bam went towards the VIP Suite where the door was wide opened unlike Bashan said it would be.

Bashan swore the VIP Suite door remained closed and Azra had backed that up saying there would be no interaction with Nefon or his guards. All Dion, Boscoe and Bam Bam were supposed to do was stand outside of the VIP Suite to make sure Azra got out the business office and up the stairs unscathed.

Dion said because the VIP Suite door was open one of the security guards spotted them and opened fire.

Azra chimed in without an invite saying she did not know why things unfolded out of the ordinary how Dion was describing. She claimed to have heard shots fired as she reached for the door of the business office but she just hurried to grab the cash.

Azra was speaking to everyone in the van but looking Dion's direction and when she stopped talking he continued saying how the plan went haywire after the younger security guard spotted them and fired his gun without a word.

Bam Bam was the first down the hall with his gun cocked and he returned fire on younger security guard but not with a fatal shot. A bullet from his gun did hit the younger security guard but the younger security guard kept firing and fired the shot that killed Bam Bam.

Boscoe was behind Bam Bam and he fired on the younger security guard killing him. He kept firing and took out the older security guard who had fired a couple shots at Boscoe when he saw the younger security guard drop but all his shots towards Boscoe missed.

Nefon fired a couple shots that hit Boscoe but Boscoe returned fire and killed Nefon.

Boscoe staggered around on his feet laughing and talking shit to Dion about increasing his cut but after a few seconds he fell dead.

Dion said when it went down like that he told Azra to go and he was last to the van because of a final sweep to make sure there were *no witnesses no mistakes.*

Big Red asked where were the bitches and Dion lied about there being no bitches.

Dion saw a woman hiding in the bathroom behind the door. He left her there because he had no reason to kill her.

By the time he noticed her he had pocketed his dark glasses but even if she had seen his face she had only seen half. The other half was covered with a black scarf across the bridge of his nose that went above his ears and tied behind his curly-haired wig.

His skin-color and his eyebrows and his eyes were visible but Azra had the entire team apply heavy foundation on their faces to distort their natural skin color. They had also glued on thick white-haired costume eyebrows and put in Halloween whiteout contact lenses to hide their true eyes.

Dion told Big Red if he was going to take a wild guess on what went wrong he would say something went wrong with the bitches but Big Red grilled him asking him something went wrong like what and Dion did not stammer. He said went wrong like Nefon and his security guard's must have just let the bitches leave and them leaving was the reason the door to the VIP Suite was open instead of closed.

Big Red did not say another word and the car rode in silence.

Bashan sat with her arms crossed over her chest pondering the discrepancies in Dion and Azra stories.

Dion told Azra to get to the van before he did a final sweep so how did she know everyone was dead.

Bashan knew that much was wrong with Azra's story and what she knew was wrong with Dion's story was there were not multiple bitches it was just Augustina for the night and he did not mention her.

Bashan wanted to say something to Dion and Azra but she kept Augustina to herself. She did not know how to speak up without putting her best friend in possible danger but she knew one other thing for sure. She no longer trusted Dion or Azra. She would have to wait until she heard from Augustina to see the truth of what really happened from her video footage.

III

Reddy drove their mini van to the Polk Street Inn and Suites in Transtown and soon as he parked Bashan decided she had something to say.

Polk Street Inn and Suites was a three-star property

managed by Augustina's friend of a friend who accepted a four hundred percent tip under the table to reserve a suite for a week.

The tip was for the friend to not look hard at the fake name and the fake identification Reddy used when he paid for the room in cash and the tip covered their being no record of Dion.

He would be the one staying in the suite with the stash as part of his role.

The agreement was to wait out the aftermath before divvying everything up and The Polk Inn as the locals called it was the best place in the city to hide.

Transtown was a place that embraced everyone with love and positive vibes but if a hate crime happened to one of their beloveds they were as well a place that could make a person disappear and they did not bother with police.

Transtown was the city's transgender community and they took care of their own to avoid being disrespected, stigmatized and not taken seriously.

Their area was a one-mile strip resident's called Tranny-Row and it ran parallel to the Tenderloin, Russian Hill and Chinatown districts.

It was a safe, clean, well-lit, upbeat posh neighborhood with twenty-four hour bars and restaurants, spas and corner stores and a full-service adult cannabis-friendly theater that people from around the world raved and gave high reviews calling it a number one bucket list destination and great place for a bachelorette or bachelor party.

Bashan asked Dion to hold up from getting out the van and she faced Big Red but was speaking to everyone except Reddy. She spoke with a sad certainty to say that night had for sure caused a war and yes she warned something like that could happen but in the context of chances being slim to none.

Big Red kept his eyes facing forward at the back of Reddy's headrest and when he shrugged one of his shoulders slowly up towards his ear and back down Bashan closed her mouth like she was finished talking.

Dion was still in position for Big Red to let him out the back seat but Big Red did not move and Bashan said distinctly no one was supposed to die. Anyone dying was the worst possible thing that could have happened and she went on about not understanding. Why the previous fourth Saturdays they tested the plan and prepared for the robbery were different and the thought someone might have said something surfaced but anyone she could have questioned about that was dead.

Azra asked Bashan why she was so sure there would be war and Bashan asked if Big Red wanted to explain to Azra what she was talking about.

Big Red said he was not about to go there. He lost his two older brothers, his one younger brother, two uncles and an aunt to the war Bashan was bringing up and it permanently destroyed his family so no he was not about to talk about it.

Reddy had put in his earphones from the moment they stopped. He was listening to his music loudly so he could not hear a thing. He was waiting for Dion to get out the van so he could hand him his room key and drive to the next drop.

Bashan looked at Dion and said he was too young to remember the days before One Frisco when the city's eleven turfs were at war with the other and warring within each other.

Dion said he was alive eight years ago and was not that young and Bashan said he may have been alive but he was too young to know intimately how bad it was.

Bashan shared that she lost her son, her fiancé and her father before One Frisco was finalized and One Frisco enacted the ceasefire to stop the gun violence. She told Dion there was no doubt in her mind One Frisco was the reason he and Reddy had lived past seventeen.

Bashan looked at Azra with tears in her eyes. She explained her and Big Red both had a past too painful to be retold but what she could tell Azra was there would be revenge and blood in the streets for what they had done. She encouraged Azra to pray when she got home that night regardless of her religion or faith. She said for her to drop to her knees and pray hard San Fran never relived Black Sunday and before Azra could ask Bashan told her Black Sunday was the city's recorded highpoint of violence that led to the formation of One Frisco.

Black Sunday was the front-page title of Sunday's newspaper article released the morning nearly the entire city's church community congregated at the Mayor's request to pray collectively for peace in the streets.
It was on a third Sunday in August and the Mayor called

for a high noon assembling of all churches in San Fran to the steps of City Hall.

What prompted the ad hoc assembly was the news article that resulted from a police officer leaking to a reporter their department had already recorded more than five hundred homicides that year and ninety percent were Black men killed by gun violence.

Azra foolishly said there could not be revenge if everyone was dead and Bashan emotionally and angrily chewed her head off saying it would not matter that everybody was dead. The story history would tell was that Boscoe, a Lake View Mobson, was murdered in Fillmoe. That right there was enough to break the ceasefire and LVM was ruthless. They would pick a turf or pick the turf of every person found dead inside Harpuzon's to seek their revenge but they would have blood for Boscoe. It was their way.

Bashan could see Azra's brain spinning and she told her not to try and comprehend gang life. Just know the way things went down in her hometown when it came to LVM was a price could only be paid in blood.

The main LVM shot callers were constantly in solitary confinement or on lock down in the state penitentiaries to lessen their dominance. It could therefore take hours or days for them to receive word of Boscoe's murder but the pen controlled the streets and when the war began in the pen the war would bleed into the streets.

Azra asked how much time they had before something crazy like that transpired and Bashan asked did she not hear her say maybe hours or maybe days. The longest they had might be a week but who would start the shit or how it would start she had no idea.

IV

Dion finally got out the van street side and Reddy handed him the key to his room through the driver side window.

Dion had not thought about his story to Lillian. There was no way to explain him being away from her and the baby. He would not be able to pick her up from the hospital on Monday morning when they were discharged and she would not and should not accept one reason for him missing their baby's first days.

Telling Lillian the truth about the robbery was never going to be an option and him lying to her would make her angry but with no other choice he had a week to make up whatever lie he was going to come up with.

Part III

ADVENTURES

Chapter 14

FUCKBOY

CoCo Marie Butler was next in line.

She had not thought of what she wanted to drink let alone was she having it with a chocolate croissant, a lemon loaf or a cheese danish.

CoCo's mind was on her co-worker who had opted to stay in the car.

He claimed to be anemic saying he was too cold to come with her inside the coffee shop but what was doing the loop-the-loop in CoCo's head was that he was in her passenger seat with her car engine running to keep her heat blasting.

If a person knew CoCo they could see the steam coming from her ears. If a person did not know CoCo they could see the steam coming from her ears.

She was standing at the barista and looking up at the menu to see did she want a soy flatwhite, a chai tea or a vanilla latte but the nigga in her car burning gas he never offered to pay for had CoCo beating herself up.

She had let the nigga get too comfy. Now he was acting like he had slipped an engraved conflict-free diamond something or another on a finger or a toe or in her ears or on her wrist or an ankle and on top of that was dicking her down with good lovin.

CoCo placed her order having determined she had kept it up with dude for too long and she did not have to feel bad about letting go. She had given him the chance to be all he could be but it was time to dismiss *Fuckboy*.

I

CoCo at first liked Fuckboy for his quickies.

The thrill of having a thirty minute lunch break to run to the parking garage, fuck in the backseat of her car, go together to get food and eat walking back to work was adventurous.

The adventure made CoCo cum to Fuckboy's rhythm most of the dozen or so times they were scheduled to work together and could manage to sneak away.

He was something in her routine workweek that made the job something to look forward to but CoCo and Fuckboy should not have moved from the backseat of her car.

They were now fucking in CoCo's king-size bed and Fuckboy was failing to satisfy every time she gave him a taste. He was finishing after three, maybe four minutes and if she was lucky he had five or six minutes in him.

It had only been a week and one day since the older woman Fuckboy was living with broke off their engagement.

She was a corporate bigwig who came home from a business trip early and discovered him in her bed with two other women.

Fuckboy missed work the day he got kicked to the curb but the next day he told CoCo his sob story and he asked to temporarily cohabitate with her.

CoCo took him in and had gone the full seven days getting a daily dose of his dick but the excitement he first brought to her life diminished with her knowing quick dick was not just at break time.

In the beginning of the week CoCo told Fuckboy how good his dick was.

She said she could not wait to have it for breakfast, lunch and dinner and originally that was the truth but fast forward seven days and Fuckboy's big fat dick was no longer the lick.

He would be hard for a few minutes before he got to convulsing as if he had exerted hella energy and the morning CoCo was in line at the coffee shop she had reached her climatic disappointment.

The night before she was lying in bed beside Fuckboy.

He was kissing and nibbling on her ear and blaming his quick dick on her saying her good pussy was the reason for his instant finish and he promised to have her wake up to him giving her hers.

He said he would not stop eating her out until her cum was oozing down her butt crack.

CoCo cared more about the stain cum would leave on her eighteen hundred count lavender-colored bed sheets and she started to tell Fuckboy no thank you. She did not believe he had it in him to give her head like that but she reached anyway to grab the large beach towel from the floor they had just sexed on top of and wiped themselves semi-clean with but when she rolled over she fell asleep.

She woke up in the morning wiping the crud out her eyes and she realized what she was feeling was Fuckboy licking on her clit like it was a chore. His promise of pleasure had turned into a daylight nightmare and the ramming of his middle finger and index finger inside her punani was not even the worse part.

She had to tell him to stop. She said they did not have enough time for foreplay she forgot she had to be early for work and he needed to get himself ready if he was riding with her.

CoCo realized after she ordered from the barista it was the first time that week she did not buy breakfast for Fuckboy.

Something that Friday morning must have told him it was best not to ask her for shit.

CoCo almost automatically ordered him his usual. A bacon breakfast sandwich double heated and a tall house roast with steamed 2% milk sweetened with one pump of classic syrup but getting in the car with that would have sent mixed signals and she was not feeling him.

Their morning commute into San Fran to go to work had the expected heavy multi-hour traffic delay but CoCo picked up a stranger from the carpool line in Oakland and with three passengers in her car they sailed by the Bay Bridge toll plaza in half the time.

The only people talking in CoCo's car were the radio

personalities on the radio.

The stranger wore headphones to avoid conversating and Fuckboy did not talk until they were waiting at the metering lights just past the tollbooths.

He asked CoCo was she mad at him and CoCo said no.

Fuckboy asked if her no meant they were on for teatime and teatime was CoCo's phrase but what Fuckboy was insinuating was he wanted them to have their morning break together.

CoCo said maybe maybe-not but him asking about teatime could have waited and Fuckboy snapped back. He said he could have waited but he wanted to ask right then and she could have answered him yes or no but she wanted to be stuck the fuck up or some maybe shit.

CoCo was ready to dump Fuckboy and kick him out her car before they drove by the Treasure Island turnoff and she could have told him to get to stepping with their carpooler at the first San Fran exit.

She had another chance to dump him before they reached the parking lot at work and she even had time before they clocked in for their shifts but she decided to wait for teatime.

She needed to think of how she was going to let him know her pussy was closed and he could not stay at her place but the money they were making together did not have to change.

II

CoCo was walking to the staff break room to meet Fuckboy for her morning break and she received the group text message from Lillian that her water broke.

CoCo was expecting Fuckboy to be waiting for her at the water cooler where they agreed to meet but he was late so she sat at the break room table to wait for him.

She sipped company provided English breakfast tea and played over and over in her head how she would break off the sex but go back to how they started.

CoCo had worked for the Bay Area Ferry Company almost five years.

She was one of the employees at the top of the seniority list.

She was a lead box office ticket seller and if needed she covered outside crowd control.

CoCo's Ferry Company ran commuter ferries, island ferries and ballpark ferries between neighboring Bay Area harbors and the San Fran Ferry Terminals.

The commuter ferries taxied passengers from Vallejo, Oakland, Alameda, Treasure Island, Sausalito and Tiburon and the island ferries went to Angel Island and Alcatraz Island.

The ballpark ferries ran seasonally to San Fran from the Bay Area harbors for national baseball and basketball home games.

Discount tickets were available for commuter ferries but the other ferry rides were priced as high as sixty dollars or more per ticket for hundreds of people per day.

CoCo had trained Fuckboy the previous summer when the company hired more than a dozen new staff.

She thought Fuckboy was cute but too young for her taste and quick as he became a thought he became an afterthought and she did not entirely notice him until months after his training.

He was laid off during the winter but he was rehired in the spring and he came to CoCo before the beginning of the summer season with the scheme of reselling tickets.

Fuckboy had become acquainted with CoCo working with her in the box office.

He recognized she had the authority to move between box office staff and crowd control staff and when she worked crowd control her job was to collect the tickets from customers boarding their ferry.

Fuckboy's proposition was for when she worked crowd control he wanted her to collect tickets from the ferry riders and not follow the common procedure. Instead of her tearing the ticket and returning the ticket to the customer for a receipt he wanted her to give him the tickets. He would sell the used tickets out of the box office window for full price and they would pocket the profit.

CoCo let Fuckboy believe he had come up with something new and she wanted in on it.

He had no idea she had been stealing from the company for years to keep up her Benicia Condo, her stylish wardrobe and her Cadillac car payments. Not to mention her lobster and crab dinners, her expensive perfume, designer handbags and her weekly hair and nail maintenance and she never missed a week.

CoCo kept secret from Fuckboy she had her own hustle that had to do with getting customer's credit card info and she was taught how to steal from the company by the best. Her former box office supervisor showed her exactly how to steal smartly to avoid being detected and the same supervisor had not only robbed the ferry company she and CoCo worked for. She boasted to CoCo about having robbed other tour agencies for decades.

CoCo's supervisor stopped stealing when she got discarded by one of the owners of the ferry company but only because her retaliation against him consumed her.

She had dated the company owner for many years. He paid for her apartment, took her on vacations and brought her around his family but a health scare caused him to suffer a delayed midlife crisis nearing his sixties.

CoCo's supervisor told CoCo that her aging blonde beauty had become too much of a reflection of the company owner's same aging blonde beauty and without warning she was replaced by a younger blonder version of herself.

CoCo's supervisor started to make many phone calls to a labor union so her heartbreak would not be in vain.
Her quest was to help unionize the ferry box office and crowd control staff with the company's other maritime employees like the captains, deckhands and concession workers. She was going to see to it that the company paid into pension plans for the senior employees and gave all employees higher wages and offered paid vacation and sick time whether an employee was seasonal, halftime or fulltime.

CoCo's supervisor was successful at getting the union interested and she became the union representative's primary point of contact.
She was the spokesperson for the employees and in the process of unionizing everyone she fell for the union

representative assigned to negotiate and finalize their union contract.

The union rep was a seasoned negotiator who was built strong and walked confident.

His chocolate head was bald. His silver beard and side-burns were well groomed. His blazers were always pressed and his trousers had a crease in every pair.

He came to town frequently from the Seattle headquarters in the beginning of unionizing different staff members.

During his union negotiation visits CoCo's supervisor noticed that the union rep wore a gold wedding band on the right ring finger instead of the left.

She eventually inquired and asked was he engaged but when she learned he was widowed CoCo witnessed her supervisor turn up the fascination.

She admitted to CoCo she was guilty of rebounding but she felt she had nothing to lose.

Her best years had been wasted on a love affair that died and the union rep was a stable man showing her genuine interest.

The union rep successfully got everyone signed up for the union and he was in town for nearly a month to be present for the finalizing of their employee bargaining agreement.

The moment the ink dried on the final version of the union contract, CoCo's supervisor quit the ferry company. She chucked caution to the wind and boarded a plane to Seattle with her union beau to enjoy a new romance.

CoCo had to be more careful with her stealing after her

supervisor quit.

She had to adjust to a new supervisor and her money was tight during that adjustment.

Fuckboy's partnership would get CoCo's money back up to what it was working with her former supervisor and what CoCo liked most about Fuckboy's plan was he took all the risk.

Nothing could trace back to CoCo unless Fuckboy told on her which she doubted him to be a snitch.

The first batch of tickets CoCo gave to Fuckboy was from the Alcatraz Sunset Ferry Bay Cruise combo.

It was the ferry company's highest priced combo ticket.

The ferry cruised the bay forty-five minutes narrating the history of San Fran while sailing into the sunset under the Golden Gate Bridge and around Angel Island.

The cruise then stopped on Alcatraz Island and people were let off on the rock to tour the prison and take pictures before they were guided back to the slippery sea-smelling boat dock to depart.

The company sailed four boats to and from Alcatraz for the sunset ferry combo three nights per week and the tickets were open tickets first come first served.

All four boats went out each night full at nearly three hundred people per trip and CoCo inconspicuously pocketed at least twenty percent of the tickets from each sailing.

She gave Fuckboy roughly sixty clean undamaged tickets from each of the four separate boarding's and he knew to sell the tickets little by little over time.

The deal between Fuckboy and CoCo was for them to split the money down the middle.

With him at work forty hours per week it took close to two months to sell a little fewer than two hundred and forty tickets and because of the tickets being so expensive Fuckboy made anywhere from eighteen hundred to thirty-six hundred each week during those two months.

CoCo and Fuckboy went three months getting money together before they had sex and they had only been having sex for two months. She felt two months was no real time invested and Fuckboy should therefore be amenable to taking it back to them being just about the hustle.

⸺⸻)((◑)) ⸻⸺

CoCo was group texting with her four best friends about when they were getting to the hospital for Lillian. She looked at the clock on the wall and her mid-morning fifteen-minute break had been over but Fuckboy still had not made it to meet her.

On Monday of that week she gave Fuckboy a new stack of ferry tickets.
He had been hustling them everyday with no days off and Friday was one of his regular days off but he put himself on-call for overtime.
He told management he needed the OT but him picking up a shift that morning was less about the OT and more about the extra day to flip tickets.

CoCo heard the box office supervisor call Fuckboy's government name over the public announcement system.
The system's reach was over half of a block and the

box office supervisor was using the public announcement system to request Fuckboy to report back to the box office immediately.

CoCo found the announcement strange.

She thought Fuckboy was in the box office because if not where the hell was he.

His favorite part of his workday was giving CoCo updates on their revenue and plus she was prepared to let him know they would not be doing anything more than tucking the ducats.

CoCo's preparation made no difference since Fuckboy never came and she had to return to her post where she was helping board the ferry to Mare Island, Vallejo at ferry terminal gate number two.

The Vallejo ferry was half boarded and CoCo heard the box office supervisor again page Fuckboy to the box office.

She could not see the Box Office windows from the area she stood in near the boat but once the ferry departed she walked over to the box office where the supervisor was paging Fuckboy a third time.

She did not want to seem too-too concerned but she wanted to find out what was going on.

She thought maybe Fuckboy was sick in the men's bathroom or maybe he was in a line somewhere trying to satisfy his sweet tooth or maybe he had a customer that was a childhood friend or a long lost neighbor and he had gone on a break to talk to them but maybe he had lost track of the time and did not care he was late.

CoCo stepped up to one of the available box office windows and the ticket-seller behind the window asked CoCo if she needed assistance.

CoCo casually asked the ticket-seller if she knew why the supervisor kept paging **William Tau**.

Tau was short for a thirteen-letter name Fuckboy abbreviated because no one ever pronounced his last name right.

The ticket-seller said maybe it was a miscommunication breakdown. She had just started her shift and had not seen him but as far as she knew he did not work Friday's so she was not sure of why he was being paged.

CoCo asked the ticket-seller if the supervisor had tried calling his cell phone or did they think something was wrong and should she alert outside staff to be concerned.

CoCo was making it a safety issue to divert any hunches of her asking for personal reasons and the ticket-seller nodded her head no at CoCo. It was like she had not a clue and did not care to have a clue about what was going on but a nosy ticket-seller seated at the box office window next to the clueless ticket-seller said she could give CoCo the tea.

CoCo stepped over to the nosy ticket-seller's window and told her to spill it then.

The nosy ticket-seller said what happened was William was in the middle of processing a transaction and when he opened the drawer to his till he had loose tickets beneath his portable metal cash holder.
The supervisor on duty asked William about the tickets he saw him pull from under his cash holder and William said the tickets were from cash refunds. He said he could

not find a supervisor or a lead team member earlier to process a void so he was reselling the tickets.

William tried to hurry to close his drawer but the supervisor asked were the other tickets also refunded tickets and William questioned what other tickets.

The supervisor asked William to lift his till from the drawer and William tried to lift the portable metal cash holder from the bottom side with two hands holding the tickets to the bottom of his till but it looked suspicious and awkward.

The supervisor said he wanted to look under William's till himself and could William please step back from his drawer and the nosy ticket-seller paused her storytelling to laugh.

She said it was so terrible how all the staff was watching. She referred to William as Bill like it said on his nametag and she said that she felt hella embarrassed for her boy Bill when he got defensive. He called the supervisor a White racist and asked why the supervisor was targeting him then he slammed his drawer and asked the supervisor why was he even over there by him looking over his shoulder fucking with him.

The nosy ticket-seller laughed again saying she did not mean to laugh but how Bill big fine ass stood up hella bigger than the supervisor was like in a hulk movie and it was crazy how the supervisor did not flinch even when Bill knocked a stack of brochures onto the floor walking away from his drawer.

She said the crazier part to her was how Bill left. He walked out the box office like he was going to the bathroom or break room but he turned around and exited the plainly marked DO NOT EXIT ALARM WILL SOUND security doors.

The nosy ticket-seller said after William set off the alarm the box office manager had to come reset the alarm because the supervisor sat in William's seat to sift through the unattached tickets William claimed were refunds.

The manager testily asked the supervisor why the alarm was set off and the supervisor ecstatically explained something fishy was going on with Bill and he justified his theory saying there was no way that many refunds were done that morning.

The manager said to let her go and investigate William's transaction records upstairs with the accounting department and the supervisor handed the manager William's drawer and his tickets.

The same supervisor that caught William approached the nosy ticket-seller's window and asked CoCo to come inside the box office to cover William's shift.

CoCo told the supervisor she had an emergency with her sister she had just learned of on her break and she could cover for maybe two to three hours but she had to leave early and get to the hospital.

III

CoCo ended up finishing Fuckboy's shift and staying overtime. She arrived at the hospital right after Lillian had given birth and when she showed up Jonny-London was at the hospital elevators. They rode up the elevators to

Lillian's hospital room together so Jonny-London was the first person CoCo told the story about Fuckboy walking off the job.

Lillian was the second person CoCo told the story but by the morning when CoCo told Lillian, she had finally heard from Fuckboy.

During Kamber putting CoCo and Lillian half to sleep telling them of her relationship woes, CoCo stepped out of Lillian's hospital room into the hallway and reluctantly answered Fuckboy's fifth attempt to reach her.

CoCo asked Fuckboy what happened to him at work and he told her he was like fuck it the gig was up. He figured he had better bounce out and he walked off the job to go to his brother's house. He said he smoked some weed, had some drank and got bent waiting for her to call but she did not call him and he asked CoCo what was up with that.

CoCo told him her best friend had a baby and the hospital had bad cellphone reception and William said he was not tripping. He asked CoCo when he was invited back to her house to give her some of his good dick and CoCo had to clear her throat and cough to cover up her laughter.

She said she did not think him coming over anymore would be a good idea and she offered to meet him to give him the few things he left over at her place.

All CoCo could hear through Fuckboy's yelling was the different types of bitches she was. Shady bitch, fat bitch, weave-wearing bitch, no-good-piece-of shit ass bitch, cum-swallowing dick-sucking bitch, dog ass bitch, hoe ass bitch, kick-a-nigga-when-he-down-bad-ass-bitch and when finally he stopped calling CoCo a million bitches he asked where was he supposed to go.

He blamed CoCo for his breakup. He said fucking with her had cost him his fine ass girl who was better looking than she was but CoCo had never met the lady and he could not tell CoCo how she broke them up.

CoCo hung up the phone in William's face laughing out loud he had made it easier for her to never talk to him again and not feel bad about it.

IV

CoCo went home after leaving Lillian at the hospital Saturday morning and she called in sick from work.

She had avoided doing laundry, making groceries or checking the mailbox for more than a week since before Fuckboy came to stay and she decided to make Saturday a reset day.

CoCo crossed the courtyard of her secure living community from her assigned parking stall and she did not bat an eye or look over her shoulder in anticipation of Fuckboy. He had put his money in a car he bought from a car auction and it was being fixed and made fancy by his cousin's chop shop. He had no other means of transportation and what he left at CoCo's place was a few dirty clothes, a toothbrush, cologne samples that actually she had given him, his cellphone charger, his electric shaver and a pair of shoes all of which she planned to toss in the garbage.

CoCo walked passed the pool, the gym and the mailboxes going from her car to her front door and she knew if she did not go and get the mail before going upstairs she probably would not go that day and another day would go by without her checking the mail.

She stood at her mailbox and sifted through her mail for what to keep versus what to toss.

She had to keep the bills for the gas and electric, water and garbage, HOA homeowner dues, credit card, car loan, insurances and phone but coupons, preapprovals and advertisements without as much as a glance went into the recycle bin.

The only thing of importance CoCo was not expecting was a handwritten letter size envelope that had the sender's name but oddly no return address. Her eyes went blank staring at the envelope from her sister but for how long she was not sure.

V

Chanel Michelle Butler and CoCo were born January twenty-third and December eighteenth during the same year.

They never met their mother and they were raised by their father who did not speak of her.

He was murdered when they were ages seven and eight and they knew nothing more about their mother than she delivered Chanel as a free woman and she delivered CoCo shackled to the bedrail of a gurney.

Their father was a fulltime tow-truck driver of his own tow company and their mother and her best friend worked for him.

Their mother's job was in the front office where she answered the phone and did tasks of that nature and her best friend helped their father get stable contracts to grow his tow company into a successful business.

Their father fell in love with their mother's best friend and he broke up with their mother to marry her best friend but their mother snapped. She heinously murdered her best friend and became property of a California prison while she was pregnant.

The prison medical nurse helped to deliver CoCo and CoCo was taken away by a state social worker and given to her father.

Their father refused to drive CoCo and Chanel the five-hours from San Fran to the maximum-security prison where their mother was serving her sentence.

He raised them as if they had no mother and he dated many ladies that came at him every which way trying to play momma but after his murder all but Gilda scatted.

Gilda stayed a few doors down from their father and she had no kids of her own.

She dated their father for the longest of any of his girlfriends and she along with Chanel's kindergarten teacher came to their father's funeral.

CoCo and Chanel ended up wards of the state.

Foster care placed them together the first three years in the custody of different relatives and sometimes temporarily with strangers but Gilda and Chanel's Kindergarten teacher kept up with CoCo and Chanel at whatever placement they lived in.

At ages ten and eleven Chanel's kindergarten teacher retired and she offered to adopt both CoCo and Chanel if they were willing to relocate to Nevada.

She had been asked by her son to move with him and his wife.

Her son was a Private Investigator with the Vegas Police Department and his wife was a Registered Nurse with the Vegas County Hospital but their paid paternity and maternity leave from work was ending.

They could not afford to extend their leaves without pay and they needed the help to raise their small children.

Chanel wanted to go where there were no places to remind her their father was dead and could never take them anywhere again but CoCo did not want to leave California. She had it in her heart to stay with Gilda and when Chanel left San Fran to move to Vegas with her foster family, she and her sister lost touch.

Chapter 15

RAGDOLL

CoCo was not sure how she made it up the stairs to the second floor of her building. Somehow she was standing inside her single-level condo with a stack of mail in one hand and her door key in the other.

She walked further inside her front door and she could only hope she closed her mailbox because she did not spend another thought on it.

CoCo's showroom-style palace was decorated with the colors, ornaments and accents of golds, silvers, teals, chestnuts, greys and yellows and her smoke grey marble kitchen counter was where she dropped the mail and her keys.

She sped to the toilet and a second after her bare ass touched the wooden toilet seat the sound of racing urine echoed from the bathroom walls throughout her unit.

CoCo came out her shoes, clothes and bra from her seat on the toilet.

Ten minutes later and about five pounds lighter she walked naked back to the kitchen counter and saw she was not imagining it. The letter from Chanel was lying face up on her stack of bills and it was folded over a glossy invitation with a picture of Chanel on the invitation.

CoCo favored her sister in light brown skin color and they had the same slanted eyes but their physical builds were night and day.

Chanel was petite and thin with defined cheekbones, a tight chin and neck and a small pointed nose. She did not have CoCo's beauty mole near her top lip but she did have the same smile with finely shaped front teeth.
Side by side Chanel looked like the younger sister but she was not.

The invitation was postmarked from a couple of weeks ago but it said Chanel was graduating in the coming week. On Thursday October twenty-ninth she would be receiving a certificate of completion from the Investigative Justice Program at the Vegas University School of Criminal Justice.

CoCo put the invitation down to rummage for her phone inside her oversized bag. She needed to check her phone calendar for if she could work a turnaround drive to Vegas into her schedule.

CoCo opened her phone to find two missed calls and three text messages. Both of the missed calls were from Kamber and CoCo had already told Kamber she could stay with her. She knew Kamber would show up at her place at some point and she was not about to call her back to hear her say that.

Kamber had also sent CoCo one of the three text

messages saying what CoCo already knew about her being dropped off later that day and CoCo started to text Kamber back to ask why she left a note if she was going to call and text about the same shit but CoCo moved on to her other two text messages. The messages were from Eliza and CoCo replied to her telling her yes Kamber could do her hair at her house and yes she could get ready for the Mayor's Ball at her house.

CoCo closed the message application on her phone and she opened her calendar app.

It was currently Saturday, October twenty-fourth and Chanel's graduation was in five days at three o'clock in the afternoon.

The graduation had fallen on the day before one of the busiest weekends of the year for two of CoCo's three jobs and getting more than the graduation day off with less than a week's notice would be impossible.

CoCo had to ponder how a turnaround trip could happen without taking more than Thursday off work.

She reckoned if she packed Tuesday night after she got home from working her double she could work Wednesday morning then go home to sleep for eight to ten hours and get on the road at two in the morning Thursday. That would put her in Vegas before one o'clock in the afternoon and after a nap in the car she could change in a hotel bathroom and make the graduation by three o'clock.

Her sister's invitation listed an email to RSVP but CoCo was not going to reply. She wanted Chanel to be surprised to see her at the graduation and she would have a few hours with her sister before she would need another nap to get back on the road by ten o'clock Thursday night. She would get home by eight o'clock Friday morning and after a couple of hours of sleep she would call her job at the start time of her shift to say she misplaced her car key but would be at work within the hour.

CoCo drafted an email to her supervisor from her phone. She requested personal time off for Thursday to deal with a family matter and she requested a couple schedule modifications for the day before and the day after. She asked her supervisor to please switch her Wednesday afternoon shift to the morning and to switch her Friday morning shift to the afternoon but before she could press the send button to email her boss the request her phone died.

CoCo plugged her phone to the power cord and went to jump in the shower while she let the phone charge.

She stood beneath the hot running water and lathered her body with a coconut and tropical blend scented soap. Her feet were aching for a foot rub and she was craving a steak served with dick hard enough and long enough to take her for a joyride.

CoCo toweled the water off her skin searching her mind for a lover who knew her body and who could make up for the lost days Fuckboy had worthlessly occupied her bed. This lover would have to be unselfish with his time with a track record to give her pussy a back-to-back-to-back type of beating.

She gently and slowly moisturized her body from her temples to her toes with pure coconut oil and vitamin E and the extra attention she gave her nipples brought a face to the surface of her thoughts.

He was the one she forbid herself from calling but who would be at her place with the quickness to eat her fruit snack like a professional fruit-snacker.

Mingus Passion Roy was a phone number CoCo could dial from memory.

She had been with many intimate partners but none matched Mingus. He lived up to his middle name and CoCo knew it was wrong to call him but he was a guarantee for multiple orgasms.

I

Mingus was CoCo's first boyfriend from childhood.

She dated him for a couple of weeks when she was a twelve-year-old virgin.

He was not the one she later gave her virginity to but for the past eleven years they had developed a friendship.

The latter two of the eleven years involved secret infrequent sexual exchanges with the occasional overnight stay but Mingus lived with his wife.

Irece Cola Graham-Roy was Mingus's high school sweetheart.

He did not dump CoCo to be with Irece but he left CoCo no choice but to accept his relationship with Irece and CoCo was admittedly jealous. She could not compete with whatever Irece had over her but jealous as CoCo was she did not want to be Irece.

Right out of high school Irece caught a case for Mingus.

They got pulled over for a broken taillight and he was riding dirty in her car.

When the cop had Irece to lower her driver window the

cop smelled weed and made her and Mingus get out the car to search her vehicle.

Irece lied to police and said the dope under Mingus's seat was hers.

The state's attorney got her to cop a plea for a reduced narcotics charge with no felony but she had to serve three years in jail and take a subsequent two years probation.

The day Irece was released Mingus was there to bring her home but in the car he blindfolded her saying he did not want her to see where he was taking her.

Mingus had asked her immediate family and his immediate family to meet them at the county courthouse and on the steps of the courthouse one of Irece's sisters removed her blindfold.

Their families were all smiles and Mingus was a step below Irece down on one knee.

He was holding open a small box with a gold wedding band and Irece's other sister was next to Mingus holding a floor length one shoulder strap white chiffon dress up to her own body.

Irece wept and was shakily amazed with the proposal and marriage spun into one.

The nonverbal rapid bobbing of her head up and down made her the lucky winner of her man's last name but it did not take long for their honeymoon phase to wear off and soon as it did CoCo was reachable at the same phone number Mingus remembered from their youth.

Out of the blue he called Gilda's phone to see if he could still find CoCo at the other end.

CoCo would have usually not answered Gilda's phone. She did not live with Gilda anymore and she did not recognize the random phone number that was calling but she answered anyway and it was Mingus.

His unexpected call ended with her giving him her cell phone number not thinking she was going to hear from him too soon but she did hear from him that night.

CoCo was curled on her couch under a blanket. She had been microsleeping in the middle of reading a graphic erotic fiction novella when Mingus texted the whereabouts to a hook up location.

She turned her book over page down on her thigh to take a longer look at her phone. The text message said to meet at midnight in Alamo Square Park and CoCo replied ok to meeting Mingus not realizing she said ok to leaving her house going hella far alone hella late at night.

CoCo knew Mingus could never be her man. Her hooking up with him could only be for a fuck and she was clear-eyed that any contact he made was to hookup for a fuckisode but their first fuckisode was not what CoCo thought it would be.

Mingus sent a second text message telling her to wear something free flowing with no bra and no panties to the park and CoCo literally laughed out loud then she texted LOL in her first reply.

She followed up with a second message saying her triple D's did not travel without a carrying case. In her third reply she told him she was already doing too much and would be wearing whatever she wanted coming out of her warm abode.

CoCo waited to see if Mingus would reply and he did not but in her rereading their text message exchange multiple times she became aroused.

The way he gave her exact commands turned her on and she decided to do precisely what he said to do.

She dug deep in her closet and found a bright colorful oversized shirt she could work with and she found a tight stretch high-waist pencil skirt she could make match.

CoCo grabbed a pair of scissors from her desk. She cut the oversized shirt collar wide to hang off her right shoulder and she cut the bottom off the shirt to stop above her diamond-studded belly button.

Wearing no bra made the areola of her left breast play peek-a-boo with every step and she put the skirt on with no panties after she cut both sides of the pencil skirt seams up to the tops of her thighs.

CoCo grabbed her jacket and purse but before she made her way out the front door she stopped in the dining area. She glanced at the time to see was she already running late and her almond stained brass vintage-style wall clock showed the time was five minutes past eleven o'clock.

Her drive to San Fran was usually forty minutes without traffic but still she contemplated when to leave to make it to the city before midnight.

She told herself leaving in ten minutes should be enough time but then on second thought she told herself she had better get going.

Crossing the Vallejo Bridge and the Bay Bridge at any time of the night always made traffic unpredictable.

II

Mingus was at the park when CoCo arrived ten minutes before midnight.

He asked did she know why he picked that location and CoCo pretended not to remember the first time they met there as kids.

She made Mingus recall the details.

Mingus stepped nearer to the front of CoCo's body and stared into her eyes.

He told her he missed seeing her beautiful face and that she was the prettiest girlfriend he ever had.

CoCo asked was he calling what they had as kids a real thing and Mingus reached for her hands to caress them. He answered maybe not as he slowly stretched his neck down to give her a kiss.

CoCo stretched her neck up to meet his lips and they both closed their eyes.

Mingus's kiss was short but when the kiss was over CoCo's lips were still puckered a few extra seconds to savor the sweetness and she opened her eyes to say that was not bad for their first kiss.

Soon as CoCo said it was their first kiss she doubted if that was true.

She quickly kidded about their childhood relationship not lasting long enough to include kissing and she asked Mingus was it their first kiss.

Mingus could not hold back his laughter.

He said he was not laughing at her question but at what he was about to say and he recalled the summer he first saw her.

He was riding his bike through the park on a sunny morning weekday with some older cousins and their friend. He was the only one of them that saw CoCo swing the highest the swing could go before she jumped out the swing, turned a double back flip and landed on her feet.

CoCo laughed calling herself such the tomboy way back then and Mingus said it was the first time he saw a girl do anything like that.

He said he even came the next day at the same time looking for her but she was not there and everyday he came back for another week until he saw her again but he watched her another two days before he finally said anything.

Mingus started laughing again.

He remembered being so captivated watching CoCo flip off the swing that he skidded on his bike and slid into the wide trunk of a giant Monterey Cypress tree.

His main concern at the time was the other boys bearing witness to him scrub.

He said luckily they were riding too far in front of him to have seen but in hindsight with how hard he hit the tree and how far he flew over the handlebars of his bike he was now more glad to have not totally broken his neck.

Mingus laughed again detailing how superfast he got up from the grass and bicycled off.

He was saying he believed no one saw him fall because of how superfast he got up but CoCo cleared her throat and said she wanted to make a confession.

Mingus told her she could tell him anything and she confessed her and her two neighbor friends did see him fly through the air off his bike.

She said they were racing over to ask did he need their help and CoCo started laughing saying but he rode off too superfast for them to catch up to him.

Mingus did not respond but his dirty thoughts were present.

He took a step back to let his eyes devour CoCo's body and he could see she wore no bra.

He reached between her legs to feel she was not wearing any panties and his fingers took the liberty of exploring the triangular space between her thighs.

He nibbled at her earlobe and whispered she deserved something special for doing what he asked her to do and at the pleasure of Mingus's strong but gentle touch CoCo dropped her head back. She closed her eyes and let the fore-play begin and naturally her thighs spread to allow Mingus's fingers more room to feel around.

Mingus placed his free hand at the back of her head and he brought her face to his. He pushed his tongue inside her gaped mouth and he sucked her lips and tongue in rhythm with his fingertips circling her clit.

CoCo gripped Mingus's forearm and pushed him in further between her legs for his fingers to penetrate and she turned her face away from the sucking of his tongue to focus on him inside her.

She became lost and she let out a loud moan when Mingus hit the right spot and he kept hitting it.

He had her wet and ready but he wanted to taste her

finish and like a magician he disappeared his face beneath her skirt.

CoCo's body was begging for more and Mingus lifted one of her thighs over his shoulder and pushed her openness further.

She gave way to the spread of her thighs and did not dare stop the immense pleasure he was giving her in sucking, tonguing and licking every crevice of her down below.

One of her hand's gripped Mingus's muscular shoulder and her other hand clinched the hair at the nape of his neck and her lower body moved in short circles.

She was riding Mingus's face fast but easy and moaning his name with oh fuck and damn and hell yea and telling him not to stop but on her way to a happy ending a car horn blared at a jaywalker who was crossing the middle of the street.

CoCo paused and her mind instantaneously left from where Mingus had her enslaved in sexual abyss.

She became self-conscious and aware they were in a public park between a tennis court and a playground and she suggested maybe they ought to go somewhere more private.

CoCo tried to bring her leg off Mingus's shoulder to put her foot on the ground but Mingus held her thigh in place and did not react to her impulse to stop.

He did raise his head from beneath her skirt but his fingers were in motion and with his words he offered to stop. He asked CoCo did she want him to stop but she could not utter the words stop nor did she push him away to stop.

His fingers kept massaging her sweet pot as he told her take a good look around.

They were alone except for very few cars on the street that could not possibly see them up on a dark hill surrounded by giant trees.

Mingus pulled his two fingers from inside CoCo and put them in his mouth. He sucked his fingers leaving her moist and throbbing and he politely offered again to stop if CoCo really wanted him to.

CoCo was biting her lip and squirming and looking at Mingus saying nothing but begging him with her eyes to please keep going.
She did not say stop but she did not say go so he slipped his wet fingers back beneath CoCo's skirt telling her she was almost there but he could stop if that was what she wanted.

Mingus put his face back under CoCo's skirt but seconds into eating her out she said she was still nervous someone would catch them and he brought his face out from her skirt to look at her.
He offered again to stop but CoCo begged him not to stop and he said he would only keep going if she did what he told her to do.

CoCo said okay and he said she had to relax, breathe deep and think of nothing but cumming on his face and in that order CoCo did what Mingus said and surely she came on his face.

What CoCo appreciated most about their first fuckisode was Mingus's generosity with his tongue and his time. He did not rush her body and what else she appreciated was that each fuckisode thereafter got better and better and the next was always better than the last.

CoCo had freshly showered off her overnight hospital stay with Lillian.

She pulled something to wear from the top of her drawer and out came a two-piece graphic knit loungewear set that fit one size too small.

She stretched the Superheroine Cipher Black boy shorts and matching tank wide across her breasts and ass and she went to check her phone.

Her phone had powered back on and she held it in her hand thinking about Mingus. He was the one who could satisfy her and she sent him a text message saying she needed to see him.

Mingus replied quickly and his message was a three-word response, on my way.

CoCo smiled knowing she was about to get what she wanted but her smile slowly faded thinking of the last text message she received from Mingus.

She had long ago deleted the message but the last thing he texted her was the three-words I am sorry and the buried memory of their last fuckisode came to the surface.

CoCo had a visceral recollection of her and him at Larsen's Peak inside Golden Gate Heights Park.

It had been months but she could still visualize approaching Mingus and noticing the emblem on his hat, the color of his shoes and the silhouette of him with his back pressed to a Blue Gum Eucalyptus with one shoe sole pressed to the tree and the other in the grassy dirt.

CoCo began to rub the tightening of her neck remembering the way her neck whipped from how fast Mingus spun her and bent her over. Without so much as a hello he started to fuck her from behind and she remembered the damp grassy dirt being not far from her face.

Mingus was holding her by the waist but the balls of her feet were not as firmly planted on the ground as were her palms and the deeper he went and the harder her bare ass got pounded the more she had to dig her fingers into the damp grassy dirt.

CoCo felt degraded initially with him not having the courtesy to say hi or ask how she was doing but for the first time they had an orgasm together.

They tapped out holding each other watching the stars and were it up to her she would have stayed embracing with Mingus past the hour their fuckisode was over.

He had her gut doing summersaults with the sensation of his dick being still inside her and the supreme euphoria she was feeling from them climaxing together left no room for her to feel ashamed she was in a public park with a married man who had just fucked her like a *ragdoll*.

CoCo learned a day late what she thought was romantic extemporaneous lovemaking under the stars was nothing of the sort.

She was a conveniently located piece of pussy up the street from the hospital where his wife delivered their first baby.

Irece had given birth to Mingus's first daughter but

she and him were saying it was the birth of both their first child.

Mingus had two sons who could pass for twin brothers and were identical to him in every way but Mingus denied they existed.

He had no part in either of their lives to continue to deny to Irece that when she went to jail for him he had two sons by two women she once introduced to him as her two good friends.

III

Until CoCo read the message from Mingus saying he was on his way she had forgotten she swore to never contact him ever again.

She felt lower than scum being with him on a night if no other night he should have been with his wife and child and CoCo started typing Mingus a message saying he was married and it was a mistake to have texted him but she deleted the message.

She did not want to be nice.

She started typing another message saying she was not fucking with no more cheating niggas and for him to not come to her house or contact her ever in this lifetime but then she deleted that message too and put her phone down.

She remembered Mingus made good steak.

Chapter 16

ON EVERY CORNER

CoCo started her childhood romance with Mingus during the midsummer.

It was a little more than a month before CoCo began her eighth grade year of middle school and Alamo Square Park was where she met up and played daily with her two neighbor friends, **Carol** and **Toni**.

CoCo went out of town with Gilda and came back too sick to play outside so she had not gone to the park for a week but the day she came back Carol pointed Mingus out to her.

He was doing flips with his skateboard on a cement path at the edge of the park and CoCo and her friends were in the playground. They could see him and he could see them but the distance was such they both could act like they did not see the other.

Carol wanted to go bust him out by asking did he see a doctor for how hard he hit that tree. She told Toni to dare her to go and say they saw him fly off his bike and wanted to know if he was okay but CoCo told Toni not to dare her to say that.

The next day Mingus walked by the park more than one time and Toni said the next time he walked by she was going to go be nice to him and ask if he had a girlfriend but he did not come back until the next day.

Toni told CoCo to dare her to go and get Mingus's number but he approached the three of them first and he asked CoCo if he could have her number.

He called that night and talked to her on the phone for hours and two days later he called her again on his birthday.
He kept their second call short but gave CoCo time to sing him a happy birthday song and he told her she could really sing. He said he was feeling her for serenading him over the phone but after that call there was radio silence from him then almost a week later he came to the park with a gift.

He knew CoCo liked to write from the night they spent hours on the phone.
She read him some of her poetry so his gift to her was a small journal with a matching pen and the gift was tied to a clear wrapped chocolate covered strawberry.

CoCo thanked Mingus and asked did he care if she shared her strawberry and he said he did not care.
She offered him the first bite but he said he was good off dark chocolate and CoCo took the first bite but she gave the rest to Carol and Toni and she walked away with Mingus.

They took turns pushing each other on the swing and on the merry go round and as the sun finished setting it was just two of them left alone in the park.

Mingus asked CoCo to be his girlfriend and when she said yes he kissed her cheek and offered to walk her home.

At the exact time CoCo and Mingus were coming out of the park, Kamber and Lillian were walking by.

Kamber was only ten-years-old but she looked and carried herself more like a teen.

Lillian was a true to size eight-year-old and in looking at the two of them together Kamber looked like Lillian's authority.

CoCo did not notice Kamber or Lillian. The two of them stood on the same corner as her and Mingus but they were crossing the street in a different direction.

Kamber and Lillian were going up the Steiner Street hill and CoCo and Mingus were going down the Hayes Street hill.

The cars kept hesitating to clear the intersection for CoCo and Mingus because they were waiting at the traffic stop sign as if it was a stoplight.

CoCo was holding Mingus's hand and smiling. She was gazing at her new cutie from around the way as though his attractiveness made it okay she knew nothing about him before making him her boyfriend.

Mingus was waiting for CoCo to come off the curb into the street but when the two of them finally stepped forward to cross over to the other corner Kamber lurched and landed both her palms in the middle of CoCo's upper back.

Kamber smacked CoCo hard enough to shove her a couple feet forward into the crosswalk in front of a car but the car had not accelerated too fast and the driver was able to slam on the breaks.

Mingus reacted thoughtlessly and pushed Kamber off balance. His strength made her fall to the ground. He then picked Kamber up by her elbow with not much less power than he used to push her down and he swung her forward in the direction she was going. He told her she had better get on before she got spit on.

Kamber spit towards Mingus but knew not to take a step any closer and she became embarrassed and ran off.

Lillian threw up both her middle fingers at Mingus but she ran after Kamber.

CoCo picked up her journal and pen she dropped when she was shoved and she continued walking in the crosswalk to the other side of the street.

Mingus trailed behind CoCo slow but stayed on her heels and he walked a couple seconds without words before CoCo turned to him. She looked spacey eyed and asked what was that about.

Mingus said he did not know Kamber or Lillian and he did not know why Kamber pushed her.

CoCo said he had to be lying because why did he think it was okay to manhandle Kamber the way he did if she were a stranger.

Mingus then changed his story and said he did not know Lillian but Kamber he saw a few times at the Hamilton Recreational Community Center where he played baseball and soccer every Tuesday and Thursday night and Saturday morning.

He said he could not remember how often or on what occasions he seen Kamber at The Rec but it could have been in passing going in or out the gym or the pool area or the park or the cafeteria and only because the locations were near to one another.

CoCo did not say anything and she stayed quiet while Mingus kept talking.

He admitted Kamber might have told people she liked him but he did not like her back and she was probably mad about that.

CoCo told her neighbor friends Carol and Toni what happened with Kamber and each day for weeks they were at the park ready to fight but there was no sight of Kamber or Lillian.

In the days between CoCo getting pushed by Kamber and the end of summer Mingus did not return to the park but he did call CoCo a few times.

He always asked how she was feeling and could he bring her anything and CoCo always said no but he stayed on the phone with her anyway through the silence and the small talk.

Mingus abnormally gave CoCo a call on a Saturday morning before the school semester was about to start and him calling over the weekend was something he did not do. He told CoCo in the beginning he could not speak on the weekends because the weekends were his dedicated family time.

His call began with their usual small talk but then Mingus asked CoCo over to his cousin's house.

He tried to entice her saying his cousin's girlfriend would be there and how cool his cousin's girlfriend was. He then said his cousin was their same age only a little older living in a house like the candy house and not just with hella junk food but with grown stuff too.

Mingus kept talking but when he stopped CoCo explained why her answer was no. She said she was cool meeting up with him in Alamo Square but she was not cool with going to someone's house even a cousin's house.

Mingus tried to invalidate them being real boyfriend and girlfriend if she did not trust him and CoCo said her mom told her she did not know him that well to trust him.

Mingus said she should tell her mom she did know him and he asked her for one reason she felt she did not know him.

The one reason CoCo gave was she did not know where he lived and she asked why was he not inviting her to where he lived instead of all the way across town on two transit buses to a cousin house she had never met.

Mingus's tone changed but not like he was dissatisfied with her saying no.

It was more like he was not interested anymore in her and had wasted enough time.

He told CoCo he understood where she was coming from and he promised to call her back later that night then click she heard the dial tone before she could say goodbye.

Saturday night came and Mingus had not called her back.

Sunday came and she got no call but on Monday she called him more than once and still he did not take her calls.

She left him a message with every call but she got no call back and that night she wrote Mingus a poem.

She had no way to get it to him so on Tuesday she called to read it to him but again he did not take her calls and he did not call her back.

After a full week of hearing not a thing from Mingus CoCo was still hanging on to plans they made in a conversation before she rejected going to his cousin's house.

The fall public school semester commenced in four days and Mingus had worked CoCo up about them dating during the school year.

CoCo told her momma Gilda of the plans she and Mingus had made and she told Gilda she believed the plans would still happen but Gilda told her not to do that.

Gilda said for CoCo to let Mingus be. Bad as she might want him as her boyfriend it was over and oh well to hell with it. She needed to think of a boyfriend like a bus stop and if she got moving to the next she would find there was a bus stop *on every corner*.

I

CoCo's first day of Middle School arrived on a Wednesday.

There had been no contact from Mingus but when the first weekend of the school semester came CoCo ignored

Gilda's advice to move on. She went to the Cookie and Ice Cream bar at Stonestown Mall at the time she and Mingus had agreed they would meet and of course he was not there.

CoCo stayed at the bar for hours reading, waiting and consuming cookies and ice cream and when she went home she collapsed in Gilda's arms and told her mom she was right. It was over between her and Mingus.

Gilda hugged CoCo tightly and she gave her forehead plenty of kisses as she listened to CoCo blame the break-up on her still being in middle school and him becoming a freshman in high school.

CoCo said they were not far apart in age but middle school and high school were worlds apart and now he probably thought he was too good for her or too old.

Gilda asked CoCo if she really thought Mingus's behavior had anything to do with her and she answered for CoCo and said no.
She told CoCo she was a fool to blame herself for that boy no longer thinking about her little hot ass and good for her he was gone.

Gilda prescribed CoCo her calgon to take her away and CoCo asked Gilda would she please run the bath water for her.

Before CoCo went to bed that night and every night of her first full week of school, she called Mingus to no avail. She did not think he would start answering the phone or calling her back but she found herself calling anyway.
She kept calling because she wanted to hear Mingus say

the words they were broken up.

She had told herself it was over and Gilda had confirmed it was over but she needed Mingus to say it was over to know for certain they were not boyfriend and girlfriend anymore.

II

CoCo's eighth grade at Muir Middle School began same as her seventh grade year. The days were familiar and routine but in the second week of school CoCo noticed Kamber was a new sixth-grader.

CoCo was not sure if Kamber had seen her yet but she was going to avoid contact with her and it was not for fear.

She did not want to be confronted by Kamber on school grounds because confrontation meant a fight and a fight at Muir Middle School meant an arrest.

CoCo did not want to be arrested.

Her middle school was the first in the San Fran school district to implement zero tolerance policies for children under the ages of fourteen.

Her school was also first to bring a police officer on middle school grounds and CoCo had befriended students she never saw again once they were handcuffed and escorted off the school grounds by the school's police officer.

CoCo had two days to go in the week of her sighting Kamber.

She got up Thursday morning and thought hard about playing hooky but there were no snacks in the house and her momma Gilda was gone from home.

She left early that morning on a daylong mission with their church pastor to do prison ministry and moms being gone meant moms could not cook leaving the school option more fun than being home alone hungry.

School had her schoolmates she hung around, her gym class she loved plus Gilda left her a little extra lunch money and she went to school with enough to buy a slice of pizza focaccia bread, a can of coke, an eskimo pie ice cream and a four pack of toffifay candy.

The ice cream she ate first before it could melt.

The pizza focaccia bread and coke she snuck and ate during class and the candy she saved for her walk home from school.

She did not have an encounter with Kamber that Thursday and her Friday was going the same way. She was walking home alone from school eating her candy with her earphones in her ear and her mind on Gilda. She was rapping the words to the song she was listening to but trying to concoct a believable story to tell Gilda when she got home.

CoCo could not just ask Gilda to go downtown to the Westfield Shopping Mall for no reason. She would ask CoCo why she wanted to go to Emporium-Capwell with no spending money.

Gilda insisted on referencing the mall but the mall's obsolete name Emporium-Capwell without regard to CoCo calling it the name it had been called for CoCo's entire lifespan.

CoCo could tell Gilda she wanted to browse Bloomingdale's and Nordstrom but Gilda would say no she did not want her tempted to steal by window-shopping at stores like that.

CoCo did not want to steal but Gilda had them on a fixed income and money was tight. She put seventy percent of the cosmetic revenue in an Individual Retirement Account and ten percent went to her tithes for the church. There was little extra left to share with CoCo from what the foster care provided after the food, rent, utilities, phone and basic cable were paid.

Gilda had to save little by little every month for CoCo to start school with a jacket, coat, a couple tops, bottoms, underwear, socks, a couple shoes, body wash, perfume, costume jewelry and cheap makeup but CoCo was told to make it last the school year not just one semester.

The holidays did not bring more than a hat, a pair of gloves, a scarf and maybe a sweater and rain boots but her favorite holiday gift was the one she got for her December birthday.

It was always two new books and inside each book was a crisp one hundred dollar bill. The two bills would be sticking up from the middle pages like a bookmark and the two hundred dollars made CoCo feel rich the last two weeks of the year.

III

CoCo was of the mindset that if she told half-truths she was not necessarily an honest person but she was not a liar if she did not tell full lies.

She decided to tell Gilda her and a classmate were meeting downtown for a school project which was not a full lie.

Her and a girl who hung around her school did agree to meet downtown just not for a school project.

The girl asked CoCo to have her back while she stole items from a downtown department store where her guy friend was a security guard.

The girl told CoCo the security guard would look the other way for her too and for being her tagalong she could steal whatever she wanted for herself.

CoCo was not a friend to the girl.

She seen her talking with different students everyday when Muir Middle School let out and when the girl befriended CoCo and invited her downtown CoCo did not give her a solid yes.

She knew getting Gilda to say yes was unlikely but she was still going to try. She figured it could not hurt to lift an outfit or two and some shoes or a coat to rotate into the small wardrobe she was building and she told the girl if she could make it she would meet her in an hour downtown.

CoCo had walked a couple blocks from her schoolyard and was too deep in thought to have seen Kamber's right fist.

It came from behind landing hard against the right side of her face near her ear knocking out her earphone.

CoCo stumbled sideways to her left where Lillian had run in front of her and got her with a right hook to the front left side of her face.

CoCo was not dazed more than a second before she grabbed Lillian who was the tiniest and she threw her in front of Kamber to block the blows Kamber was landing.

CoCo got them both into view and she wasted no time swinging her punches fast with all her strength to defend herself. She landed two punches on Lillian who quickly dipped out the way and a third and fourth punch landed on Kamber.

Kamber stepped into CoCo's blows but she was swinging too wild to land any solid punches and her getting her face bashed in by CoCo's punches made her step back to readjust her fighting stance.

CoCo quickly pulled off her earrings, stuffed everything in her jacket pockets and dropped her backpack and jacket to the ground.

Kamber and Lillian charged CoCo at the same time so again CoCo directed her energy at Lillian and took her out first with the least amount of effort.

CoCo' punch to Lillian's face was hard enough to make her back up and she ran to check her face in a parked car window.

Kamber got a couple punches in that landed on CoCo but when Lillian ran off CoCo was able to go at Kamber with everything she had feet and all.

CoCo took Kamber down to the ground but she could hear Lillian screaming bitch, bitch, fucking bitch.

CoCo had busted her face up but the parked car window revealed Kamber getting her ass beat and Lillian got over herself to return to the fight.
She karate kicked CoCo in the head and knocked her off Kamber who was losing the fight getting her face rearranged by CoCo's fist.

CoCo fell off Kamber onto her elbow and Kamber was able to scurry from beneath CoCo but both got to their feet at the same time.

CoCo's shirt was ripped and her elbow was bleeding. Her lip was also busted same as Lillian and she had a small open gash bleeding over her eyebrow from where Lillian had just kicked her.

Kamber's brown skin was not showing any bruising but her nose was bleeding, her eye was puffed and there were bloody fresh red scratches on her face.
She was calling CoCo a bitch and a hoe and saying how her and Lillian were about to fuck her up and Lillian was going crazy. She was yelling over and over to God about the swelling of her busted lip and the bruising showing on her cheekbone.

Kamber and Lillian were using their trash talk to get their strength to come back at CoCo but Jonny-London stepped in. She had run over from where she and other by-standers were watching the fight across the street.

Jonny-London got in front of CoCo who was breathing heavily but not saying a word.
Instead of talking CoCo had tied her hair back and was ready to defend herself again.

Jonny-London was also a new sixth grader at Muir Middle School but she knew CoCo from Raphael Weill Elementary.

Jonny-London was a kindergartener when CoCo and Chanel left her elementary school but she remembered playing with both sisters at recess.

Chanel helped Jonny-London get into the upper yard to play with her and some other second graders and she was the first person to teach Jonny-London how to jump rope and hopscotch.

Jonny-London never knew what happened to the sisters or why they left school and she did not even recognize CoCo at first.

It had been five years since she last seen CoCo's face but when CoCo pulled her hair back, Jonny-London immediately recognized her.

Jonny-London did not know Kamber before they met two weeks prior in sixth grade student orientation but she knew Lillian. Their families had a connection that brought Lillian to Jonny-London's home more than a few times and she had played with Lillian and her brother.

Jonny-London told Lillian and Kamber they were wrong for jumping CoCo and they were not about to keep jumping her.

Jonny-London was oversized for her age much like Kamber. She was an inch or two taller with bigger breasts, a plumper midsection and more hips but CoCo still appeared the biggest out of the four of them.

Jonny-London asked CoCo if she wanted to keep fighting and CoCo said she did not want to fight in the first place.

Jonny-London asked could somebody tell her what they were fighting about and CoCo said she did not know what the bitch Kamber problem with her was but she knew it was over a boy named Mingus.

Kamber said she caught CoCo mean-mugging with her nose in the air thinking she was all that because her boyfriend was Mingus and Jonny-London asked Kamber why did she care about a boy that was CoCo's boyfriend.

CoCo blurted that Mingus told her he did not know who Kamber was and Kamber became furious telling Jonny-London Mingus was a fucking liar. He did know her and Lillian echoed Kamber with the same intensity yelling to Jonny-London the lying ass nigga know he knew her.

Jonny-London turned to Lillian and asked was her little eight or nine-year-old ass fucking with the same boy too.

Lillian said oh no no no but Kamber was her best friend and if a bitch came for her best friend they came for her.

Kamber was bigger and older but Lillian had taken on the role of her guard dog.

Lillian was one of those gifted students in school who got selected in her third grade year as a peer tutor for the fourth and fifth grade Special Education class.
She was paired with Kamber who was in Special Ed for her learning disability and from day one the two became inseparable.

CoCo was irritated and ready to go home but she had to have the last word. She rolled her eyes at Lillian and turned to Kamber to ask would she stop lying and tell the truth. She had never a day in her life seen her to mean-mug her and she told Jonny-London she believed Mingus when he said he did not know Kamber.

Jonny-London gave CoCo the side-eye. She said maybe she ought not be trusting Mingus and she asked did she know where he could be found while she was there getting jumped over him.

CoCo said Mingus was her man in the summer but now he was in high school she did not know anymore and Jonny-London said since before school started her neighbor Irece was fucking with a boy named Mingus.

Jonny-London acknowledged it could be a coincidence. She said maybe Irece was dating another boy of the same name but Jonny-London asked CoCo to tell her realistically, how many niggas from Fillmoe did she think were named Mingus.

Chapter 17

SQUAD

Jonny-London Lois Jones lived only blocks from Alamo Park High School where both Mingus and Irece were newly attending freshman.

Jonny-London mentioned Mingus had been coming over to her apartment building everyday and was probably there with Irece while Kamber, CoCo and Lillian were fighting over him.

Lillian clarified that she was fighting for Kamber and not over a stupid boy.

CoCo clarified that she did not start the fight and she was not Mingus's girlfriend anymore if he was with the girl Irece everyday.

Jonny-London invited CoCo to her house to run into Mingus and see how he treated her with Irece around and CoCo was with it.

Kamber and Lillian were invited too but Jonny-London

made them agree to be cool and not bring any drama to her house and they both agreed.

On the short walk to Jonny-London's home they walked in two pairs.

Jonny-London had CoCo alone long enough to bring up how she knew her and her sister Chanel.

CoCo did not remember at first but Jonny-London called herself by the nickname Chanel gave her and they both laughed and hugged as CoCo remembered.

She thanked Jonny-London for having her back and she asked to still call her the nickname Lundy Bundy but Jonny-London said only without the Bundy part.

The four of them reached the corner of Jonny-London's apartment building and it was as Jonny-London predicted.

Mingus and Irece were hugged-up and horsing around at the public transit stop outside the six-unit residence where Jonny-London and Irece both lived.

Jonny-London had lived there the eleven years of her young life but Irece and her two older sisters had moved there before the summer.

They came to stay with their grandparents who lived in the building for many more years before Jonny-London's mom, **Donna London Fox-Jones**.

Jonny-London and CoCo quickened their pace and once they were walking at the same pace as Kamber and Lillian their two pairs became one *squad*.

Their squad got close enough to Jonny-London's building to hear the exchange between Mingus and Irece. She was doing most of the talking and Mingus's responses were nervous shy boy laughter and short answers.

They were into each other like they were the only two people in the world and no passerby could distract them from sharing the chemistry they had.

Jonny-London's main entry to her building was a metal gate that opened outward from a short marble staircase about seven feet from the public transit stop.

Jonny-London unlocked the gate with her key and she held it open for CoCo, Lillian and Kamber to go inside. She told them they could have a seat on the marble steps and CoCo sat on the top stair near the apartment doors.

Lillian and Kamber sat down by the gate and Jonny-London took a center seat above the two of them but below CoCo.

Lillian said the stairs was the spot. They could spy on Mingus through the diamond shaped holes in the gate and not get noticed but she asked how were they supposed to get his attention with him being all eyes on Irece.

CoCo scuffed at not wanting his attention ever again and Kamber smirked and told CoCo to not be mad she was getting a taste of how it felt to be in her shoes.

CoCo said she knew nothing about them boats on Kamber's feet because she was actually Mingus's girlfriend and Kamber was never that.

Jonny-London asked could they not see Mingus was worried about neither one of them.

She questioned why they still had any beef and CoCo said she had no beef with Kamber.

Kamber rolled her eyes and scooted down another step to move closer to the gate. She was staring at Mingus and Irece and she saw them get up from the transit stop holding hands.

She said to everyone sitting on the stairs that the lovebirds were on the move and they were walking towards the corner store. The corner store was thirty or so feet away and Kamber suggested they walk to the corner store too for Mingus to not be able to avoid seeing them and they all agreed that was a good idea.

CoCo said they should wait a couple minutes and give Irece and Mingus enough time to buy whatever they were buying and Lillian said that was smart. They could catch them coming out the store for him to for sure for sure see them.

Kamber, Lillian, Jonny-London and CoCo came out the gate in that order and in a staggered line they walked towards the store.

They entered the intersection to cross the street at the same time Mingus and Irece entered the intersection coming towards them.

Mingus saw Kamber first but it was like she was not there. He did not acknowledge her with his eyes or with a slight turn of the neck.

Lillian was completely blocked by Kamber but Irece

slowed to speak to Jonny-London and Mingus saw there were four girls. His eyes bulged at the sight of CoCo and his face expressed worry for what was about to happen but Irece could not see his anxiousness.

Jonny-London had Irece's attention asking Irece about her grandfather making his bomb-ass gumbo again and Irece said it was crazy she asked about gumbo.
Her middle sister had turned seventeen that week and her grandpa promised to make some that weekend for her birthday.

Jonny-London joked saying a birthday portion sounded like a personal size and she asked Irece what did her sister's birthday gumbo have to do with her getting gumbo.

Irece guaranteed that her grandpa only made one portion size and that was double double extra large just like him and he would do as he always did and give neighbors a bowl.

Jonny-London asked Irece to pinky-swear she and her mom would at least get a bowl and Irece locked pinkies with Jonny-London but she asked what about a bowl for her dad.

Jonny-London's face grimaced to show her confusion. Her dad had never come around and she had never mentioned him to anybody.

She thought maybe Irece had been to the Ferry Building lately where her dad could be found half painted in gold and half painted in silver.
His half gold half silver paint pattern went from his hat to his shoes to his face and hands and extended to his radio, his milk crate and his umbrella.

The radio played his eighties and nineties music from cassette tapes and his milk crate was for him to have a standpoint above the crowd.

His giant standing umbrella he used against the hot sun or for light to medium rainy days and everyday he set up in the same spot to break-dance and strut for change.

Irece could have known the painted man in his fifties performing street-acts to earn a living was Jonny-London's dad. He was a San Fran legend she would not say she was ashamed of but he rarely left his post and if she or anyone wanted to see him they had to go to the Pier 1 Ferry Plaza.

Irece saw Jonny-London's facial expression. She asked was the man that was always with her mom Donna carrying the groceries and coming in and out of their house with a key not her dad and Jonny-London's face straightened. She explained to Irece that he was not her dad.

Vincent Angelo Manning was her mom's boyfriend and Jonny-London said yes he loved her grandpa's gumbo too.

Everyone had gravitated back to the front of Jonny-London and Irece's apartment building but while Jonny-London and Irece were talking Mingus made brief eye contact with CoCo. He glanced one time intentionally to be sure it was her and twice he glanced by accident trying to keep his cool when Irece introduced him as her boyfriend.

Irece looked at Jonny-London then she looked at Lillian then she looked at Kamber then she looked at CoCo and she told them she knew her man was the finest they had ever seen. She said it was okay for them to lift their heads and eyeball her goods they just better not touch.

Irece turned to Mingus to see his reaction to her offering up his looks for free and he was blushing and mainly looking only towards her.

Irece rubbed up from his shoulder to his neck and she whispered in his ear that no other girl better be what was making him blush and Mingus assured Irece with a kiss on the lips only she was making him blush. Instant they were back in their own world and they walked away from Jonny-London, CoCo, Kamber and Lillian like an encounter with them never happened.

I

The coming Monday Jonny-London stayed home from school sick with a stomachache and CoCo and Kamber walked home from school together.

On their walk Kamber shared a story with CoCo about her cousin's cousin who was a seventh-grader at Muir Middle School with them. She got arrested Friday for boosting downtown claiming she was set-up buy a shady bitch that hung outside their schoolyard afterschool but she was not a student.

Kamber asked CoCo did she know what shady bitch her cousin's cousin was talking about and CoCo said she knew what the shady bitch looked like but she did not know her.

Kamber said the story going around her family was the shady bitch invited her cousin's cousin to come downtown. The deal was for the cousin to have the shady bitch back and for having her back the cousin could steal whatever she wanted.

The cousin said she would not have stolen shit if the shady bitch did not tell her that the two security guards were her friends and they were willing to look the other way.

It was too late once the cousin realized she was the sacrifice and come to find out both security guards were not the shady bitch friend.

Only one security guard was in cahoots with the shady bitch.

So as long as the shady bitch security guard friend let his coworker follow and catch one person, basically keeping the coworker distracted, the shady bitch security guard friend could make sure the shady bitch stole what she wanted and got away.

CoCo kept it to herself that if Kamber had not picked a fight with her Friday after school she could have been the idiot sacrificed and set-up and arrested for boosting.

———)((◉))———

CoCo was sitting on her three-cushioned microfiber couch the colors of teal and cabernet.

The side of her body was near the armrest and she had her elbow propped on a cylinder shaped custard colored pillow.

Her legs and feet were stretched out in front of her and she was sipping a Shiraz that paired well with the dinner Mingus prepared for them.

CoCo had just finished a juicy medium-well done steak

with smothered potatoes and onions and broccoli with melt-ed cheese and she was waiting for the brownies to cool.

Mingus was in the kitchen washing the dishes he made and he was about to serve CoCo brownie a la mode while he kneaded the soreness out her aching feet.

He had asked that when he finished giving her mas-sage she serve him his dessert in bed and CoCo cheerfully obliged. She spoon-fed him bites of strawberry ice cream with fudge brownie, whip cream, chocolate syrup and nuts and before Mingus finished his dessert, she was sucking the whip cream and chocolate syrup from his nuts.

Not long after CoCo swallowed his dick a couple times to the back of her throat they were breaking her headboard.

She got her first orgasm from him giving it to her dog-gy-style and her second orgasm came from his tongue. She was missionary for their final go-round and at the apex of her third orgasm she wailed a pleasure screech that could have awakened the dead before she erupted into a human waterfall.

Mingus pulled his dick out and yanked it a couple times back and forth until he ejaculated himself on CoCo's belly and collapsed on top of her.

He had landed his sweaty muscular breastbone on her breast and it hurt but she did not push him off. She adjusted her body to free her smashed tit and in a matter of minutes his labored breathing and heaving turned to snoring.

CoCo found his breathing to be calming and when she heard Kamber enter her house she was halfway sleep breath-ing in iteration with his calm snore.

Kamber coming over was the plan but CoCo thought it would have been later and she would have had the time to get rid of Mingus.

Kamber had not seen Mingus's face in many many years but she knew CoCo and Mingus were fucking on an on-again-off-again basis. What Kamber did not know was they were on again and CoCo did not want to have to defend herself about that.

CoCo had blabbed to Kamber and the rest of her squad how she felt low fucking Mingus in the park the night his daughter was born.
She knew one if not all four of her confidants would not shy from reminding her of what she told them about never fucking Mingus again.

CoCo closed her eyes and decided to sleep on it but she overheard a man's voice outside her bedroom door. She wanted to go see who Kamber brought in her house without permission but Mingus's limp sticky dick on her thigh and his warm body against hers felt too good to get up from.
 She was enjoying him pressed to her body. His face was pointed at hers and his nose was right under her chin.
She traced his beautiful features with her finger close to the touch but without touching she traced over his brow bone, the length of his eyelashes and the natural line from his temples down his cheeks to his chin.
She was in a moment she wanted to last and she drifted off to sleep lying there beneath Mingus's muscular welterweight body.

CoCo was out for however long before the house phone woke her.

The house phone was affixed to the wall near the front door in the living room but Kamber let the phone ring longer than necessary before CoCo heard her say hello.

The house phone gave visitors entry to CoCo's condo community from the main gate and she was only expecting it to be one of two people.

Eliza was coming to get her hair done by Kamber and Jonny-London was bringing Eliza and Kamber the weed they paid her for at the hospital.

CoCo enlarged her eyes and stretched her arms to find Mingus had rolled onto the bed beside her.

She did not know the hour she had fallen asleep but she knew it had gotten late and for however much time she was sleep it must have been a deep sleep.

She slipped on her robe to cover her naked sex-funky body but she was not ready to be apart from Mingus.

She nestled herself back beside him and he did not flinch. He was comatose and snoring like he had not had a good sleep in days so CoCo instead of waking him and telling him he had to leave she watched him.

His face was turned in her direction and pressed into the pillows next to hers and she watched his smooth brown sugar brown back rise and fall.

He rested so peacefully CoCo reached for her phone to capture a picture of his perfection.

She took a picture of him by himself then leaned in for a kiss and snapped a picture of her lips on his cheek.

She slid her robe from her shoulders to free her arms and show her naked upper body and she snapped another picture of her looking up at the camera with her head touching his head on the same pillow.

CoCo snapped two more photos from a side angle that captured Mingus sleeping in her background. She was exposing half her boobs from the areola up to the top of her long messy weave and in one photo she was looking demure like an innocent freshly fucked housewife.

In the second photo she had her middle finger up to the camera. Her top lip was arched in one direction with her tongue stuck out the opposite side of her mouth and she was looking like nan-nan-na-nan-na lullaby-baby had done gone and fucked the next bitch man to sleep.

CoCo put her robe back over the top of her body and she slipped her phone into her robe pocket.

She laid her head down to continue watching Mingus but she fell back to sleep and when she woke up the second time she heard music playing and voices chatting.

Mingus was in a new position and was now wearing his underwear.

CoCo decided to finally rise up and see what was going on around her house but first she stopped at the bathroom inside her bedroom.

She was too lazy to shower but she was not leaving her bedroom without washing the dick from her breath and cum from her belly.

She brushed her teeth and rinsed her stomach thinking she was finished but she made a turn and got a whiff of herself and had to fill the sink with body wash and hot water for a birdbath.

It took her two-minutes to soap and rinse under her breasts, her stomach, between her legs to her ass crack and under her arms.

She came from her bathroom wearing an old too small but clean robe and she went over to where Mingus was sleeping.

She reached slowly under his side of the bed to slide a decorated card box from beneath and quietly she tiptoed out her bedroom holding the box tightly under her armpit.

Chapter 18

LIFE IN A DIFFERENT COLOR

Kamber Diamond Perry had always fantasized of what she envisioned to be a real family.

It was the family that ate together, watched movies together and went to church together. They went on family vacations every year and spent holidays cooking meals, buying gifts and wrapping presents together.

It was a family that slept under one roof they could all call their home and this was the family Kamber wanted to someday create for herself.

Witnessing Royal enter the world and watching Lillian's vagina widen to the size of a cantaloupe to drop a fat brown bloody baby body out it tore Kamber in half.

Part of her still held the dream of her picture book family but she did not know if the childbirth part was something her body could take.

The sounds of Lillian's screams, the putrid smell of her insides, her blood on everything and the look of agony on her clammy face made Kamber question ever becoming a parent.

Even after Lillian and the baby were bathed and smelling winter-fresh, Kamber was still traumatized but then she saw Reddy.

He trailed Richie into Lillian's hospital room and he eased up next to her and asked her name and before thinking Kamber said her name was Diamond.

That was the name she automatically gave to men she did not know but she opened up their small talk saying he could call her Kamber and she asked did he ever go by his middle name.

He said he did not use the name Lawrence for anything and soon their small talk became about him knowing Dior from way back.

He said he did not know for hella years she was his little brother's mom and he was shaping the conversation to chop Dior up for being a mistress but Kamber redirected the conversation back to him.

She bluntly asked him to tell her his plan for life and she shut her mouth to listen.

She did not know why she asked him that or where it came from but he answered saying he had businesses already lined up and he gloated on his mom.

He called her a boss lady who co-owned a boutique and barbershop with his dad and he said matter-of-factly how raw he cut hair then he jumped to saying something about an inheritance and being an only child.

When Reddy mentioned his barbering Kamber remembered seeing a picture of his face on the San Fran Times. He was a cover story for the magazine and not just once. He had been holding the title for top urban barber of the year for two or three years.

Kamber drifted momentarily from her attentive listening to process her opportunity. She was getting macked on by the notable Reddy Rich. Here was a hood celebrity smiling in her face and she was partially not listening but she heard him say her eyes were pretty and matched the color of her crystal brown topaz earrings.

He asked was brown topaz her birthstone and she said no her birthstone was aquamarine.

Reddy looked stumped but as Kamber explained March's birthstone was an aqua colored crystal he came close enough to relish the lingering traces of perfume she applied early that morning.

He asked how she stayed smelling so good all day and as bizarre as she found his question she answered like she was being quizzed.

She said she put a dab behind the ears and she pointed to a spot behind one ear.

She straightened her arm downward and turned out her leg as she pointed to where she put a perfume dab in the creases of both her elbow and her calf.

She lifted one wrist to his nose to show where the dab of perfume went on her wrists and she said she also wore scented lotion on her body and she sprayed a scented mist over her hair and outerwear.

He said that was how he applied his cologne too and he asked Kamber did she think he smelled good and Kamber laughed and said yes he smelled real good.

Reddy kept talking about all he had and all he did and Kamber gazed at his mouth movements like he had her attention but she was measuring him with an ocular inspection and thinking so what. He had money, and. He did not seem any different than her. He was attractive to look at but so was she. He was a couple of years older but whoop-de-do. He was no better spoken. He knew what topaz was but he did not know about aquamarine.

They were both Black and both native to San Fran but she wondered did he think his four one five area code was brighter than hers or did he think he was made better because he was born of a better set of circumstances.

Of course him having money put him in a vastly different income bracket but the idea of him being made better came from something Kamber's oldest sister forever said about herself.

I

Kamber grew up between the homes of her two grandmothers.

She knew her mother and father and all her siblings but they were just never one family.

Kamber was the youngest of both of her parent's children and she was the only one of her siblings to share both parents. She had two siblings she shared with her mother and three siblings she shared with her father and both parents were on drugs their entire adult lives.

Before Kamber's parents met they were both separately always in and out of jail or a drug treatment program.

The story told to Kamber was that from the moment her parents met in the street they became each other's shadow and they wanted to get clean for each other.

They entered a coed drug treatment facility together and within a year they became pregnant with Kamber but seven months after Kamber was conceived her very pregnant mom relapsed.

She left Kamber's father in rehab and went back on the streets.

Kamber's mother could not be found the rest of her pregnancy and when her water broke she was smoking a crack pipe inside a tent pitched beneath the US 101 freeway.

Fortunately someone had the sense to go for help.

Kamber would have been born on the cement curb but she was born in the ambulance on the way to the County General Hospital where her mother vanished from and abandoned her at less than a day old in the world.

II

Reddy on the other hand was an only child with a momma who loved and worshipped the ground he walked on. That made Kamber certain of one thing. If she had Reddy's children they would be loved and doted on by his momma.

Kamber wanted to ask Reddy more about his mom's money since he brought it up but she would have been asking too much for an initial conversation.

She wondered the amount his mom was sitting on but without having to ask he mentioned his mom made well into the six figures annually on just her investment portfolio alone. He called her a natural born hustler and Kamber said she too was raised by natural born hustlers like his mom.

What Kamber also said in the nicest way was contrary to his mom those that raised her had to raise more than one child.

Kamber shared that she came from a big family but she got separated from some of her siblings when their mother died.

Reddy did not let Kamber's death comment make the moment awkward or stop his pursuit. He replied with a sincere apology for her loss but he wanted to know what part of the city was she from and he asked to know more about her big family.

Kamber said she was from two separate parts of the city. Christmas break and a portion of the summer including the Fourth of July she spent in the Hunter's Point District with her paternal grandmother, **Victoria Perry-Marcus**.

The school year except for Christmas break and including the latter half of July and the full month of August she spent in the Fillmore District with her maternal grandmother, **Lucy Graves**.

Her Grandma Tori was a retired city administrator but she ran a twenty-four hour weekday childcare from her garage and Grandma Lu was a Travelling Beautician. She custom made wigs for a shortlist of regulars but she worked as the editor-in-chief for a popular online beauty blog. She and a partner co-founded OCTOBER to glamorize the lifestyles of women and men after the age of sixty.

Kamber had Reddy laughing with a comment on her grandmother's raking in decent earnings and owning their homes but if something was not broke it did not get fixed and if the wheels were not falling off their hoopty they were steadily putting miles on it.

She said they both had and handled costly responsibilities

but any extra they blew on their expensive habits.

Grandma Tori liked to drink her Japanese whisky and play the lotto. She took frequent weekend casino vacations and she liked to hold weekend bingo and blackjack tournaments in her in-law apartment behind her house.

Grandma Lu liked her imported black and gold menthol cigarettes and she only smoked the top shelf weed. She had to have a custom made suit to wear with a new wig and she lived to go on the road for a hair show. If she was not styling in the hair show she went to do interviews and take pictures for her blog and she often hosted local wig showcases and contests.

Grandma Lu had full custody of Kamber and one other of her daughter's three children but Kamber told Reddy only about herself and her mother's oldest son, **Solace St. Claire**.

Her mother's middle child **Nathan Mann Jr.** lived with his dad fulltime since infancy so Kamber glazed over his existence to tell Reddy about her big sister who lived with Grandma Tori.

Grandma Tori had full custody of two of her son's children and every summer Kamber got to be with her half-sister, **Justice Perry** and her half-brother **Jamison Perry III.**

Justice and Jamison both lived with Grandma Tori but Kamber failed to speak of Jamison to Reddy.
It was Justice and Jamison's mother who had died before Kamber was born but Kamber thought of her sibling's

tragedy as her tragedy and she did consider her mother dead. She did not believe coloring her truth with a sibling's reality was being phony or that her implying her mother's death to Reddy was farfetched. This was just a way to paint her *life in a different color.*

Kamber could have stopped going on about her siblings but not before mentioning her father's oldest daughter, **Boston Perry**.

She wanted to leave Reddy feeling she related to some of his world through her sister living that only-child-apple-of-her-mother's-eye type of life.

Her sister had been raised on a lie but the lie was what Kamber shared with Reddy.

Boston's social media following starred her having fun times with rich kid's relishing the panoramas of San Fran Area but Boston and most of her stuck up horde lived twenty or more minutes from the city on the other side of the Golden Gate Bridge.

Boston's mom told her daughter she was made better than the rest of the Perry family.
This was a mom who wiped down tables and cleaned dirty dishes for a living but who was in Boston's ear saying she was too good to spend more than a day or two a year around her father's side for her Grandma Tori's birthday.

Boston's mom was a dining attendant at the headquarters of the worlds largest technology company in Mountain View where every employee received the same company perks. She got box seats to major league games, five hundred dollar gift cards for shopping sprees, first class airline tickets, cash tips everyday, free cooked meals from her job and the list went on. She could do it big at no cost but she had Boston's head full of fluff thinking momma was at the company level of a software engineer when in truth momma was secretly banging a couple of them engineers to get her daughter whatever she could not get her on her own.

Boston and Kamber were not on speaking terms after the day Kamber had to tell Boston the factuality she was not better. Her township was rich and her neighbor friends lived high up on them rolling hills in rich people homes but she only went inside those homes to visit. Her ass lived at the bottom of them same rolling hills and her momma's flossy platinum blonde Land Rover SUV could be found parked at the front door of their low-income public housing project.

⸺⸺◦((◦))◦⸺⸺

Big Red told Reddy it was time for them to leave the hospital right when Kamber told him she did not populate second place in her relationships with her man and she was not going to start with him.

Big Red opened Lillian's hospital room door for Dior and Richie to walk out and when Dion walked out the door behind them he held it open for Reddy who was slow to follow.

Kamber stood with Reddy at the open door and asked how would his mom react to a new sheriff being in town and Reddy asked was Kamber about to give him her number to find out.

Reddy left Kamber with the suspicion she would hear from him.

She felt they had a genuine connection but until he made his move her next move was to crash with CoCo however long it took for her to find a place to live.

She had earnestly had enough abuse from her boyfriend, **Baku Hawes**.

Baku was a legit charmer.

He did not let Kamber want for nothing and no matter how hard she tried she could not quell the dirty thoughts of her last time riding his saddle due to it was not a distant thought.

When Kamber got the group text message from Lillian about her going into labor she was bouncing on Baku's big-ole-thing.

Their sex was what she did not regret about their relationship.

He was a square with no diseases and no addictions and he never cheated.

How controlling and possessive and violent he could get at times was outweighing his good clean loyal dick but his head and bed game made Kamber have to fight her urge to give him an umpteenth chance.

She might have given in and went crawling back to Baku had Reddy not swooped in and made her ponder smashing him that night if he called and came to pick her up from the hospital.

Kamber fucked Baku the first night they met on some drunken hoe shit leaving the club together and that was over three years ago on her eighteenth birthday.

It was not until more than a year into her living with him he became over possessive and would not go anywhere without her, including work.

Baku was the manager of a San Fran homeless shelter not far from his high-rise.

He showed up every morning on time and he had Kamber wait in the car while he took about two hours to check in with his staff.

He did his necessary paperwork and conducted his meetings then he told his staff he was going in the field but he was actually crossing bridges to go on dates with Kamber.

Baku left the city where he worked and he took Kamber to the Eastbay, Northbay and Southbay for recreation and to relax, shop, eat or go to the movies and before he returned to work they always stopped at home for some late afternoon bed play.

Kamber would again wait in the car for him to finish the final hour or two of his ten-hour shift. He wrote and discussed false field reports and told his staff tales of him aiding and abetting in the care of former occupants as required by an aftercare management contract his shelter had with the city.

Once he was off the clock he took Kamber wherever she needed to go to do whatever she wanted and he paid no matter what it was.

Baku's Thursday's at work were his Friday's and after he and Kamber ended their Thursday date night they were usually in the house for the next three days.

He liked to sleep when no one was paying him to get up and any food he ordered in and the sex they had over and over and over until Monday morning they were back on his four-day workweek schedule.

III

Kamber enjoyed being spoiled by Baku and for their first eighteen months of living together she thought it was the perfect situation.

Marriage became a topic and soon as Baku thought he had her the abuse started.

First it was verbal with him calling her stupid or idiot or dork.

Slowly came the slaps to her face for giving her opinion and the choking he did to her in private was to make her believe she was powerless when he embarrassed her in public.

The first time Baku punched Kamber in the head and knocked her to the floor she started to tell him then she was pregnant.

She had known for about a week but she was waiting to say anything because of the abuse and she had not decided to keep the baby.

A few days after the punch to the head they were entering their home and Baku was walking up the stairs in the lead.

Kamber was not even sure what she said when his elbow came towards her mouth but she leaned back to dodge the blow and fell down the stairs.

That was when she told Baku she was pregnant and had planned to surprise him but he had probably just killed their baby.

Kamber threw Baku the papers from her purse showing him the positive pregnancy test results from the clinic she visited.

Her most recent visit was actually to schedule the abortion but now she could tell Baku she miscarried from the fall he caused her to have.

Baku stopped the abuse after that incident and their relationship was back to perfect for maybe eight or nine months.

Kamber got pregnant again but her gut told her to keep it copacetic and not say anything then one night out of nowhere Baku beat her down.

He gave Kamber senseless reasons saying it was her fault. She was talking too long to the corner store man she bought candy from and he said he saw her waving at that bus driver which Kamber said was her way of thanking the bus driver for allowing her to jaywalk in front of his bus when she was leaving the corner store.

IV

Kamber terminated her second pregnancy without Baku knowing she was pregnant but she knew it was time to leave him. She just did not know how she was going to make her move because she depended on him for everything.

She gave her phone number to Reddy hoping he would be her lifesaver but she was not expecting to be saved so soon.

Reddy was texting her like an hour after he got her number.

They texted back and forth until Kamber dozed off but he later called her when everyone in Lillian's hospital room was asleep.

Her cell phone ringer was on vibrate so it would only disturb her but she answered quickly to make sure the vibrating did not wake Royal, Lillian or CoCo.

Kamber kept her voice low enough to answer the call inside the hospital room but she kept it brief.

She said it was her bad she forgot to text him about picking her up but Reddy acted like she had not dropped the ball.

He said he wanted to see her but Kamber asked him what did he want to see her so badly for and Reddy said he wanted to create his tomorrow with her.

Kamber called him hella corny then said it sounded romantic but to let her think on it and she would text him her response.

Chapter 19

NOT YET

Kamber went outside the hospital emergency room entrance and she paced the smoking area a few paces in one direction. She puffed her cigar and waited to see Reddy pull up but when she walked a few paces in the opposite direction she saw Reddy was already waiting for her.

He was leaned against the passenger door of his car parked in the white painted passenger zone.

He had his window's down and the music playing.

Reddy must have called from outside the hospital to be there that fast and Kamber ducked out of view.

She tossed her cigar and used her water bottle from her purse to rinse her hands. She let her hands air dry and she sprayed her hair and body with perfume.

She put a stick of gum in her mouth and rubbed on her scented lotion while she walked towards Reddy.

She got close enough to see the diamond-studded license plate read MAXRICH and she could hear the words to his soft music playing.

The music was not disturbing the peace loud just loud

enough to be heard by someone approaching his vehicle.

Kamber assumed Reddy was trying to impress her driving a Bugatti Chiron. When she Googled him from her phone the article she found online said Reddy drove a matte black Camaro and not that his momma's money could not afford him a Bugatti but the article was recent.

His Camaro would have impressed her more because she would not have been guessing whether it was borrowed or rented and she could have asked to drive and he would have let her and that would have been a turn on.

I

Kamber stepped up to the Bugatti and caught Reddy off guard looking down at his phone. She said the music he was playing was from an old souls' era and she asked was he an old soul.

Reddy said yes he was an old soul and he asked Kamber if she was familiar with the song.

Kamber tilted her head and waited a second to join in sync with the tune.

She finished a line in the song about a midnight train and she held the note then told Reddy she was not one of those people who thought the only music in the world was rap music.

She said she was raised to appreciate funk, disco, soul, pop and even soft rock and she could probably name more melodies than him from the seventies and eighties.

Reddy asked was that a fact and Kamber said he could bet on it.

Reddy opened the passenger door for Kamber to get in the car and he said their first date would be karaoke.

Kamber sat in her seat slowly and asked him what to call them hooking up at that hour and Reddy said for her to call it a warm up.

He pulled Kamber's seatbelt from the base and handed her the buckle to make it easier for her to fasten and she cracked a smile. He closed her door and came around to his car door and as he was getting in she told him that with the love song thumping through his car speakers and with the chivalry on top he had them living a dreamy scene from an eighties cult classic film.

Reddy comically said he done good then yes and Kamber said yes done good he had.

Kamber rested her head back against the headrest of her seat and closed her eyes while Reddy set the car for takeoff.

She asked him to raise her window and turn on the heater and if her eyes were open she would have seen him about to steal a kiss but after Reddy stole the kiss she opened her eyes.

His face was still in her face and she let him steal one more kiss before she told him his kiss was nice but uninvited.

Kamber politely acknowledged Reddy for his manners with her car door and the seatbelt. She was even polite saying she could leave him and go be with a man who might not know to open her car door or hand her the seatbelt but who knew to ask and wait for permission to touch, kiss or suck any part of her body.

Reddy pulled himself back against his seat. He was stunned speechless but he apologized.

Kamber asked did he want her to leave. She said that would give him room in his two-seater car to pick up a tramp maybe two if he stacked one bitch on the other bitch lap but Reddy said no. He wanted to be with her and Kamber said for her it was late and she was tired.

II

Reddy left the hospital going straight to the Union Square hotel where he had a reservation booked through a family hookup.

Anytime he needed a room he went to his uncle Maxim who had his girlfriend Saba handle it and she did anything for him. He was her young rich boyfriend that took excellent care of her and her two grown kids and a hotel suite at the last minute for his nephew to impress a lady was nothing. She had the clout to call on her almost-brother-in-law **Bluebird Johnson**.

Bluebird was her children's uncle.

He was the General Manager of a hotel chain where Saba used to work for years in Human Resources. Her HR job paid her way through Barber College but before she resigned to become a Barber she hired everybody she could.

She got her daughter Morningstar hired at the Front Desk as a supervisor and her son Eagle she got him hired to run Bellman Services. She got a younger cousin hired to work in Security and her two older cousins she got hired in Housekeeping.

Bluebird she got hired as a night Manager On Duty with no experience and he continued to feel indebted to her.

Long after she broke off the engagement to his brother

he often hooked her up with special room request at the friends and family rate or at no charge.

Kamber and Reddy walked in their hotel room to find a bottle of champagne chilling in an ice bucket on the side table.

In the center of the king size duvet bedcover was a silver tray displaying chocolate covered mixed fruit, cheese cubes, wafer crackers, butterballs and sourdough bread.

Illuminating beneath the desk lamp was an envelope Kamber opened to find two complimentary ferry tickets for a champagne brunch to be redeemed before the end of the year.

Kamber looked at Reddy and he did not know it but he had her validly rapt.

The first thing Reddy did after their walk-thru the suite was search for an electrical outlet.

Kamber knew Reddy's phone was dead. He mentioned in the car how he was mad at himself for forgetting his charger when he switched cars knowing his uncle Maxim's car charger did not fit his phone.

Reddy was able to borrow a charger from Morningstar at the front desk when she gave them their room key but no sooner than Reddy plugged his dead phone in Kamber handed him her cellphone to connect to the same cellphone charger.

She could see Reddy gravely wanted to charge his phone but her cellphone had also died.

Reddy heard Kamber's soft voice ask him to please charge her phone too.

If he was her type of man he would want to satisfy her first before himself and after Reddy showed Kamber he was her type of man she invited him to help her take off her jacket and shoes.

He hurried to do what Kamber asked but she told him to take his time. It was the closest he would get to her all night and again Reddy did not know how to respond except to behave as Kamber wanted.

Kamber went into the bathroom and started running warm water to fill the Jacuzzi tub.
She added the bath soap and sat at the edge of the tub long enough for the tub to fill halfway with an overlay of white bubbles.
She pressed the button for the Jacuzzi jets to come on and she began to daydream watching the bubbles bubble up even more.

She was still contemplating would she fuck Reddy and she told herself no.
She wanted Reddy on the team but not mad, jealous or trying to beat her because he got sprung on the sex and wanted to own her.
He was crushing on her big time for some reason but if she fucked him too soon she would lose her advantage.
She wanted him to know she was interested but not easily impressed and they had the kind of chemistry that made Kamber's stomach dance but she could not show it.
He had to do more than get her a room and feed her some cheese and crackers. According to the gospel of her

Grandma Tori the harder she made a man work for her affection the more her affection would be worth.

Kamber hoped to one day snag a quiet hardworking husband like her Grandma Tori and Grandma Tori getting married did not make her the monogamous type. She told Kamber her golden years had not suppressed her sexual appetite. She said it took three men to satisfy her and when the hubby and his goods went out of commission she interchanged him with her debonair boyfriend or her playboy play-brother.

III

Kamber appeared from their hotel room bathroom naked and she walked to the window.

Their room was on the thirty-third floor with the curtains drawn apart and she could see the vivid lights down Market Street.

The people, cyclists, taxis, trolleys, food stands, street kids and panhandlers were microscopic from her view.

Reddy did not notice Kamber at first.

He was occupied with filling their glasses with champagne.

He could sense she had entered the room but he noticed she was naked when he turned in her direction holding both their glasses of champagne.

Kamber faced Reddy and he froze momentarily to watch her.

She leaned half her naked body against the cold window and before Reddy took a step he absorbed every inch of her from her toenails the color of pink sprinkles to her mocha areolas nearly the size of his palm.

Reddy moved close enough to grip one of Kamber's big breasts.

He had the urge to let at least one boob fill his large hand to see did his palm cover her whole areola but Reddy knew better than to touch. He was glad he had the champagne in both hands to control his whim to reach and fondle.

Kamber accepted her champagne flute from Reddy and said cheers.

He said cheers then clinked the edge of his glass to hers and they each took a silent sip.

She glided away from the window across the room towards the bathroom and at the bathroom doorway she asked Reddy did he want to join her for a bubble bath.

Reddy said no thank you and he turned from Kamber quickly to wipe the slobber from his mouth.

He saw a brief moment of insecurity spread through her vibe from her reflection in the window but the window reflected him too.

He might have said no thank you but Kamber could see the temperature had risen below his belt and she came walking briskly back towards him downing her champagne.

She touched her empty glass to his pectoral and after he cupped her glass she arched her pear shaped ass around to give him a show.

She walked to the bathroom switching her chunky cheeks side to side and she asked him would he be a dear and bring her some mellow music for her to soak alone.

Kamber took her purse in the bathroom and pulled out her silk scarf to wrap up her weave.

Her scarf was a colorful pattern of pinks, purples and

blues mixed with a black and white cheetah print and she tied the scarf turban-style with a twisted side knot.

She slipped into her hot water very slowly and leaned her neck against the top of the porcelain tub but before she could close her eyes Reddy appeared.

He was naked and holding the hotel room radio and Kamber eyed his dick like his dick was the one telling her she knew his phone was dead.

Reddy said radio music would have to suffice and he confidently walked to the electrical outlet with his dick leading him by about seven inches but Kamber was giving him a half an inch longer for if the hook shape straightened out when it got harder.

Kamber asked Reddy why he was naked but the music came on soon as he plugged the radio into the wall and he acted like he did not hear her question.

He came over to the tub and he asked Kamber could she move forward but as he placed his feet in the water behind her he gave her no choice but to move forward.

Kamber suggested he sit opposite of her so his dick was not sticking her in the back but Reddy did nothing with her suggestion. He continued into the tub and when he was seated he said if she wanted to do something about his dick she could.

Kamber held Reddy's gaze and leaned sideways gently into his open legs.

She wrapped her right forearm around his neck and her breasts floated just above the surface of the water. She smoothed the white bubbles from her hand over his speckled brownish straw-colored chest hair and he smoothed the white bubbles over her breasts.

Reddy's dick grazed below the jeweled piercing in Kamber's bellybutton and as he played with her nipples he started to suck her tongue.

Kamber started rubbing his dick and she heard herself moaning from how amazing his tongue felt in her mouth and her moaning made Reddy kiss her more aggressively. He sucked from her tongue and her lips to her earlobe and neck and Kamber pulled away to make his eyes pop open. She wanted to stare in his brown eyes and she wanted him staring back at the face of the girl jerking his dick up and down and round and round.
She told him to keep his eyes on her and he did for a few seconds before they rolled into his head.

Kamber slowed her hand movement almost to a stop and Reddy looked at her widened her legs for him to explore the inside as well as the outside of her body freely.

Reddy gripped his dick and Kamber let him circle the tip of it on her clit. She knew he wanted her to slide down on it and she knew she wanted to feel him inside her but she still had not decided to give him any.
She kissed his neck and sucked the same spot hard enough to give him a hickey then she whispered in his ear *not yet.*

Reddy pulled Kamber's head back by her scarf knot for her eyes to point down at him and he placed his other hand around her throat.
He gently caressed her throat and told her to open her

mouth and when she did he spit in her mouth.

He pulled her face forward by the chin and he sucked his spit from her tongue and Kamber did not show it but she was thrown off guard by how fast that happened.

Reddy placed her hand back on his dick and his fingers slid between her lower lips.

They both chased their orgasm helping one another get there but Reddy got Kamber first to the finish line and unintentionally she left him hanging.

She rested her body on his chest but he had no qualms helping himself along and he choked the chicken at top speed until he busted cum in the water.

He fell with Kamber into a snooze but their snooze got disturbed with her announcing she had to pee and Reddy admitted he had to pee too. He told Kamber to pee in the water and she said that was not okay.

Reddy told her it was okay because pee was natural and they could just shower each other clean and Kamber laughed but she let go in the water.

She asked Reddy did he feel it and that made him laugh harder than her.

He still had his eyes closed with his head leaned against the porcelain tub but he asked Kamber was it not his leg she was peeing on.

Kamber rose up onto her knees to face him. She waited for him to look at her before she said his chill mode was sexy as fuck.

He thanked her and she said it was now his turn and Reddy asked if she was telling him to pee on her.

Kamber said yes she wanted to see his aim game and he said okay he was aiming for her mouth and she had better open wide.

Kamber was cracking up as she leaned her head back.
She yelled fire in the hole and she waited but when she felt pee hit her chin she screamed and blocked her face with both hands.

Reddy told her not to cower now she knew his aim game was strong and he kept spraying and his pee hit her palms, her neck and shoulders, her breasts and her stomach before he was done.

IV

Kamber and Reddy shared a long, hot and soapy shower.
They cleaned each other and toweled each other off quietly and they let the love songs on the radio say everything for them.
She lotioned him then he lotioned her and both of them were content wordlessly satisfying the other.

Kamber asked Reddy to carry her to the bed. She said she did not want her clean feet to touch the floor and he bent his knees to scoop her in his arms.
She gripped him around his neck and as if her five-foot-seven-inch two hundred-plus-pound-body was light as a feather he toted her like he was carrying his bride over the threshold.

Reddy sang dun-dun-da-dun, dun-dun-da-dun and Kamber found the moment amusing.
She laid her head at his shoulder and told him she felt

safe in a way no one had ever made her feel. She said she knew the night was coming to an end and there was the possibly it would never happen again but she could say they had made the most of it.

Had Kamber said more of what she wanted to Reddy it would have been she could imagine forever with him.

Reddy reached the edge of their king-size bed and Kamber loosened her grip on his neck letting one arm come down to his chest but her other arm stayed around his neck.

She was lost in his mesmerizing eyes and out of nowhere came a gust of excitement inside her. She attempted to act and she lifted her head towards his face to kiss his full lips but he tossed her suddenly from his arms onto the bed.

Kamber's arms flailed and she shrieked and grasped ahold of her breath.

She could not catch her bearings until she bounced on the soft pillowtop mattress but Reddy did not give her time to get fiery. He pulled at her feet and friskily bit at her toes causing Kamber to giggle and shrink her feet up the bed.

He promised he would stop tickling her if she let him pull her feet back out and she did.

She let him straighten her legs and he crawled from the bottom of her body licking and smooching each leg one by one to the tops of her inner thighs but when his lips lightly touched her pubic hairs, Kamber reminded him he did not have permission to eat her Patty Cake.

Reddy smirked and said he knew the rules of her body. He thought for a second and asked himself had she just called her pussy a piece of cake and he told her he was not eating her piece of cake or whatever she called her twat.

Kamber laughed as he locked eyes with her and drifted over her body and he hovered but he did not kiss or touch her.

He rolled onto his side of the bed and they tucked themselves under the bed covers.

They shared a simple kiss with their goodnight and right when Kamber got comfortable Reddy rolled over to nestle up next to her.

He wrapped her in his arms and legs and asked her to sing him to sleep.

Kamber asked him why and he said because he could not sleep outside of his bed at home and Kamber sniggered. She told him not to deny he had been with many other women outside of his bed at home and of course he had but not overnight. He said he got on before morning and he never brought a piece of ass to where he lived so that wherever he fucked a female he could leave her wherever he fucked her at.

Reddy swore to Kamber were he in that moment with another woman he would have already left or he would have been in the process of leaving.

Kamber asked why was he not leaving her and he said he did not want to leave her. She cleared her throat and asked him if he wanted her to sing a cradlesong and Reddy told her to sing whatever.

Since he did not say no to a cradlesong Kamber opened her mouth to sing you are my sunshine but what came out was a remixed version of somewhere over the rainbow.

Chapter 20

FREEDOM

Reddy gave Kamber a ride from San Fran to CoCo's condo upon leaving the hotel late Saturday afternoon.

Along the drive Kamber asked Reddy to pull off the freeway in the city of Richmond for her to run into the mall.

She assured him she was running in and running out and she did.

She went to one department store to find a couple days worth of chic threads on clearance and to her surprise, at the register, Reddy refused to let her pay.

I

It was not Kamber's plan to let Reddy into CoCo's place.

Kamber knew CoCo was against strangers in her house but Reddy had to use the bathroom and Kamber did not know if CoCo was home. She called to ask permission for Reddy to come inside but she kept getting CoCo's voicemail.

When Kamber reached the gated entrance of CoCo's

property another resident was entering.

She instructed Reddy to bypass the guest entry protocols and follow the resident inside and they parked his Bugatti in an open stall marked for guest parking.

Reddy walked behind Kamber up the stairs to CoCo's front door and he carried the small bag of clothes he insisted on purchasing for her.

Kamber let herself in using the spare key taped beneath the doormat and she walked Reddy to the bathroom but she went to wait for him by the front door with it open.

Reddy told her before they left the city had he not somewhere else to be he would have stayed all day and night with her but when he rejoined her in the living room he did not seem to want to leave.

Kamber did not want to be apart from him either and her stomach started growling which made her think they had only eaten the fruit and cheese platter left on their hotel bed. She entered the kitchen and offered to make them some fresh hot coffee with fried biscuits and honey and Reddy happily took a seat.

Kamber filled a skillet with oil and she turned on the stove but when she reached to grab the coffee from the cabinet she spotted CoCo's keys and mail on the kitchen counter.

She second-guessed having the coffee and biscuits knowing CoCo was home but she had already begun heating the oil in the skillet.

She could have turned the oil off and told Reddy to leave but what she told him was to keep his voice down because the keys on the kitchen counter meant her roommate was home.

Kamber assumed CoCo was with company in her bedroom because her bedroom door was closed and that was not usual if CoCo was home alone.

Kamber's nosiness carried her from the kitchen down the hall to listen briefly at CoCo's bedroom door and she heard faint snoring. She knew CoCo did not snore and her being home with a man snoring in her bed should have made Kamber uneasy about having Reddy in the kitchen but no. Her mind told her CoCo was boo'd up and she had all the time in the world to be boo'd up too.

Reddy was content waiting at the dining table near the kitchen entrance and he let Kamber know when she came back in the kitchen he was trying something new with her.
She asked him what was that and it was that he had never thought to pan fry biscuits.

She said the challenge was on then and she had better make them good but he said not to feel challenged. He was just grateful she was making him some coffee for his long night ahead, which he did not mean to say.
Of course Kamber asked him what he had planned.
She did not pry earlier when he mentioned he had something to do but when he mentioned it a second time she thought whatever it was he must have wanted her to know about it.

Reddy was not a good liar or a quick thinker.
In the fewest words possible he said he had nothing special planned it was just some shit he had up with the fam no big deal and with the same lungful of air he asked was it anything he could do to help in the kitchen.
He got up from the dining table before Kamber could say

if she wanted help or not and he had switched the subject but it was not that he could slip up on any vital details. The most he knew about the Harpuzon robbery was the three locations he had to be at later that evening and the times he had to be there but he knew not to say shit about any of that.

Kamber had set the can of biscuits on the kitchen counter beside the skillet and she was pouring ground coffee into the coffee filter when Reddy came in the kitchen to help.

She told him the canola oil was hot and ready and she said if he could not sit himself back in his chair and wait to be served he could finish making the coffee while she tended to the biscuits.

He said okay and she told him to pull the coffee pot from the base and fill it to the max with cold water. She pointed to where he had to pour the water into the coffee maker and she showed him where to push the red button to start the brewing.

Reddy had a delayed reaction to being told how to make the coffee and he stood there like he had nothing to do.

Kamber turned the water on at the kitchen sink to rinse her hands but the water was also for him to fill the coffee pot. She asked Reddy did she need to explain again what to do and he said no he got it.

He hurried to fill the pot from the tap and Kamber popped open the can of biscuits and started frying.

II

It was a cold late afternoon with remnants of light still outside.

The living room fireplace was lit with artificial flames

that only heated the plush area rug in front of the fireplace and the couch area right behind the rug.

Kamber and Reddy cuddled up on the floor in the one warm spot against the edge of the couch and they sipped their coffee and ate their honey-dipped biscuits until the early evening became complete darkness.

Reddy did not overstay his welcome after his second cup of coffee.

He had to get home to drop his uncle's Bugatti. He had to get to the rental car agency to pick up the minivan. He had to get to the Polk Street Inn and Suites to pay for the room and then he had to go meet up with Big Red.

Kamber politely sent Reddy off with a to-go cup of coffee and she let him give her the sweet kiss farewell that he asked for.

His stopover lasted a little under two hours and he missed Eliza by maybe three minutes.

She called the house phone from the entry gate right as he would have been exiting but probably neither one remembered the other from the hospital.

Kamber thought the house phone would have awakened CoCo and brought her from her bedroom but CoCo did not come out.

Eliza came to CoCo's front door dragging a carryon-size two-wheel roller bag.

She tried to zip through the doorway like she was some prima donna but one of her wheels spun to the side.

The doormat had briefly stopped her short of a grand

entrance and Kamber remembered CoCo's spare key was in her back pocket.

She was going to hang on to the key but she put it on the kitchen counter next to the mail to not appear presumptuous when she did ask if she could have the key during her stay.

Eliza sat on the couch and started trying to rush Kamber but Kamber told her to have several seats. She was not about to get put the fuck out before she could get a foot the fuck in and she told Eliza her hair would get done after she cleaned CoCo's kitchen and did the dishes.

Eliza said she would have been there earlier but she was being cheap and did not want to pay the full fare to take a single ride from the city.

She chose the fare that pooled with others and ended up being the first picked up but the last of three stops to be dropped off.

Kamber asked Eliza how late did her boyfriend work on Saturday's for her to not wait on him to get a ride and Eliza told Kamber her boyfriend was at home. She laughed saying he would be at work on a Saturday all day long if his company needed him. They paid him triple pay for overtime but he blocked that Saturday off. He did not want to risk being late to the Mayor's Ball.

She said he tried to bring her to CoCo's but he would have wanted to stay waiting for her and she did not want to get ready in front of him. She wanted him to be surprised by how she looked when he picked her up.

The invitation to the Mayor's Ball said costumes were suggested but not required and Eliza was not doing a full costume but she was wearing a distinguishable mermaid look. She had decided on a red goddess braid with a short sexy emerald-green dress and a pair of nude super-pointed snakeprint closed toe high-heeled shoes.

Kamber told Eliza she should ride back to the city with Jonny-London. Her hair would not take long and getting ready at her momma's house would save Mali the long ass trip to Benicia to pick her up.

Eliza said no. Her mom would find a way to ruin her night and just because her mom's house was nearer the Treasure Island venue did not make her mom's house a good idea. She was not about to get played by her doing some shit like making Eliza give back her ID knowing she needed it to show she was over twenty-one to get in the Mayor's Ball or disappearing for hours and leaving Three-D with no one else to watch him.

III

The Mayor's Ball was important to Mali but more important to Eliza.

She had only ever read reviews about the Ball being attended exclusively by the top of the San Fran food chain making it the unforgettable party of the year but Eliza was not shy about seizing such an opportunity.

She could see opportunity in any situation and her excitement with going to the Ball was for whom she might meet to open future doors for her.

The Mayor's Ball honoree was Mayor **Sirisol Sunya**.

The City Supervisors appointed Mayor Sunya a little

more than a year after the election.

His predecessor became ill with Amyotrophic Lateral Sclerosis and before his predecessor succumbed to his ALS symptoms he was able to support Mayor Sunya in an advisory capacity for several months.

Prior to becoming Mayor, Sirisol was the face of the San Fran's District Attorney's office.

He got his start in law enforcement working for the Sheriff's Department as a Deputy in the County Jail while studying criminal justice in college.

He had connections all over the city and he was known as The People's Mayor.

Sirosol's voyage to America was as a small child with his family from Thailand and he was campaigning to be the first Thai immigrant elected Mayor in the city's history.

He grew up in the San Fran's South of Market District on Shipley Street and in his late twenties he became a part-time law student.

He attended law school at night for many years and he fell in love with a classmate from Zanzibar who graduated and became his professor.

He had never seen a woman more beautiful but her beauty was not her greatest asset.

He believed she was the only person he met in law school who could outwit him and her spellbinding brilliance was why after he graduated he made her his wife.

Zuri Njeri Mwanakombo Sunya became the first African First Lady of San Fran when her husband became Mayor and he was arguably the most powerful man in the city.

Eliza had it in her head the Mayor's Ball was her shot to get next to the Mayor or any of his affiliates first, second or third removed. She knew she would not be the prettiest woman in the room with First Lady Zuri in the same room but she could undeniably be the best dressed with the best hair and the utmost swag.

Kamber applauded when Eliza pulled her dress from her roller bag.

The top half of the dress was a sequin beaded sleeveless wide-strap V-neck.
The bottom half of the dress was flared quadruple layered tulle that stopped mid-thigh and the middle of the dress had an attached three-inch high waist diamond studded belt.
The sequin and beads on her top were bold different color greens dominated by emerald green and the tulle on her bottom was iridescent dominated by a pastel green.

Eliza accessorized the dress with a diamond choker and a diamond bracelet that matched the diamond studded belt perfect. Her earrings were pastel bows made of the same iridescent tulle as the bottom of her dress and they dangled from her earlobes to just past her chin.

Every detail of Eliza's fit was immaculate and Kamber had the vision for her hair. She was dying it red velvet and styling it in one long plait or fishtail braid or twist coming from the crown of her head.

Kamber called Eliza into CoCo's kitchen to start on her hair and she asked what the deal was with her makeup.

Eliza said she could apply her own makeup but she was going to ask Jonny-London to do it who was better at it than her.

Kamber said CoCo was even better at makeup than Jonny-London but Eliza brought up how CoCo did not like to do anyone's makeup but her own.

Kamber made the point it never hurt to ask and Eliza said she did not need to ask CoCo with Jonny-London already on her way but if CoCo came out her bedroom before Jonny-London got there she told Kamber she should be the one to ask her.

Kamber washed Eliza's hair in the kitchen sink. She sat her in a chair to apply the hair color but as she was about to turn on the handheld blow dryer to dry the color quicker she admitted to talking not very nicely about Eliza to Lillian the day before at the hospital.

Eliza asked Kamber what she said and Kamber told her what she said was not as important as her apology. She wanted Eliza to know she knew she was wrong and she was asking to be forgiven for being on some hater shit.

Eliza thanked Kamber for the apology but she said she was not sincerely asking for forgiveness unless she admitted what she said that was so fucked up.

Eliza was not surprised or hurt by Kamber saying her light skin color made her less Black. This was something she had been hearing for as long as she could remember.

She told Kamber she had to hear that shit in school, in lock up and it followed her around the streets but her being a lighter-skinned Black girl did not make her hunger pains go away. She still had a momma who got high and forget to feed her but then Eliza faked a laugh and said that might have flew over Kamber's head because she knew Kamber had never missed a meal.

Eliza's voice dropped low but Kamber could hear her say her Blackness was always being checked for battle scars to prove how Black she was but bitches only cared about the battle scars they could see. If only being lighter-skinned protected her from neglect or erased her memory of being child molested but having lighter skin did none of that.

Kamber asked Eliza was there more she could do to apologize. Did she want her to kiss the ground she walked on or wash her feet with her weave or go and kill herself because if not she needed them to change the subject.

Eliza said granted and she told Kamber she was bored in her relationship with Mali. It had grown stale in their short three months living together and she blamed it on how it began.

Kamber asked Eliza how did she end up with an old ass nigga in the first place and what was the big hush-hush about their relationship.

Eliza claimed Kamber knew the story of how she met Mali and Kamber told her to not try and bullshit a bullshiter. She said it might have been a story she told Lillian but she knew damn fucking well she had never told her.

Eliza shrugged and curled her lip to signify the possibility of Kamber being right. She may not have told her but it was not to try and be secretive because she did not mean to keep a thing from her especially about Mali. She was happy to tell her the Mali story but she could only tell her Mali's recollections pieced together with her own spotty memory and she warned Kamber not to get her hopes up. Their story was certainly nothing majestic.

IV

Mali was out on a Saturday morning jog before sunrise.

This had been his custom for many years and although the mountain temperatures were icy he was focused on the final strides of his sprint and he was sweating.

He was taking the hill at top speed but as he came inches from where he usually stopped to stretch and wait for the sun to rise he spotted a child on the ground. She was wearing a thin floral gown and her arms and legs and face were pale and she was alone.

Mali did not think twice to wrap Eliza in his sweater.

He had no phone to call anyone and the streets were like a ghost town due to the hour so he scooped her in his arms and he carried her almost a mile to his home.

Mali tenderly laid Eliza on his couch and called his housekeeper who was not yet scheduled to arrive for almost two hours.

His housekeeper answered sleepily and Mali apologized for waking her.

He said he urgently needed her to come right away and within the hour his housekeeper was at his home.

When she arrived she saw Eliza's long frail body on the

couch resting soundly and she asked nothing. She hung up her coat, put on an apron and walked to the guestroom.

On the way to the guestroom she turned on the central heat and Mali followed his housekeeper. He explained Eliza being there and the housekeeper told Mali not to worry. She would make Eliza comfortable until he instructed her what to do next and Mali left his housekeeper to do her thing.

Inside the guestroom the housekeeper plugged in an electric blanket. She threw back the covers on the bed to lay the electric blanket on the fitted sheet then she covered the electric blanket with the top sheet to quickly warm the bed.

The housekeeper returned to the living room to look Eliza over for any signs of harm. She appeared fine except for her filthy black-and-blue feet that the housekeeper gently washed with a mixture of warm water, peroxide and soap.

The housekeeper had Mali to carry Eliza to the guest bed and the housekeeper tucked Eliza in snuggly.

They left her to sleep undisturbed and Eliza slept for hours.

Eliza opened her eyes as she was repositioning and there was a tray by her bedside. The tray had a bowl of soup with a spoon and some crackers on a napkin beside a teacup but Eliza closed her eyes and did not eat.

Her eyes opened again when she moved her body to another part of the bed and she seen the bowl, crackers and tea were still there but night was falling outside her window.

The next time Eliza woke she reached for a cracker but it

was gone and she lifted her head to look around.

The door to the room where she slept was open wide.
She could hear the sound of a choir singing and a preacher worshiping through a television or radio and she smelled fresh blueberry pancakes.

Across the hall she saw the gentle giant who whispered his name and promised her safety when he scooped her up from the street and rescued her.
He was seated at a desk wearing headphones over his head that covered his ears and he was facing a computer screen.

Eliza felt her bladder about to burst.
She knew better than to urinate in a bed but she could not hold her bladder and she told her body to get up but her body acted paralyzed and she drifted into sleep peeing a waterfall.

A woman different from who tucked Eliza in sat another tray by her bed and there was an aroma coming from the plate.

Eliza waited for the woman to leave the room before she checked for what she had been given to eat. There were scrambled eggs and fresh berries sprinkled with powder sugar at the center of a fluffy pancake with butter and syrup.

Eliza ate more than half her breakfast lying on her side but she fell back to sleep and the housekeeper who washed her feet and tucked her in bed woke her up.

Eliza's plate of food had spilled in the bed. Her face was

stuck to a piece of pancake and syrup and berries were on her sheet and pillowcase.

The housekeeper helped Eliza out the bed and walked her down the hall to the bathroom.
She asked Eliza what was her name. She asked had she suffered any abuse and if there was someone she could call but Eliza did not say a word.
In Eliza's mind she was responding to everything but in actuality she had said nothing.
As far as the housekeeper knew, Eliza could not speak.

The housekeeper said Eliza had a warm bubble bath waiting for her and on their short walk to the bathroom Eliza did not see or hear anyone else.

The room where Eliza saw Mali at his desk was empty and the other housekeeper who brought her breakfast was not around.

Eliza would have rather no one knew she peed on herself but she was grateful just the one housekeeper would uncover she had soiled the bed.

The housekeeper closed Eliza inside the bathroom and behind the bathroom door hung a hooded white robe zipped closed on a clothes hanger.
On the bathroom sink was a folded white thermal pajama top with the matching bottom beside a pair of black fur lined calf-length house slippers.

Eliza spread her hands over the robe's soft polyester fabric and with her fingertip she followed the robe's design pattern.

Out of bunch of smiling gold-filled black-lined honey bears and honey pots, Eliza's fingertip traced one of the honey bears licking their red tongue at a mini honey dipper dripping with honey.

The two articles of clothes had the same honey bear pattern as the robe and everything had price tags.

Eliza soaked in her bath until the watered cooled which was not that long because the water was not that hot.

She knew the housekeeper would be a while tending to her pissy sheets and she toweled off considering should she stay or should she go.

She finished dressing in her new pajamas and slippers and she decided to leave without so much as a thank you, goodbye or well wishes.

Eliza left Mali's front door wide open.

She walked two miles in her new slippers to get home and nobody at home asked where she had been.

Her new pajamas and slippers did not get noticed and she wore the same thing for days.

She went to school wearing the pajamas with the robe and the slippers and the child psychologist who pulled her from class said it was fine to wear her PJ's if they made her feel safe.

The psychologist asked did she get the clothing from someone who made her feel safe and Eliza said yes.

The psychologist asked if that someone had a name and Eliza said Snow Cake was their name.

The psychologist wanted to know how long did Eliza think Snow Cake would want her to wear their gift but Eliza said what she had on made her feel like it was Christmas on her birthday and she did think Snow Cake would want her to take off her presents.

V

Eliza's rescue by Mali ignited her truancy from school.

She was in the seventh grade at a middle school located in The Marina District and one day at passing period she skipped school from a side door. She left the building mid-day when the street artists, food vendors and other pop up merchants took over the The Marina.

She blended with the waves of tourists and locals traversing the waterfront looking to buy things like paintings, lobster and crab chowder in bread bowls, coffee beans and fruit, handmade jewelry and candles, flowers and plants, cats and pups needing a home and vintage clothing and books.

Eliza was always alone when she bucked from the school grounds. She knew no one would get why she spent her days and hours returning to Mali's street to stalk his building.

She learned from her stalking he was a driver for a parcel delivery service and he came home daily in his company truck and uniform to have lunch.

She watched him on different days for weeks and finally she got up the nerve to say something to him on his way in the house for lunch.

He found it odd Eliza was outside his house saying she was in the neighborhood but against his better judgment he invited her inside to join him for his afternoon meal and Eliza impulsively accepted.

She walked in his home behind him but she wanted to

unaccept his lunch offer seeing that the housekeeper who had to clean her piss-berry-syrup-stained sheets was in the kitchen.

Eliza was so embarrassed she ate her chicken enchiladas in silence and she did not answer more than one question using her words.

She said her name was Lizzy but when asked how old she was she shrugged.

When asked where she was from she shrugged.

When asked was she in any danger she shook her head no and when she was done with lunch she avoided stalking Mali for two weeks.

Over the next few years Eliza hung out with Mali for a couple dozen lunchtime popups but her first dozen and a half popups were in the first few months.

Her visits were sporadic but the irregularity kept Mali looking forward to them. He was stirred by Eliza's youthful enthusiasm and joys. They were encased in the simplest of things like buying advance tickets for a new movie coming out or spending Saturday mornings practicing for a performance in a parade months away or going to the beach county fair all day everyday during the weeklong citywide Juneteenth cultural celebration.

Eliza's greenness worked as magnetic energy with Mali and his show of appreciation for their encounters was his re-gifting her gifts he received from his rich customers who liked to share their travels and interest with him.

Whenever he was given a gift card or was something newly invented, expensive or sparkly and appropriate for a young girl he passed it on to Eliza but unbeknownst to him

Eliza was a liar.

She was not in some special private school for artists who were given a three-hour lunch and reflection period to go off campus and be inspired by nouns.

For the first few months Eliza got away with lunchtime at Mali's until finally she was noticed sneaking off school grounds and was arrested by a school police officer.

The judge released Eliza with court-mandated conditions she did not meet and she ended up locked up in juvenile hall for months.

Eliza was released but she cut school again and did something the judge said not to do and a status offense got her locked back up for her second time.

Eliza's third arrest included fighting, her fourth arrest included theft and her fifth arrest was for the possession of her mom's narcotic painkillers at school.

At Eliza's juvenile court hearing for her fifth release she swore to the courtroom her eighteenth birthday that had just passed would be her last birthday in a cage.

The judge wanted to know the cause for Eliza's change in attitude and choice of terminology and Eliza said she had been attending her court-mandated educational programming. It was facilitated by a community organization that came in three times per week and had her entire juvenile pod read and interpret a musical play called The Melody of Black Consciousness.

The play was about systems of oppression and slavery and the criminalizing of youth.

It made her conscious about her ancestors and elders who died so she would not have to wear chains. She now and forever had a responsibility to them and to the future of Black people to only sing the chorus of *freedom.*

VI

Mali and Eliza knew each other for six years but there was not much in common between them. She was growing up twenty-first century and had never heard of most of the music, movies or events that shaped his world.

Mali had no way to get into contact with Eliza and he never tried.

He knew she was too young and that a man more than half her age had no business allowing a relationship to take shape.

He thought of her all of the time wondering was she safe and eating regularly, was she doing her homework, being prepared for college or a trade, would she join the military or remain a civilian and so on and so on but he kept his cares buried to fight any feelings of attraction.

Eliza was not interested in fighting her feelings.

Before she left child prison she had made up her mind that Mali's kingdom would be her first stop and not during his lunch hour.

She came to see him late enough on a Saturday night for his hired help to have gone home and for him to be alone.

Eliza's cellblock rehearsals of what to say when Mali answered his door made what came from her mouth sound natural.

She stood at his doorway in no jacket wearing a short,

low cut dress with an open back and she told him about the morning he found her.

She said she had escaped a horrendous and violent night and she just wanted to curl up and die but he brought her into his home and brought her back to life. What he did for her made her feel something she only felt around him and why she showed up for his lunch hour the way she did was to feel what only he could make her feel.

Eliza touched her hand to where Mali's heart was beating beneath his chest.

She told him now that she was no longer a little girl it was up to her where she wanted to be and with him was where she wanted to be.

She had his attention in a way she had not before and Mali stepped back to further open the door clearing the way for her to come in. He said he was just about to have dinner and she was in time to join him.

Halfway through dinner Eliza uncorked an open bottle of red wine on the table and she took a swig.

She poured some of the wine into the wine glass already sitting in front of Mali and he thanked her for pouring him a drink.

He lifted his glass and he clinked it with the wine bottle in her hand then he took him a sip.

Eliza took her another swig and she complimented his wine being tasty. She said it was not awful or tart like what she had before which she said was probably some cheap shit and Mali commented that the red wines he purchased were usually of the pricier tastier of brands.

Eliza chugged her fill of Mali's tasty expensive wine from the bottle while he indulged from the refills she kept pouring in his glass.

They finished the bottle and Mali showed Eliza how to use the corkscrew to open another and for the first time they held a conversation that went on for hours.

She asked him why he ran every Saturday morning and he said to stay fit to deliver packages. She asked where in San Fran did he deliver packages and he said on the hills of Laurel Heights, Presidio Heights and Pacific Heights districts. She asked how long had he been a delivery guy and it had been twenty years for the same company. He said it had taken that long to become a vested employee and vested meant his benefits included shares of the company stock and his annual compensation was at a six-figure pay he was satisfied with.

Eliza told him to keep talking but she said and was walking to the living room couch from the dinner table. She asked him about children and he followed her to the couch saying he was old fashioned when it came to family. He told her he went to church on Sunday but he was no saint and he loved to have a good fuck but he wanted to wait for marriage to have children.

Eliza's next question was why and she asked why was he unattached living alone in a fat ass Diamond Heights condo but he said his dog and his housekeeper's were good company.

Eliza looked around then asked where was there a dog and Mali said the dog rotated between the two housekeepers.

Eliza laughed extra hard saying that dog was the house-keeper's dog then and Mali was laughing too but he said he had yet to meet the lady for him and being single was better than being tied to the wrong mate.

Eliza continued listening and kept Mali's wine glass full but she took fewer and fewer swigs from their second bottle.

Mali got to rambling about high school where according to him he was an icon and a beast on the football field.
He blamed his parents for him failing to have a longer football career and he said his parent's never cared to understand him.

Eliza asked where his parents were and he said they had long retired overseas.

Mali lifted his wine glass to circle the glass slow and wide around the top of his head for Eliza to look at the surroundings he said his parents left behind with him in it.

He brought his wine glass to his lap and paused before he said his parents forced him to give up on his dreams and then they deserted him.

Eliza was warm and fuzzy inside from the wine but she was catching the unspoken truths Mali's ramble had disallowed.
He was the former high school football star who never got over he did not go pro and would never play pro football but he refused to own that shortcoming for himself.
He was the spoiled only child from two hardworking parents that forced him to grow up and who by the time he was twenty-three had left him their property and the help.

The same two housekeepers that helped his parents raise him from the time he was a preteen was his housekeeping staff six days per week.

Their jobs were to shop for his household, cook every meal, clean daily, handle the laundry and dry cleaning, feed, walk and keep the dog, empty the trash, take care of any household bills and be the conduits between Mali and his parents.

Mali's parents did not want to talk often they just expected to see him once every year.

They faulted him for being lazy and mediocre but they said saying less meant he could not accuse them of only ever putting him down since they were not willing to mask their disdain for his life choices.

Mali's housekeeper's ceremoniously booked his travel to be in the presence of his parents by the third Sunday of January and for fifteen years since the year after his parents left the states the housekeeper's handled his itinerary.

The location of their family vacation often changed but the date never changed and how long Mali stayed each trip depended upon how well he got along with his parents.

Eliza asked Mali where did he and his parents last vacation and it was at a two-story village cliff house on Aegean Island in Santorini Greece.

They had the place for fourteen days but the topic that ran Mali off on day eight was the same topic that ran him off early most often.

They were badgering him about settling down and giving them grandchildren.

The secondary topic they liked to badger him about was going to business school at night.

They were against him being the delivery guy his entire adult life but they wanted to invest in his training and education so he could manage a business or run his own parcel service.

Mali started drifting to sleep talking about his parents but Eliza leaned into him and allowed a little wine from her mouth to pour down his lips and chin.

She lapped the wine from his skin as she straddled him and she took control with no theatrics. They were slow grinding and wet kissing then she stood up and danced to no music.

She stripped naked while Mali fondled his Johnson and watched her perform and when she climbed back in his lap he fucked her and fucked her until the morning sunrise illuminated their lovemaking touching every inch of his living room.

Mali had a surge of glee after they finished having sex.

He told Eliza his weakness was betting on horses and Sunday's were his day at the races.

He said later that day the racetrack was where he had to be to see his undefeated thoroughbred Thundercat. He had been following her career and felt connected to her from the moment she arrived in California. He said each night since reading such a perfect beauty had come to town he closed his eyes and Thundercat was in his sleep neighing at him in every dream.

Eliza cackled at Mali's horse obsession and she told him he sounded like one crazy nigga.

He teasingly agreed there might be truth in him being on some crazy nigga shit but Eliza said Thundercat sounded like a fellow bad bitch she needed to meet.

Mali got Eliza's meaning after she asked if he wanted her to join him at the racetrack and he said if she wanted to come she could.

VII

They were en route to the city of Berkeley to see Black Thunder and Eliza sidetracked Mali with getting off the freeway in the Emeryville shopping area.

She voiced her need for daywear and clean lingerie to change out of what she had on the night before but she ended up with enough gear to stay with Mali the rest of the week.

Mali said his wallet had no complaints about her buys. Her stuff was reasonably priced and he was feeling her sticking around a few more days but he did complain about her making them late to the racetrack.

By the time they found parking to enter the gated racetrack entrance the races had started and the afternoon sun was overhead in a position that had the only available seats on fire.

Mali was scowling having to cross the crowd and pass his regular seating area but Eliza was turning the head of every man, women and child.

The scowl left his face and he hooked Eliza on his arm soaking up every bit of every stare feeling like the one again but he kept checking Eliza out too figuring it was her clothes.

She was dressed in distressed denim blue mini shorts and a white half top shirt with rainbow suspenders.

The suspenders were lined with gold bells down the front and Mali guessed it was the jingle in her walk or the clickety-clack of her bright yellow two-inch-heel sandals but as he watched her like the others were watching her he saw it was not her clothes. What was bringing him the type of ogling he had not had in two decades was how confidently Eliza's five-foot-eight-inch perfect-ten body was slaying the outfit.

Mali brought Eliza back to his home after the racetrack and he let her stay the week but at the end of the week he did not ask her to leave.

⸻ «(◦)» ⸻

Eliza told Kamber that in less than thirty days she went from living in a cold locked cell as a so-called juvenile delinquent to driving a man's corvette and having not one but two maids at her beck and call.

Kamber said she had never heard nothing like her and Mali's story and she did not know what Eliza considered majestic but their duet sounded pretty fucking majestic to her.

Eliza said Mali was a good man, great actually but he was old news and she hoped to meet someone better at the Mayor's Ball.

Kamber started laughing like Eliza told a joke.

Eliza asked what was so damn funny and Kamber laughed saying her nigga Mali and again she said her nigga Mali and again one more time she said her nigga Mali but she could not stop laughing to finish the sentence.

Finally she said her nigga Mali was old news but old literally like ancient and because Kamber's laugh was infectious she forced a small snicker out of Eliza but Eliza defended her man and said yes he was older but she would not call him ancient.

Kamber was more than half way through Eliza's hair when CoCo entered the living room and with her voice pointlessly amplified she said good evening how you hoe's doing.

Eliza's hair had been dyed to match the weave hair. It had been blow-dried and Kamber had sewn the weave hair into Eliza's hair giving it more length and volume.

The ponytail had been secured at Eliza's crown and Kamber was about to fishtail the ponytail to hang from the right side.

Eliza and Kamber's four eyes landed on CoCo. Her mane was looking a hot mess and their eyes went down to her robe. It was tied at her waist and stretched to her calves but it looked painted on her naked body and with every move the fabric accentuated her hip and butt dimples and with each step her tits giggled.

CoCo took a seat next to them smiling and with minty fresh breath she asked what the fuck were they staring at.

Kamber asked why did she feel the need to hide her dick breath from them and Eliza said for her to cough up the details.

CoCo asked did they need details while the nigga was

still in her bed and Kamber talked low telling CoCo to use her inside voice like her and only the three of them and God would hear.

CoCo said they knew the man in the bedroom and there was nothing to tell she just needed to release some stress after wasting time with Fuckboy.

Eliza was surprised it was not Fuckboy and she could not guess who else it might be.

Kamber asked why was Coco making them play the guessing game instead of saying who the fuck had dicked her down but CoCo said he was a no good person and it was embarrassing to say his name. She wished she had not given him any pussy but she did and her guilt was enough without them knowing who he was. She asked them both to forget about it because if she told them they would have something to say and she already knew what she did was wrong.

Eliza asked if CoCo needed a hug and Kamber interrupted and said no she did not need a hug. She needed a man who did not give her guilt-dick.

CoCo told Kamber that was why she was not telling her what nigga was in her bedroom.

Kamber got to rolling her neck saying she did not want to know who CoCo's guilty dick ass nigga was anyway but then she jumped out of her skin startled by the sudden ring of the house phone.
Her impulse was comical and CoCo laughed saying it was just Jonny-London at the door.

CoCo handed Eliza the card box she pulled from beneath her bed and she walked to the house phone to buzz Jonny-London into the entry gate.

Eliza opened the card box to find credit card vouchers inside where CoCo had hand written full name, security code, date of birth, address and phone number on the voucher already pre-printed with the credit card number and expiration date.

Eliza counted the vouchers and she closed them inside the card box. When CoCo came back to the couch Eliza returned the box to her and told her Mali was picking her up to go straight to the Mayor's Ball. She would have to come for the vouchers in a couple of days with the money and CoCo was square with that. She said she just wanted Eliza to count the vouchers like she just did to know how much dough she would need to bring.

Chapter 21

SORORITY BITCHES COULD WAIT

Jonny-London came inside CoCo's place around eight o'clock at night with a blunt already rolled.

She knew her best friends would be ready to smoke but before she fired up she disclosed she had only come to bring them their weed.

She said Lillian delivering Royal the night before was everything and a bag of chips but it was unexpected and she had shit to do and could not stay.

Jonny-London sparked the weed but she did not take a seat.

She passed the weed to Eliza who hit it and said she appreciated her coming in firing up.

Eliza passed the blunt to CoCo and CoCo hit it twice before she passed it to Kamber and bolted to the kitchen.

She said the occasion called for her to mix everyone a whisky ginger with a twist.

Jonny-London started divvying weed to Eliza and Kamber based on who spent what.

Kamber stopped hitting the weed to look at her sack. She sniffed it and said it was loud and she agreed with Eliza who said their sacks were fat.
As Kamber passed the blunt back to Jonny-London she told her stop walking around like the pusherman and she asked why had she not sat the fuck down somewhere.

Jonny-London stayed standing with her coat and scarf on and she said she already told them she could not stay.

Kamber asked was it because she had to go stomping the yard and Jonny-London told Kamber she could call it what she wanted.

Jonny-London walked over to the kitchen to pass the weed to CoCo and CoCo slid her the first drink she mixed. She told her she could take her jacket off to have a toast with her best friends and she said her *sorority bitches could wait.*

CoCo walked three drinks over to the living room and Kamber and Eliza grabbed their cocktails from her hand.
She told everyone to lift their glass for a toast and Kamber asked why were they toasting.

CoCo said they were toasting because she felt like it but then she thought of Lillian. She said they could not toast without her and she had Eliza to call Lillian and get her face up on the phone screen.

Lillian answered the video-call with her face too close to the camera and Eliza could see Lillian's lips and teeth talking a mile a minute thanking her for calling.

She said Eliza must have been reading her mind to know the hospital had her depressed and in need of contact from the outside world to keep her sanity.

Eliza waited for Lillian to take a breath to tell her to back her face away from the camera and rebuke the depression demon in the name of Jesus. She said Lillian knew the scripture God so loved the world he gave his only begotten son and whosoever believeth in Him, Eliza paused and said again whosoever believeth in Him shall what she asked Lillian.

Lillian angled her phone for a view of her face that included the top of Royal's head on her chest and she said shall not perish and Eliza asked not only shall they not perish they will have what and Lillian said everlasting life and Eliza repeated they shall not perish but have everlasting life.

Lillian told Eliza fuck depression and she said her gangster ass quoting the bible had got her all the way together and Kamber shouted at the phone asking Lillian did she think she would she be discharged after the weekend.

Eliza pointed her phone at Kamber's face and Lillian said hi to Kamber and that she likely would be leaving Monday but it felt hella far away. She made a request for Kamber to pray on that with Eliza and pray she not get cabin fever and jump from the hospital window before Monday morning.

Eliza circled her phone around the room for Lillian to see their whole squadron there and she told her they called for a toast.

Lillian complained she did not have any drank for a toast and CoCo yelled for her to grab some damn water.

Lillian took a few minutes to put Royal down. She needed both hands to hold her phone and her water cup.

She got back on the phone and asked what were they toasting for and Kamber yelled out they were toasting because their highness CoCo felt like it.

CoCo said in that case it was only right they did what her highness said and she had everyone to again lift their glass.

She suggested they each contribute saying something thoughtful and not just toast for the sake of toasting.

CoCo went first. She toasted to their sisterhood and said being their bestie and sister had been a highlight of her life and would be for infinite.

She put her fist to her chest to show her small infinite tattoo on the outside of her wrist and everybody including Lillian robotically did the same gesture showing they had the same tattoo.

Jonny-London toasted to their new edition to the sisterhood. She said their firstborn Royal Dior Hayes had turned their fabulous five into a super six and they all called out, ayeeeee.

Lillian chimed in from the phone. She said she was toasting to her daughter too and she thanked God for her daughter being blessed with four aunties to help raise her.

Eliza said her toast was to their sisterhood same as CoCo and to her baby cousin same as Jonny-London and Lillian. She would just add to it by asking God to keep Royal from the types of struggles they had endured for most of their young lives.

Kamber cleared her throat loudly to get their attention and to tell them they were still living their young lives. She said her toast was to Royal for sure and their squad too but also to them as individuals and she asked for God to keep a hedge of protection over each of them.

Lillian tapped her water cup to the phone while the four in CoCo's living room clinked their glasses together and in roll off fashion they responded different one after the other with amen, word, hear here, for real for real and cheers.

I

Jonny-London got coerced into doing Eliza's makeup for the Mayor's Ball but after Eliza left she had a second drink and a third blunt with CoCo and Kamber.

She was two hours late for a sorority obligation with the other women aspiring to pledge the same sorority as her.

She came speed walking into the ground level garage area of the house they were using for their Pledge Headquarters. She was rubbing both shoulders to knock the outside chill off but she was smiling in good spirits and she gaudily apologized for her tardiness as if being late was the thing to be.

Her being giggly made it obvious she was high and tipsy and she expected to hear the other aspiring pledgees complain that she was always late but she did not expect a sorority member to be paying them a surprise visit.

The sorority member yelled over Jonny-London's gaudy entrance and said that clearly heifers were not ready and had come there to waste the sorority's precious time.

The sorority member said she was sent to check on their studying and to see if they were prepared for their pledge line interview scheduled on Monday afternoon.

She asked for aspiring pledgee number five to tell her what the fuck was her ass so damn dandy about and it took more than several seconds for Jonny-London to realize the sorority member was speaking to her. She was the number five but she was stuck and did not know how to respond to the sorority member's question.

She and the other aspiring pledgees received their pledge numbers a couple nights before but they were told not to use their numbers until after their pledge line interview.

The sorority member by now was screaming in Jonny-London's face.

She asked was she a fucking imbecile or something worse and aspiring pledgee number three said nothing was wrong with aspiring pledgee number five they were taking the process very seriously and they found nothing dandy.

The sorority member told aspiring pledgee number three to shut the fuck up. She had not granted her permission to speak and without permission to speak she should only speak when she was spoken to.

The sorority member walked away from Jonny-London towards aspiring pledgee number three to ask if aspiring pledgee number three understood how to either ask for permission or to not speak unless spoken to.

Aspiring pledgee number three shook her head yes to say she understood.

The sorority member raised her index finger and pressed the tip of her index finger into the dead center of aspiring pledgee number three's forehead. She asked was shaking her head the proper way to respond to a question and aspiring pledgee number three stumbled backwards from the amount of pressure the sorority member used to poke her head back with a finger push.

The garage was full with stuff surrounding them everywhere and Jonny-London saw a fraternity member appear out of the thin air from a spot near a broken washer blocked by an old box-spring.

He stepped up behind aspiring pledgee number one and whispered something into her ear and aspiring pledgee number one blurted out affirmative. She then explained affirmative was the proper way to respond yes to a question.

The sorority member backed away from aspiring pledgee number three and told aspiring pledgee number one her answer was good.

The fraternity member came forward from the shadows and asked did they feel ready for Monday.

Aspiring pledgee number two looked in both directions to see if anyone else was going to answer before she said, affirmative.

The fraternity member asked why if they all knew the answer did they not say it together as one and he pompously demanded they not hesitate again.

The sorority member asked the aspiring pledgees if they

had their interview outfit together and in unison they all said, affirmative.

She nodded pleasingly and said she was looking forward to seeing what they had selected as their unity piece for the interview.

Aspiring pledgee number two offered to show the unity piece right then but the sorority member said no. Their unity piece was sacred and it was a secret to be kept only amongst sisters. She said something they had better keep in mind if they knew what was best for them was that their fraternity brother's did not need to see or know everything.

The fraternity member told them they sounded good when they said affirmative in unison and he asked were they going to fuck up reciting the Omicron Creed.

In unison the aspiring pledgees said no and the fraternity member said negative. He was correcting them by saying the proper response back to them and he asked if they got that and all five in unison said, affirmative.

The sorority member asked them to recite all sixteen lines of the Creed and she barked the command go.

Jonny-London stomped her left foot and she called out Omicron Creed.

Her foot stomp signaled them to begin and in unison they recited the words slowly:

The decision is ours to pursue sorority membership.
No matter the reason we are brought together by choice.
Together we have chosen the Omicron Zeta Omicron family.

It is only together we will take our first step into the Black Greek world.

It is in our pursuit we will be tested. It is in our humility we will be brave.

We trust the process. Our paths have been paved.

By the first and the only Black Greek Family we are bonded.

We pledge to follow our three Founding Mothers and two Founding Fathers.

By the bonds of Sisterhood and Brotherhood we are made.

We stand on the principals the Founding Five believed.

In our hearts these principals are engraved.

We stand for Scholarship. We stand for Liberation. We stand for Humanity.

These are the principals we are boldly proud to uphold.

Omicron Zeta sorority, she is the greatest sorority.

Zeta Omicron fraternity, he is the greatest fraternity.

The Omicron Zeta Omicron family is forever ours by choice.

The fraternity member gave them kudos for reciting the Omicron Creed with precision and enthusiasm and he told them to get out their notebooks to take down a few notes.

They wrote down the on campus meeting location for their pledge line interview and were told to bring two forms of identification with the third and final increment of their payment towards organizational initiation dues.

They were told if their interview went well they would not be going home Monday night. They would participate in an overnight orientation and needed to bring an overnight bag with whatever in it was necessary for them to go to class or work Tuesday morning.

Their final notebook entry was a reminder of The Stone and Pearl Feast.

They were already told should they be selected for initiation they would have to host a feast but the fraternity member told them what being hostesses involved.

The sorority member said she was not nice enough to give out information too early for them to have. Their feast planning time was supposed to be two days to find a dinner location, invite every active undergrad member of the sorority and fraternity and come up with a three-course meal and beverage.

Their countdown to start planning was after their pledge line interview and she called them lucky muthafuckas. Her frat brother feeling generous gave them a two-day advantage but she warned them not to be over the top because the feast was not about them spending an enormous amount of money.

The fraternity member reminded them the pledge process was an expensive one and they would need to hold onto their funds for the unexpected.

The sorority member snapped her fingers three times in Z formation and the five aspiring pledgees stood at attention. Their hands were at their sides, their lower backs were arched and their chests were stuck out.

The sorority member said her and the fraternity member were leaving and she summoned Gone With The Wind to get the door.

Aspiring pledgee number four rushed to unlock and open the side door of the garage and the fraternity member started laughing.

He asked the sorority member if aspiring pledgee number four was the OG she told him about and the sorority member said yes.

Aspiring pledgee number four was more than a decade older than the other four aspiring pledgees on her pledge line and she came to San Fran University through a second chance program for people with a criminal record.

She had to take online classes while in jail to demonstrate her behavior and grades were up to par with the jail's donor sponsored life enrichment program.

For her completing the program she was granted an early release with student housing, work-study and a full academic scholarship to finish her education.

The fraternity member was still dying laughing at the name Gone With The Wind.

The sorority member said the aspiring pledgees had earned their names from a visiting alumnus of their chapter who was in town for a night on business and came to meet them.

The fraternity member asked to hear the names of the other four aspiring pledgees and aspiring pledgee number one went first. She told him her name was Muppet Baby.

Aspiring pledgee number two had to wait for the fraternity member to stop laughing so loud before she could tell him her name was Plastic Surgery.

The fraternity member fell down onto a worn-out couch at the name Plastic Surgery and with tears coming from his eyes he yelled stop he could not take anymore.

The Sorority member told him the other two names were not as funny.

She kicked aspiring pledgee number three in the shin and she yelled at her to keep going and not be so easily distracted.

Aspiring pledgee number three said her name was Pet Cemetery and Jonny-London said her name was Hamburger.

The fraternity member was bent over in laughter. He had to lean on the sorority member to make his way through the side door but once they finally left pledge headquarters Muppet Baby lit into Hamburger for always being late and coming to headquarters high off weed.

Plastic Surgery agreed with Muppet Baby and asked was Hamburger trying to ruin everything for everybody continuing to act like the pledge process was a joke.

Jonny-London's defense was that the process was not a joke but it was just that, a process. Not real life. They were being tested on could they commit to the sorority no matter the situation or circumstance and she told Muppet Baby and Plastic Surgery they needed to loosen the hell up. They were annoying enough without complaining.

Muppet Baby looked at Plastic Surgery and said wait. She asked did the hungry-hippo-high-bitch just call her annoying.

Muppet Baby turned to Jonny-London to ask who the fuck was the Hamburger calling annoying when it was her big ass being hella lazy that always made them look bad.

Muppet Baby did not let Jonny-London respond because she immediately asked did she actually come to pledge or was her ghetto ass trying to skate in on their backs and take credit for their hard work.

Jonny-London turned to Gone With The Wind to ask why did ugly bitches always want to question some shit and Plastic Surgery took offense. She asked why did fat bitches always want to eat some shit and that comment made Pet Cemetery take offense.

Pet Cemetery asked Plastic Surgery who the fuck did she have the nerve to call a damn thing when she made the bitch Hatchet Face from Crybaby look good.

Jonny-London calmly said she could take being fat and ghetto and anytime she wanted to do something about being fat and ghetto she could anytime she wanted but they were screwed.

She said Muppet Baby could not diet away her terrible figure and Plastic Surgery was stuck with dragon breath from being a headbobba.

Gone With The Wind got between Jonny-London and Muppet Baby when Jonny-London said Muppet Baby wearing layers of clothes did not hide her bad body nor did her bad weave hide them bald edges on her scalp.

Pet Cemetery was already between Jonny-London and Plastic Surgery when Jonny-London said unfortunately no clothes could cover botched lip injections but she thanked the heavens for shirts because with them Plastic Surgery could cover up her terrible fake titties.

Gone With The Wind told the four of them they were wrong to disrespect one another.

She said if they did not let go of the tension and start getting along they would not get past the interview Monday and she reminded them the process was about bonding as pledge line sisters, becoming one line and having sisterhood.

Gone With The Wind explained that as far as she was concerned they did not have to love each other or even half like each other. They just needed to start acting like it before she beat everybody ass for ruining her one chance at sorority life.

Jonny-London said she was not tripping off none of the hater shit Muppet Baby and Plastic Surgery were talking about.

She grabbed her purse and invited Pet Cemetery and Gone With The Wind to the backyard for a smoke break before they returned to their study session.

II

The three of them went outside in the freezing night air and were shivering while Jonny-London searched her purse to find her partially smoked blunt.

Jonny-London's cellphone was illuminated and she pulled it out her purse with the lighter and the blunt. She passed the weed and the lighter to Pet Cemetery and told her to fire up she needed to check her cell phone.

Eliza had sent her a group text message.

Jonny-London opened the text to find a bunch more

messages all reacting to a picture of Eliza hugged up with a man. The subject of the text message was JACKPOT and Kamber had made the first comment in the group. She said the man Eliza was hugging was too fine for Eliza and he was damn near the finest man she had ever seen.

Lillian's message to the group asked who the man was with a line of exclamation marks.

CoCo's message said he looked too old to be hugging up on Eliza and she asked where was Mali.

From Jonny-London's reaction to her phone, Gone With The Wind and Pet Cemetery asked what she was oohing and awing over and Jonny-London could not help but show them the picture on her phone.
They both agreed the man in the picture was worth the oohing and awing over and Pet Cemetery said his girlfriend in the picture was very pretty.

Jonny-London paused typing her message to the group to correct Pet Cemetery and say the girl in the picture was her bestfriend not the dude's girlfriend then she finished typing her message. It said the fine ass man in the picture did not look older than Mali old ass and she put a row of question marks after asking was Mali not like forty or fifty.

Gone With The Wind told Jonny-London she went to high school with the man in the picture. He was a basketball star back in her day and he was known by an unusual name she could not think of.

Jonny-London asked Gone With The Wind and Pet Cemetery what they thought he was mixed with. She could see he was Black but from his complexion and the shape of his eyes and that hair texture Black was not all.

Pet Cemetery stared at the picture and could not tell what he was mixed with. She said he had that racially ambiguous thing going on but whatever he was made of made him breathtakingly beautiful.

Gone With The Wind said possibly he was mixed with Taiwanese. She said not to quote her on it but a million years ago she either read something or heard somewhere he might be related somehow to the their Mayor.

Chapter 22

THE NEXT NIGGA

Eliza Bethany Kerry walked into the Mayor's Ball hand in hand with Mali.

The cameras were flashing and everyone wanted a picture of Eliza with her bright red braided hair, sexy dress and faux snakeskin shoes.

She heard the people saying wow and calling her a green goddess and she was sopping up those first fifteen minutes of fame.

The different media outlets complimented Mali on Eliza's beauty and asked for his connection to the Mayor but after he proudly said he was the Mayor's deliveryman, the media person snapped his or her photo, thanked him for his time and turned away without another word and some did not bother to thank him or snap a photo.

Eliza tried to get Mali to move slower through the crowd to allow the onlookers time to take in all her beauty but he went on a mission to the open bar.

Eliza stood at the bar with Mali only to tell him what to

order her and she left. The reason she gave for leaving was to go to the ladies room but in truth she had come to stunt on hoes and mack on moneymakers and the bar was too far off to the side of where everyone mainly gathered.

On Eliza's way to the bathroom she laid eyes on a man she asked about to a cocktail waitress who apologetically bumped her in passing.

The cocktail waitress told her the man's name was **Sur Liberty Morgan**.

Eliza learned from a media person in the bathroom that Sur was a Special Assistant to Mayor Sunya.

The man serving the appetizer cheese toast bites said he agreed with Eliza, Sur and Mayor Sunya did favor in facial features and build but he believed there to be no known relationship outside of a working one.

The server with the Swedish meatballs said there were rumors about Sur and Mayor Sunya having possible blood ties but there was nothing that had ever been proven.

Eliza followed Sur around about twenty-minutes inquiring about him to everyone who crossed her path but eventually she made eye contact and gave him a smile.

Sur smiled back with his eyes and he looked Eliza from head to toe. He clearly liked what he was seeing until his line of sight was obstructed by Mali and his horrible timing.

Mali kissed Eliza's cheek in handing her drink to her and where he came and stood directly blocked her from Sur.

Eliza knew Mali probably saw Sur checking her out and was purposely cockblocking.

She asked Mali to get her a drink to keep him at the bar waiting for her to return and he was killing her action by coming to find her.

Her intention was to stroll the party alone to see what other fish she might find in the sea.

Eliza took a sip of her drink and frowned.

She told Mali her drink was hella gross and she called him a foul ass nigga for how bad it tasted.

Mali told her she was overreacting and Eliza asked why did he not taste the shit before even thinking it was okay to hand it to her or did he taste it but bring it to her to be funny.

Mali said she could stop with the coming at him crazy. He was drinking his Manhattan so no he did not taste her punk ass Lemon Drop. He said her shit would not have tasted right to him anyway and he accused Eliza of doing too much to get attention from *the next nigga.*

Eliza said what if she was trying to get attention from the next nigga her drink was still gross and that was his fucking problem and was he going to fix the problem or not.

Mali said hell to the not. She needed to go and tell the next nigga to get her a better drink and he snatched Eliza's drink from her hand. He gulped it down and sat her empty glass on the table in front of her and walked off sipping his Manhattan.

Eliza pulled her mirror from her purse and checked her face.

Her makeup still looked flawless. Her hair was still perfectly in place and she had marvelously distanced herself from Mali. Her night officially belonged to her.

Eliza put a mint in her mouth touched up her lips with her lipstick and walked over to Sur.
He had a handful of guests around him and she stood close enough for him to see she was waiting for his attention.
She stood off from the line a bit to not seem obvious but her patience was a clear signal she wanted more than thirty seconds with him for a smile, handshake and a photo.

When Eliza stepped to Sur he acknowledged her like he did the other party guests who stepped to him before her but after the smile, handshake and photo she asked to buy him a drink.

Sur said yes to the drink but he asked Eliza did she know the drinks were free and he chuckled at Eliza saying yes of course she knew.

Sur trailed her to the bar and she was carrying her phone in one hand. She got ready to put her phone away but before she dropped the phone in her purse she texted the photo of her with him to CoCo, Kamber, Jonny-London and Lillian.

I

Eliza and Sur got their drinks then they moseyed their way to a corner to occupy an oversized plush loveseat in front of a beautiful window view of the Bay.

Eliza listened to Sur's story growing up in San Fran's foster care system and she could tell he had told the story a gazillion times.

Every word was enunciated completely and synchronized to his easy tone and poignant gestures.

Sur kept leaning close enough for their shoulders to touch and Eliza became putty under the spell of his sweet cologne. She hung on his every word but she questioned his truth after he said he was raised in Potrero Hill and spent the early part of his childhood in the Swamp.

Eliza cut him off and shared she was born and raised in the same low-income housing as him. She said before her mom moved to her own housing project in the Valencia Gardens she had Eliza living in Potrero Hill for a couple of years after they left in the Swamp.

Eliza was about to keep going on to say she only knew the Swamp to produce people like her momma not polished professionals like him but that would have been too much information and she told him to please continue about himself she would not interrupt again.

Sur said listening to her beautiful voice was in no way an interruption but he was quick to get back to talking about himself being orphaned by a mother who died in childbirth and how Mayor Sunya rescued him.

In his eyes he owed his life to the Mayor and his wife. They found him a stable foster family and saw to his upbringing and when he was old enough to be baptized they became his Godparents.

Sur said his appointment to the Mayor's cabinet was how he did not take for granted the love he had been given by his foster family and his God family. His way to pay it forward was by being the head of the Office on Urban Community Affairs and it meant more than a job to him.

Sur told Eliza he declined the Mayor's Ball invitations in the past but this was the first year they were naming a Guardian of the City and he had been nominated.

He explained he was the behind the scenes person in the Mayor's office. Contrary to what she might have extrapolated from the attention she had observed him getting most of the people she saw him talking to and shaking hands with were part of the City's Nominating Council. He said no one actually knew what he did for the Mayor's office and anyone who knew him from his high school days called him what was on the back of his basketball jersey.

He began telling Eliza why his jersey read Liberty but Eliza was only half listening.

Her view had taken her thoughts to other places. There was the calm dark Bay waters and San Fran's colorful buildings and bright billboards and above it all was a glowing full moon.

She was not following Sur's reasoning of the school board having his middle and last name juxtaposed in their system and she was not ready for him to ask her a question but she heard his last two words and she asked what about her story.

Sur repeated himself and asked Eliza again what was her story and as she searched her mind for where to start she filled the quietness with movements.

She touched her hair, straightened her posture and she leaned away from Sur to press one elbow into the armrest. She clasped her hands together and she looked at him.

She studied Mr. Goody Two-Shoes and did not know

what she could say.

She could not be honest and say she was part of an identify theft ring that bought and sold people's credit card information for personal gains.

She could say she was in the process of getting her General Education Degree but that would reveal she did not already have it.

She could say she was undecided on whether to go to junior college or intern with her cousin at the San Fran Times and her GED story would have been the most real but Eliza went with her story about the internship. She said she worked in reception monitoring general email traffic and was also a print model for the company's urban fashion blog.

Eliza's cousin did say he could probably get her the internship months back when she was freshly released from incarceration. He said he could probably get her placed in reception where he got his start but she never followed up with him. She therefore did not technically intern for the SF Times but the print modeling could be considered true. Her cousin was the chief editor of the urban fashion blog and Eliza was in a picture of them having lunch. The blog post recognized the restaurant's snazzy display of their meals and the picture captured one of Eliza's hands holding her fork lifting a portion of her food from the plate.

Eliza took a couple of minutes on the topic of her story and was glad Sur asked for her phone number so she could give it to him and walk away.

She thought they had spent enough time together and she wanted to go see if a fish bigger than Sur had joined the Ball.

Eliza stood from her seat right as a slow jam came on by one of her favorite male signers.

She started to sing the song word for word like she was on stage and Sur was her audience and between versus she told him the song was a couple of years old but still one of her favorites.

Sur said he was pretty sure he had heard the song before and he asked Eliza to allow him a dance before the song ended.
She reached her hand for him to take it and the two of them danced in their corner but for longer than the song played.

Sur held on a few extended seconds after Eliza thanked him for the dance and she had to lightheartedly pull herself away to get him to let go of her.

II

The Ball was emptying and Eliza had to go outside the venue to call herself a ride.

She saw Mali dirty dancing with the same woman the whole night. It was apparent to Eliza the big booty-shaking hoe had got her nigga dick dumb hard and he had left with her to take the hoe no doubt to a hotel.

Mali did not let his bed-buddies know the type of money he had by bringing them to his condo and he knew Eliza considered his condo her home but Eliza was pissed he bailed without letting her know he was leaving her to get home on her own.

Sur found Eliza outside in the process of using an app on her phone to access Mali's rideshare account to get home on his dime.

She was so hell-bent on charging the most expensive vehicle to his account out of spite she almost did not detect Sur walk up on her and make her an offer.

Sur invited her to an after-hour locale for a bite to eat. It was going to be him, the Mayor and his wife and a couple of their close friends.

Sur waited a second for Eliza to say something but he did not want her to say no and before she could speak he said of course it was his treat.

His treat, were Eliza's two magic words and she put her phone in her purse to pay attention.

Sur said he enjoyed the time with her earlier in the evening and he reached for her hand saying he wanted to spend more time getting to know her.

Eliza had not given Sur a yes or no to his invite but he was caressing her hand and staring deeply in her eyes and he made his invitation so enchanting Eliza did not want to tell him no.

She ended up at a hole in the wall cigar bar in Chinatown known for their special brewed tap beer and the best dim sum in the city.

Eliza hated tobacco and beer and had never eaten dim sum but no one could tell. She simply mirrored whatever Zuri did even down to how Zuri ate and how Zuri sat in her chair.

Zuri shared a superior feminine energy outwardly with the table and she showed the Mayor consistent affection.

She would randomly touch the Mayor's thigh, brush her finger across his chin, ask for a kiss, slip her hand in his hand and hold it, rub his shoulder, caress the back of his neck and head and it was natural and hardly noticeable.

The third woman at their table did nothing but bat her long false eyelashes and smile with her juicy red lips. She nibbled at her food and she sipped her drink and her chair was cozily close to the third man at their table.

Eliza had her suspicions the third woman was a Side Chick.

She did not know for sure until the third man whom the third woman was nestled against mentioned his wife being too ill to attend the Mayor's Ball.

The third man was clearly not referring to the third woman sitting to his right.

What also gave away the third woman's Side Chick status was the third man wore a wedding band and the third woman wore barely anything.

She was all long hair and high heels. She had the smallest figure an adult woman could have and a sixty-year-old face under mounds of makeup that took off about eight golden years.

Zuri excused herself to go to the ladies room and Eliza excused herself to follow. She asked Zuri was she okay with other women fawning over her like Eliza had been since they met and Zuri said yes. She knew she was a rare kind of a women one could only read about in those timeless romance stories and Eliza said that was on point with how she would describe her.

Eliza returned with Zuri to their table close to ten minutes later because of a wait for the bathroom stall and the
staff was speedily clearing their table of remaining food and
drinks.

Eliza followed Zuri outside to find the three men each
on their own phone in the street yelling and trying to put the
pieces of a story together.

The third woman was talking to the third man while he
was on the phone and she was pulling at his arm trying to
get the phone from him.
She was screaming it was not just his son It was her son
too and she had a right to hear what was going on.

The third man was yelling back at her to stop screaming
if she wanted him to hear whatever the person on the phone
was saying.

The third woman was arguing for the third man to put
his call on speakerphone and the third man said then neither of them would hear the person talking over the street
noise.

Eliza could make out from the different conversations
that something bad had happened to someone close to them.
A few minutes later Eliza knew the calamity was about
Sur's brother and the son that the third man shared with the
third woman.

Sur told Eliza he was sorry but he had to cut their night
short and he offered to call her a ride home but Eliza refused
to leave him.
She asked him to please allow her to be of support and

help in any way. She said she too had a brother. He was her heartbeat and she could only imagine how he must feel to learn something might have just happened to his. She promised to just be there and not to get in the way or ask any questions and Eliza's plea got her a companion pass to the next stop.

III

Eliza was one of five people in the Mayor's black eight-passenger SUV but she and the driver were the only two people not on a cell phone.

Even Zuri was on a call and from what Eliza could make of Zuri's one-sided dialogue she was speaking with the third women who left the Chinatown cigar bar in a car with the third man.

Eliza was listening to the different voices but she took notice of when their SUV crossed into the Potrero Hill neighborhood.

Sur's family resided only a few blocks from where Eliza spent some of the formative years of her childhood and as they rode her streets she peered out her tinted window.

What peered back were her childhood memories and the good, the bad and the ugly began to come alive in her mind.

The driver had to stop for a pedestrian at the corner where she had her first girl-fight. She could see the faces of the crowd gathered to watch her fight to win and she could see the same faces turn away when they seen her lose.

She got a glimpse of her aunt and uncle's building and she got a phantom smell of her hair stinking from a fresh press and curl that got wet in a water balloon scrimmage on a hot day.

Looking at the dirt lot where a water gun soaked her for the kill evoked the feeling of her arm and leg skin welting from her aunt who did her hairdo and gave her the extension cord beating of her life for ruining it.

The neighborhood liquor store was a block down from the dirt lot.

The liquor store sign was covered in graffiti and Eliza had to turn her neck to keep staring at the sign. It was above where her aunt's husband set up his table and sat for hours with his domino buddies playing bones.

Once Eliza could no longer see the store behind her she had to turn forward but not without the lingering taste of a sugarcoated pie in her mouth from a particular domino buddy.

Her aunt did not allow her to have sweets but anytime this same domino buddy trapped her alone he gave her flavored pies with either a cherry or a lemon filling.

To get the pie he would say all she had to do was let him look at her with her panties down and if her pie was gone before he finished touching himself she got a second pie to keep her panties down until he did finish.

Chapter 23

NIGHT TO REMEMBER

Sur entered his family home with a key.

His parents were up out of the bed and they were sitting in front of their living room television.

Mr. Justin Sr. and Mrs. Noni Morgan were watching the news live on the scene of what read across the bottom of the TV as a suspected robbery.

The news reporter was saying a handful of neighbors from a multiunit apartment building heard what they believed to be gunshots. One neighbor saw what they called in and told police was suspicious activity coming from the alleyway they shared with a row of local business. The Police had arrived to find the backdoor of the Harpuzon Shoe Museum ajar and they entered to find multiple gunshots had been fired inside but they would not release any further details to the media.

The media was made aware so soon because the girlfriend of a primetime journalist was one of the building occupants that heard the gunshots.

The journalist happened to come inside their girlfriend's apartment right after police arrived and they seized the opportunity to be first on the scene.

The Morgan's had been awakened at that hour by a call from a neighbor-friend.

The neighbor-friend had a daughter Bam Bam's age who after seeing the news told her mother of a rumor she heard from a friend that shared a mutual friend with Bam Bam.

The friend said Bam Bam told their mutual friend he planned to hit his first lick that weekend.

The neighbor-friend's daughter felt what she heard was relevant because of a wise crack her friend told her was made about the lick being a waste of time and only a dumb nigga would think they could get solid bread knocking off a shoe store.

The neighbor-friend offered to come over and comfort Noni while she waited to hear from Bam Bam but Noni said that would not be necessary. She was sure the rumor was nothing and that her son was fine.

That was what Noni told her neighbor-friend but the neighbor-friend's call had Noni and Justin Sr. sitting on the living room couch staring at the television news in a trance.

They did not even move when Mayor Sunya, Zuri, Eliza and Sur came into their home.

With no call from police confirming anyone was dead and no definitive information yet coming from the news, the Morgan's could do nothing but wait.

They left their two daughters upstairs asleep seeing no need to wake them with false news of their big brother being in trouble. It was not like it was unusual for Bam Bam to stay out all night sometimes for days.

He had a family. He had his two sons nicknamed Biscuit and Baby Bam born only one year apart and Baby Bam was just learning to walk.

His two boys lived with their mom and her grandfather in the Lake View neighborhood of the city. The grandfather's garden studio was hers rent free for her and her sons on one condition.

She had to leave Bam Bam alone. Her grandfather told her he would gladly provide for his kin forever but were he to catch Bam Bam in his house, kin or no kin he would put an end to her cushy life and offer her no more provision.

Bam Bam had to sneak to be with his family and the grandfather had no way to know how often Bam Bam frequented his home.

The grandfather made his living on the road as a truck driver. He stayed gone for weeks before he took time off and his time off was usually in a liquor-induced slumber.

Justin Sr. called Bam Bam's baby-momma when they first heard from their neighbor-friend. He did not repeat what he heard he just said he was looking for his son and needed to speak with him. He figured his son would be with her.

He went as far as to tell his son's baby-momma she and the boys had nothing to worry about then he held his breath. He waited for her to rule his son out of danger but she could not.

Justin Sr. hung up the call with his son's baby-momma and went to sit on the couch next to his wife. She asked was their son safe and he told his wife he did not believe their son's baby-momma had not seen their son since the day before.

His wife said she had no reason to tell him a lie and there was no reason not to believe her but vilifying the baby-momma was the only thing bringing Justin Sr. any comfort.

I

Sur led Mayor Sunya, Zuri and Eliza to his parent's living room but they stopped behind him and because he did not enter the room they all watched his parents from the doorway.

Noni had her eyes closed and was rocking back and forth.

She was squeezing her brows together, wringing her hands and praying hard giving all glory to God asking the creator to return Justin Jr. home safe.

Everyone in and near the living room could hear her declare her baby imperfect but still her baby, her oldest child and also God's child with so much more life to live. She told the lord her son had always been a handful but it was not his time to leave her and his sons needed their father. She begged the lord to be merciful, consider her loyalty, her obedience and hear her prayer in the name of the father, the son and the Holy Spirit.

The news coverage had begun to show the Harpuzon's storefront.

The television camera zoomed in on the maroon awning that read Harpuzon Shoe Museum in metallic copper letters.

The camera zoomed out and switched angles to show around the storefront that had been secured with black and yellow crime scene tape for no one but authorized personnel to cross.

Inside the crime scene tape was police, crime scene investigators, forensics specialists and two black coroner vans blocking the alleyway.

Outside the crime scene tape random people were interspersed and multiple news crews were arriving.

The reporter the Morgan's had been watching unfold the story was bundled up.
He wore a knit cap and scarf and he said he had been on the scene a little under an hour. He shared that it was certainly a record freezing cold Sunday morning and he hoped the sunrise in the next thirty minutes would warm things up a smidge.

Justin Sr. turned the channel in time to hear another reporter say there could have been an argument amongst friends or foes or there could have been a robbery or something else but so far there were no witnesses to identify a culprit or culprits that may have fled the scene.
The reporter admitted to not having learned much but said whatever the case might be things surely had taken a turn for the worse inside the Harpuzon Shoe Museum.

The reporter did release one name in reference to the Shoe Museum being a popular one-off designer shoe company owned by Mr. Nefon Harpuzon.

The reporter called Mr. Harpuzon one of the city's most successful small businessmen but could not say if he was a victim. Investigators were not officially saying there were

any victims but when the reporter pointed out the two coroner vans they were able to get an investigator to confirm
there were victims involved.

No conclusive statements were being made but the reporter said by pairing the investigator's information with
what witnesses told police earlier about hearing gunshots it
would appear there had been a possible shoot out.

The reporter mentioned surveillance cameras and
pointed to them mounted on and around the shoe Museum
saying there was the possibility of video footage soon allevi-
ating speculations.

Justin Sr. turned off the television and stood from the
couch.

Sur immediately came to his father for a hug and they
held together for seconds. It was enough time for Justin Sr.
to ask Sur what brought them there but it was not enough
time for Sur to say why before Justin Sr. walked into a handshake and embrace with the Mayor.

Mayor Sunya whispered he was sorry about Justin Jr.
and Justin Sr. told him not to be sorry unless he had come
there with proof something had happened to his son.

Mayor Sunya nodded his head apologetically for jumping the gun and he stepped back.

Sur sat in Justin Sr.'s seat on the couch next to Noni who
had opened her eyes when her husband asked if there was
proof. She was looking at Mayor Sunya for an answer even
after he stepped away from her husband reluctant to say
anything further.

Sur wrapped one arm around his mom's shoulders and his other hand rested on her knee.

Noni griped both Sur's hands with her hands but she did not for a second take her eyes off Mayor Sunya and he glanced over his shoulder for Zuri.
She was standing by Eliza until she caught her man's eye and she instantly stepped forward to be at his side.
She grabbed for the crease of his arm above his elbow and she held him there. She slipped her hand in his hand and she glued her body to his as if her touch gave him the power and the will to go on.

Zuri gazed at the side of her husband's head and Mayor Sunya asked Sur to please share the news they received from their sources including what their source inside the police department said.

Noni sharply turned her head and her teary eyes to look at Sur.

Sur became choked up and was struggling to find his polished delivery.
He cleared his throat a couple times and began his narration with, word on the street but he stopped to clear his throat again and again.
That was when Eliza saw a box of tissue on a side table and she thought to stop holding up the wall and take the tissue over.

Eliza pulled two pieces of tissue from the box and handed them first to Noni.
She pulled two more pieces of tissue from the box and pushed the tissue into Sur's hand.

She placed the box nearest him and went immediately back to her corner like she never moved.

Sur used his tissues discreetly and began again with word on the street was Boscoe pulled Bam Bam in on a lick that must have gone wrong.

Eliza knew who Boscoe was. She had learned from her ear hustling before they left the front of the Chinatown cigar bar Boscoe was the third couple's son.

Sur told his parent's their police contact was one of the first to go in Harpuzon's after the police were called. They found five people dead on arrival but they could only officially identify three of the five and the notifying of the next of kin for the owner of Harpuzon's and his two security guards was underway.

The police could not notify Boscoe and Bam Bam's next of kin. They had no identification and more time was needed before their identities would be confirmed but the Mayor and Sur's police contact recognized Boscoe and another source tied Boscoe to Bam Bam.

Justin Sr. asked Mayor Sunya was their son really dead and the Mayor could not answer simply yes. His reply was that Justin Jr. was said to be inside Harpuzon Shoe Museum and everyone inside Harpuzon was dead.

Noni spoke of having seen Boscoe.

She described him as the older flashy fast-money having type from the street that boys liked to follow. She said on occasion Boscoe picked Bam Bam up from their home.

He was related to Bam Bam's baby-momma and for some reason he took Bam Bam under his wing but Noni said she made nothing of it.

She had only ever taken one look in Boscoe's eyes to know he would be trouble for their son but she kept her low opinion of him between her and her husband.

Noni told everyone that nobody could be sure her son was inside or anywhere near the Harpuzon Shoe Museum and she refused to believe her son was dead.

She ignored the twinge in her chest from her insides screaming Boscoe and her son were probably together but she did not let that come from her mouth.

Instead she said her son might not have been with Boscoe. He just as well could be coming home soon and she asked everyone to please leave so she could get breakfast together. Her girls would be waking up soon to get ready for church and she did not need them wondering why there were visitors at that time of the morning.

Noni rose off the couch and walked a few steps away from it. She thanked them for their concern and she said she loved them but on the Lord's Day her family was routine. She said she needed to get her house in order and she hoped they could respect that. She asked for them to excuse her she was going to the kitchen and she told her husband to see everyone to the door but Mayor Sunya told her that would not be necessary.

He waved to Noni and gave Justin Sr. a head nod then he turned to leave with Zuri still glued to his arm.

Eliza remained in her corner waiting for a move from Sur who looked perplexed. He could not believe his mom did not believe him but part of him wanted to believe as she believed.

Sur got up from the couch to kiss his mom's cheek on his way to the door.

He stood with her a moment and used his half-smile to silently agree she was right and everything would be okay.

Eliza moved to the front door and stepped outside to give Sur some privacy but she heard his mom ask him to stay. She invited him for breakfast and to church and he said no thank you he was going home to get some sleep but he promised to be back to see her later.

II

The driver of Mayor Sunya's SUV was waiting at the back passenger door for Eliza and Sur to load into the row in front of where the Mayor and his wife were already seated.

The truck was dark inside and the jazz station played low on the car stereo.

None of anyone's faces could be seen behind the tint of their windows and as they were being driven away from the Morgan's home no one knew how to break the silence so no one did.

Sur did not think to ask Eliza if she needed to be dropped off somewhere.

She was ready to tell him the only place she needed to be was with him but she did not have to say a word.

The driver of their vehicle pulled up outside Sur's apartment building and came to a complete stop.

Eliza remained seated until Sur stepped out the car curbside.

She had to come across the seat to exit Sur's door but

he blocked her standing inside the door like he knew Mayor Sunya had something to get off his chest.

The Mayor told Sur to be mindful he had urgent pressing matters of top priority that should have his attention and the Mayor looked at Eliza.

Eliza raised her brow at the Mayor and looked towards Sur who stepped out her way for her to step out the vehicle.

Eliza waited beside Sur close enough to hear Mayor Sunya ask when should he expect Sur to be at his house.

Sur said he needed a shower and a couple of hours sleep and would be at his place before evening, maybe earlier but maybe not.

Mayor Sunya did not give Sur any response like he was waiting for Sur to say more but Sur closed the door to the truck like he really did not care what the Mayor was on.

Eliza walked from the vehicle to the sidewalk and she stopped for Sur to take the lead.

He opened his building entrance for her to follow him inside and the two of them were quiet on their walk together to his apartment.

Sur unlocked his oversized apartment door and automatically hit the light switch on the inside wall.
He stepped back out of the entrance into the hallway and gestured for Eliza to enter into what he described to her

earlier in the evening as a city-leased junior one bedroom.
Nothing fancy.

III

Eliza stood in Sur's doorway and from what she could
see right off the bat he had totally downplayed his city
accommodations.

She entered his lushly furnished Russian Hill apartment and told him he had definitely inhabited the residence
they showed pictures of online to get people to rent their
overpriced furnished apartments.

Sur thanked Eliza for her compliments and told her to
make herself at home.

Eliza pulled off her high-heels and asked could she use
his shower.

Sur told her she could use anything she wanted but he
asked was there not someone looking for her and not somewhere she needed to be.

Eliza smiled and asked Sur to unzip her dress.

Sur did what he was asked and Eliza let her dress drop
to the floor.

She got out of the dress and picked it up as she faced
him in her panties with no bra. She told him the only place
she needed to be was with him and she turned to walk away
slowly for him to fully enjoy the view of her bare square bubble butt that swallowed up her G-string.

Eliza tossed her dress on the couch and went to open

one of the few doors in the room.

She found the washer and dryer behind door number one and Eliza looked at Sur. He was undressing while watching her so he saw she opened the wrong door but he did not say anything and Eliza laughed to herself. She went to another door she thought was too close to the kitchen to be the bathroom but she did not see another door.

Eliza opened door number two to find the walk-in pantry and she laughed but she covered her mouth to not be so overdramatic.

She looked at Sur who was down to no shirt in his underwear and he laughed at her laughing but he picked up his television remote and said nothing.

He turned on the living room television to the sports channel and the surround sound came on loud enough for tenants across the hall to hear the voices of the sports commentators.

Sur threw the remote on the couch and walked past Eliza.

He stepped down one step into where his bed took up the entire alcove but he went along the side of his bed further into the alcove and voilà. There was the bathroom beyond the bed.

Eliza heard the shower water come on and she waited a few seconds to see what Sur would do but he did not come back out the bathroom.

She sat on his bed and gave him another couple of minutes but then she walked into the bathroom to find him crying over the bathroom sink.

Eliza decided against saying anything.

She let her panties fall on the floor and she unobtrusive-
ly entered the shower.

Eliza liked her water hot with the steam engulfing her.
She enjoyed the wet heat for an extended amount of time
before she lathered Sur's bar soap on her body and let the
suds melt and runaway.

Sur opened the shower curtain naked ready to step in
and he was surprised to see Eliza and he quickly apologized.
He admitted to forgetting she was even there.

Eliza also apologized for staying in the shower long.
She told Sur she was finished but as she attempted to
step out the shower leaving the water running for him he
kneaded her shoulder and her neck and uttered in her ear
not to leave him. He spoke so softly Eliza did not know if
that was what he really said until his all consuming tall powerful presence eased her back into the shower.

Eliza could see the gloom in Sur's eyes. He was in pain
and bewildered by his mom saying it was not true his baby
brother was not dead and him knowing it was true his baby
brother was dead.
He desperately a needed distraction and in that moment
his desired distraction was Eliza.

Sur kissed her deeply and with his big strong hands he
groped her thighs and her breasts passionately. He hoisted
her by the ass in full penetration mode and Eliza thought to
stop him.
He had not put on a condom and had not washed his
dick.
She wanted him to meet her in his bed when he was

done with his shower giving her the time to get the condoms from her purse if he did not have any but she did not turn her thoughts to words quick enough.

Sur had her backed against the shower wall with his dick inside her and before she knew it he was in a zone fucking her too rough and too fast.

He had his tongue down her throat and she could not speak to tell him slow down, back out and start again but she wanted to be of comfort to him so she turned her face from his mouth and held on.

She closed her eyes and told herself she could take that dick. It was smaller than Mali's but it was still big enough for it to hurt with no real foreplay and his tongue on her neck felt good and it loosened her up a little but she wanted it to be over.

Eliza crossed her ankles around Sur's back and she squeezed and pulsated her pussy for him to cum quicker. She spoke into his ear telling him to go deeper, do it harder, fuck her faster, make her cum and it was working.

Sur let out a moan and said how good Eliza felt and his breathing got heavier. She knew he must have been finally focused on chasing his nut so she started bucking and bouncing her titties at his face.

He watched her body as she fucked him back and as his strokes got more intense Eliza moaned louder and louder to make him think he was that good.

She was almost about to fake an orgasm if Sur had not swiftly gripped both sides of her hips, pushed her body away and yanked his dick out.

Both of Eliza's arms remained crossed behind Sur's neck

but the intensity of his push unlocked her ankles from behind his back.

Her legs fell clumsily to the shower floor and Sur collapsed his body onto hers.

He smashed her to the shower wall and as he jerked his dick he exploded semen on her thigh.

IV

Sur had a luxury city-leased car to match his luxury city-leased apartment.

He told Eliza he did not use the car for personal reasons but taking her home late Sunday afternoon was on his way to his scheduled appointment with Mayor Sunya.

During her ride home Eliza asked was Sunday not a day of rest and reset and could politics not wait until Monday but Sur said his meeting would not be long. It was just he and the Mayor discussing the key players in the city's formal response to the Harpuzon violence.

Eliza asked Sur was there not someone else to handle the Harpuzon situation since it involved his family and he reminded her his brother's murder was not public and the source that told him about Bam Bam and Boscoe was off the record.

Sur asked Eliza had she heard of a sworn duty and she gave him a blank look.

He said as the city's head of Urban Community Affairs he had a sworn duty to respond to violence in the community.

It could be in hours or another day before his brother's name would be released but the news had made the matter public.

The public would be and should be expecting an immediate statement about the city's response but a response required the affected communities to be convened. His job was to make that happen and he was not saying he was a spokesperson but he was the liaison between the community and the office of the Mayor.

Sur pulled up in front of Mali's Diamond Heights condo and he asked Eliza how was she living so large at her age.

He was insinuating Eliza had lied to him at the Mayor's Ball and really she had come from money but Eliza told Sur flat out it was her boyfriend's condo.

Sur was surprised at her response and he asked how could she have had the night she had with him and claim to have a boyfriend.

Eliza said nonchalantly she and her boyfriend had an open relationship but she said being with Sur was the most amazing experience that she ever had.

Sur admitted it was amazing for him too but he said if Eliza was his girl there would be no open relationship bullshit with him and she would not be allowed to fuck no other nigga.

Eliza got out of Sur's car and closed his car door.
She leaned into his open passenger window and said lucky for him her boyfriend was the other nigga or they may have never shared their *night to remember*.

Sur laughed being so taken aback by Eliza. He asked when he would see her again and reminded her she was one of the very few people to have his personal cell phone number.

Eliza agreed. Having his number made her feel extra special but she graciously reminded him. The phone worked in both directions and he was one of the very few people to have her personal cell phone number.

Eliza glided to the entrance on Mali's condo with her sexiest swag each step of the way and all Sur could do was watch her leave and he watched until he could not see any more of her.

Sur had delayed his morning into the afternoon with Eliza for as long as he could before he took her home.

They did not fuck again outside of the shower but they did lay conformable in his bed both getting rest here and there but mostly pretending to sleep.

Sur had food and drinks delivered.

They ate bits and pieces of their cuisine in bed but him sipping his chai tea latte or her sipping her almond milk decaf café au lait were the only sounds that broke their silence when one or the other was not chewing.

They watched and re-watched a cult classic of his choice and were nestled together both gazing at the romance happening on the television screen but oblivious to the romance spawning between them.

Eliza did not have a problem being quiet with Sur.

She could keep her mouth shut and her opinions to herself and she assumed Sur's mind was on Bam Bam and she was partially right.

What she could not know was Sur dreaded meeting with Mayor Sunya more than he dreaded getting confirmation his brother was dead.

Sur knew Mayor Sunya would be looking for him to fix whatever damage Bam Bam had gone astray and did.

That was how it had always been since Bam Bam was a young boy.

If Bam Bam did anything wrong, Sur was the person the Morgan's and the Mayor held liable to fix it and Sur usually did. He cleaned up Bam Bam's mess-ups every time but something about this time felt beyond his capacity to fix.

Bam Bam had operated outside the family and for what and why was the mystery and Sur had nothing but the words of a known thief to go on.

The known thief told Boscoe's father the owner of Harpuzon was an old muthafucka but he was a brute. He would not let his store get hit without hitting back and the known thief claimed Boscoe approached him about the Harpuzon lick first but he told Boscoe no. His main concern was they would be dead before they could spend whatever they stole. He said Boscoe was his partner in crime but there was no way a place like Harpuzon was going to allow any nigga to pull a jack move and get away with it.

Another reason the known thief said he told Boscoe no was because Harpuzon was a pillar of the Fillmoe community and he and Boscoe were affiliated with the Lake View Mob.

Them robbing Harpuzon would start a war and the known thief said he was not a warrior.

He stole only what he did not have to pack a real pistol to steal.

Sur did not want to believe Bam Bam would get entangled with the Harpuzon robbery.

The idea seemed outlandish even for Bam Bam. He was not the shiniest star in the sky but he knew Mayor Sunya orchestrated the One Frisco initiative when he was working for the DA's office. Without One Frisco the influence of the Unknown Dynasty would diminish and to shield the Unknown Dynasty from demise The Mayor was invested in keeping One Frisco under his thumb.

Bam Bam notoriously did not think beyond money, pussy or street credit but he was one of the six people in the entire city who knew the success of One Frisco and the Unknown Dynasty were intertwined. He had to know a move against Harpuzon would destroy the truce and Sur had no desire for his baby brother to be dead but he felt the weight lift as he let it settle in he would not have to clean up after the little nigga ever again.

V

Sur left Diamond Heights on his way to meet the Mayor but he stopped at a bar in the Haight-Ashbury area for a cup of courage.
One drink turned into two and two drinks turned into three and after the third drink he walked four doors down from the bar to the cannabis club for a smoke.
He bought a pre-rolled joint and finished it before he got in the car to drive to the Mayor.

It was nightfall before he arrived at the Mayor's mansion.
He was grateful he was high off weed and had as many drinks as he did because were he sober he may not have excused the slap to his face the Mayor greeted him with when he finally showed up.

Anyone else, sober or not, Sur would have knocked them the fuck out.

He was tempted to knock the Mayor out after he pushed the Mayor and told him to calm down but the Mayor swung another punch that fortunately for him missed Sur by a good inch.

Mayor Sunya reeked of liquor.

He was stumbling and grumbling about he had talked to Boscoe's father again who he had talked to the known thief again who again confirmed Bam Bam was with Boscoe on the Harpuzon burglary.

The Mayor said he also talked to a couple of his sheriff friends who said the news had reached the northern California jails. The inmates had already got word and retaliation was on the brink, talk of riots had sparked, blood alliances were being formed and promises were on the verge of being broken.

Mayor Sunya was furious one of his own he raised and nurtured and whom he considered a nephew had betrayed him but Bam Bam was not there for the Mayor to take his fury out on.

He was not there to get slapped in the face, swung on or slammed against the wall because of the Mayor feeling that with every passing moment he was losing control of his city.

The Mayor did not want his legacy tied to turfs being at war. He wanted to be remembered for keeping the peace and controlling bloodshed, uniting warlords and keeping crime down but the greed of others had recklessly ruined his hard work.

Sur looked in his godfather's eyes and he could see that his eyes were red with rage.

He knew the Mayor had not seen his beloved godson come through his front door.

The Mayor was seeing what was once his younger self. He was a man that had given decades to building his name and his anger was fueled by him thinking it could have all been for nothing.

It was not like he had gone looking for melee but because of Boscoe and Bam Bam, melee had found him.

If he allowed countless unexplained deaths to line the streets of San Fran, he would face the threat of his name being irreversibly tarnished.

The Mayor knew there would be no do-over for those long ago days of his youth but he was not about to let his age force him to turn a blind eye. Never had he ever felt more ready to play the long game no matter the cost.

He was not giving up on his city and he had no fear of retiring from his spotlight at the podium. With the increasing power and influence of the Unknown Dynasty, he would remain in control of the city from the shadows.

To Be Continued...

ACKNOWLEDGMENTS

O Lorr William is a native of San Francisco, CA and holds an M.F.A. Degree in Writing & Consciousness from an accredited academic institution.

This work of fiction is dedicated to those who relate to the struggle of poverty and systemic oppression all over the world. You are the light of truth and your existence is God's gift to humanity. Your scars are perfect and your wounds are my wounds. May you find joy with every footprint you leave on this earth.

To my mom. I love you. You are the fire that burns in the pit of my stomach and keeps me pushing through this thing called life. To my father and to my grandmother. Thank you for being two of my archangels. To my oldest big brother. My thousand mile journey started with you. I owe you the world. To my other big brother, my sister-in-law his wife and my other two older sisters. Thank you for unconditionally loving me, for listening to me and encouraging me through life's storms. To all my other family including my cousins, nieces and nephews, aunts and uncle, my friends and best friends and my godchildren. You know how much you mean to me. To my publisher. Thank you for giving me my first shot. To my readers. Thank you for reading my book and for supporting my work. God Bless you. God Bless everyone that has ever crossed my path in life and may God Bless the future and everything that it holds!